*Their eyes met, and she ventured a smile.*

"I must admit, you have a nice way of making ordinary things special," she said.

The red on his cheeks got ruddier. "Uh, ordinary things like having supper together in town? It's pot roast Monday at the diner. Their cook makes the best pot roast in the West. We've all had a trying day, so it's my treat. Say, seven o'clock?"

His offer surprised Jenna, but she only hesitated for a second. "Sounds terrific. I'm not sure how long my errands will take. How about if Andee and I meet you there?"

"It's a da—" He stopped short of saying *date*. Jenna could tell Flynn knew it, and so did she.

Unwinding Andee's arms, he chucked her under the chin and made good his escape, with his dog loping through the open screen door at his heels.

Jenna gave a start when Andee piped up to say, "We love Flynn, don't we, Mommy?"

Dear Reader,

Parts of this story have percolated in my mind for quite a while. There's an ostrich ranch off the highway between Tucson and Phoenix. A few years ago the ranch was in the news. Hot air balloons taking off from an empty field frightened the birds, and many were hurt when they broke down fences. I wanted to feature an ostrich ranch in a story, but I didn't want them hurt. I decided to set my story in a neighboring state. I wanted my main characters to love animals. And because *An Unlikely Rancher* is a love story, I decided my ranch owner, who isn't looking for love, falls in love accidentally. I hope Jenna Woods and her daughter Andee's second chance at happiness with ex-military flyer Flynn Sutton is a story that touches your heart.

Sincerely,

Roz Denny Fox

I love hearing from readers. Contact me via Facebook or my website, korynna.com/RozFox.

# HEARTWARMING

## *An Unlikely Rancher*

—

*Roz Denny Fox*

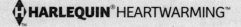
HARLEQUIN® HEARTWARMING™

Recycling programs
for this product may
not exist in your area.

ISBN-13: 978-0-373-36711-5

An Unlikely Rancher

**Printed in U.S.A.**

**Roz Denny Fox**'s first book was published by
Harlequin in 1990. She writes for various Harlequin
lines and for special projects. Her books are
published worldwide and in a number of languages.
She's also written articles as well as online serials for
Harlequin.com. Roz's warm home-and-family-focused
love stories have been nominated for various industry
awards, including the Romance Writers of America's
RITA® Award, the Holt Medallion, the Golden Quill
and others. Roz has been a member of the Romance
Writers of America since 1987 and is currently a
member of Tucson's Saguaro Romance Writers, where
she has received the Barbara Award for outstanding
chapter service. She's also a member of the Desert
Rose RWA chapter in Phoenix, Midwest Fiction Writers
of Minneapolis, San Angelo Texas Writers' Club and
Novelists, Inc. In 2013 Roz received her fifty-book
pin from Harlequin. Readers can email her through
Facebook or at rdfox@cox.net.

### Books by Roz Denny Fox
### HARLEQUIN HEARTWARMING
*Hearts Entwined*
*The Western Dare*
*The Boss Next Door*
*The Hope Dress*
*Annie's Neighborhood*

### HARLEQUIN AMERICAN ROMANCE
*Too Many Brothers*
*The Secret Wedding Dress*
*The Perfect Tree*
"Noelle and the Wise Man"
*The Maverick Returns*
*Duke: Deputy Cowboy*
*Texas Dad*

For more titles, visit Roz's website
at www.korynna.com/RozFox.

# CHAPTER ONE

JENNA WOOD SAT at her sister's dinner table and draped a napkin across her lap. "I have news. Today I finalized buying the ostrich ranch in New Mexico I told you about last month. Movers will collect our things from storage tomorrow. Andee and I will leave at the end of the week. Salad, anyone?" She forced herself not to wince as she passed the bowl across the table to her brother-in-law, but finally set it down when he didn't take it.

Jenna's sister, Melody Carter, and her husband, Rob, both dropped the rolls they were buttering.

"You can't be serious," Rob, a JAG attorney stationed nearby at the Pentagon, sputtered through a laugh.

"I am. I know you guys thought it was a passing fancy." Jenna picked up the salad dressing, bracing herself for the full onslaught of their reaction. "My funds were wired and I've received confirmation from the seller's Realtor. I'm now the proud owner of 300 acres, 1,500 birds, a two-story home, plus a single-story, three-bedroom rental in a town near my ranch. *Our* ranch," she stressed, smiling down at her serious-faced six-year-old daughter.

Rob frowned at Jenna. "Look, Mel and I know it's been rough on you to have the Air Force investigating Andrew's collision with that Navy flyer. Thorough investigations take time. Especially when the planes had to be fished out of the ocean. I can get your contract voided on the basis of your being a grieving widow."

Jenna stiffened. "I don't want out of the contract. I want a clean start for Andee and me before her school starts." She glanced again at the girl, who'd been too quiet and withdrawn since her dad's accident.

Melody reached across the table and squeezed Jenna's hand. "I assumed we'd talked you out of this folly. You've always lived on a military base. What do you know about ranching?"

"I'll learn, Mel."

Rob finally slid the salad bowl over. He

gestured with the tongs. "Mel's right. I hate to say it, Jenna, but you aren't thinking straight."

"Mom thinks it's a good idea. It's why she stayed on after the funeral, so I could visit a local ostrich ranch. Get a sense of what I've got ahead of me." Jenna poured the salad dressing.

"How reliable is Mom or Dad? They moved lock, stock and barrel to Costa Rica weeks after Dad retired," Melody argued.

"That's exactly right. That's why they're reliable in this—they're proof that you can make a dramatic new start at any age. They researched and chose a place where their money will last. And they're the ones who recommended this place in New Mexico."

She stopped to study them, acknowledging their concern. She couldn't—wouldn't—listen to her own self-doubt. "Look, I can't thank you guys enough for helping move us off the Florida base and for letting us stay here temporarily. But even here—"

Jenna had to break off, catch her breath, before she said slowly, "Everywhere I turn I see men and women in uniform. We've been here ten months." She lowered her voice, looking hesitantly at Andee. "I think the commission is bent on proving pilot error. They're discounting Andrew's countless missions in war zones." Jenna idly split her roll, barely murmuring, "You know about the reports saying he and the Navy pilot argued. Should that destroy his career?"

"War can mess with a man's head," Rob said.

Melody nodded. "Yes, we all saw a marked change in Andrew after his last tour in Afghanistan. You said he refused to go for a physical. Whether or not the commission finds him at fault, you need family now, Jenna."

She tensed. No one knew how strained her marriage had been at the end.

"Andee, honey, I forgot your milk. Will you go to the kitchen and bring the carton from the fridge?"

Jenna waited until after she'd gone to put a finger to her lips.

Oblivious, Rob continued, "Some chest thumping goes with being a fighter pilot. And rumors always circulate after a non-combat accident. They fade away, so it's no reason to uproot Andee. Let the commission finish its work."

Jenna added a dollop of dressing to Andee's salad. "He was three short years from retirement, Rob. We discussed leaving the East Coast. I've always wanted land where I could have animals and plant a garden. Mel, you know how much I loved the Army base in Germany when we were kids and Mom raised chickens."

Rob ate his salad as Andee scampered back with the milk. "Ostriches aren't chickens," he said. "They're big, powerful birds. They kick and bite."

After pouring Andee's milk, Jenna set the carton aside. "Ostriches only act out if they're frightened, according to the American Ostrich Association website. They're curious creatures who like shiny objects. The people I bought from advised against wearing jewelry when I work with them. Plus, the couple who owned the farm I toured in Georgia has raised birds for ten years and they're doing really well."

"Even so, New Mexico is still the Wild West," Rob said.

"Please be happy for us," Jenna begged, suddenly blinking away tears.

Pretending to fuss with Andee's hair, she

gently cupped the girl's ears and said quietly, "Mel…if we stay here, there are bound to be negative comments about Andrew." Jenna dropped a kiss on the child's forehead and smiled because Andee had clearly taken an interest in their conversation.

Melody and her husband exchanged guilty glances.

"Of course." Melody hastily passed Jenna the meat platter. "But you call us the minute you get there. And if… Well…our door is always open if you want to return."

FLYNN SUTTON WATCHED his newest customer jockey a four-passenger Cessna Skylark into the hangar he'd just rented out. It was Flynn's third rental since he'd finished clearing the runways of the old airpark he'd bought while serving in the Air Force.

That had been before he'd been shot up and landed in the military hospital with a new knee and shrapnel wounds in his hip and thigh.

The cloudless blue sky and shimmering heat of his native New Mexico helped to cleanse the stench of war and dull the painful loss of his best friend.

Chip Talbot had flown the search-and-rescue mission that bitterly cold afternoon when their chopper had been shot down in Kandahar province. Only dumb luck had let Flynn crawl out of the wreckage alive.

He counted himself lucky again that he'd invested in this airpark over the twelve years he'd served Uncle Sam. It gave him the fallback he'd needed when his career with the Air Force was over.

In the beginning it had been his intention to stay in for twenty, retire with a good pension, come here and teach flying in his golden years. He'd had to cut those plans short—or move them up, depending on one's view of his current situation.

Disability pay covered the cost of his renting the house in town. He'd have money enough to keep his dream alive, providing he filled his hangars and lowered his blood pressure so he could pass his next physical.

Imperative if he hoped to teach flying.

But maybe he was asking for too much. Unlike Chip, he had his life and a future.

Shading his eyes, Flynn tossed a wave to the pilot of a red-and-white, single-engine

Piper Cub taxiing to the caliche runway from another stall.

Travis Hines, the twenty-year-old son of a local land developer, was a bit of a grandstander. Or maybe the kid just made him feel old at thirty-three.

Still watching the plane, Flynn idly wiped his greasy hands on a rag. He grimaced as the Piper lifted off in a wobble of wings and a full-throated growl.

Dropping his mirrored sunglasses over his eyes, Flynn dismissed the show-off and limped into his makeshift office. He tucked his client's check into the bank deposit bag for when he and his dog went home at lunch.

JENNA TIMED THEIR arrival in Deming, New Mexico, to coincide with the moving van hauling their worldly possessions. Over her sister's continued grumbling, Jenna had traded her compact car for a Jeep Grand Cherokee. The purchase had seriously depleted what was left of her savings, but as she pulled up outside the realty office, she felt a renewal of hope.

Hope had been missing from her life for longer than she had admitted to anyone.

The office looked like so many other buildings she'd seen in the virtual tour. It was flat-roofed, beige stucco and blended with the sandy landscape.

Taking Andee's hand, Jenna stepped inside.

The only person in the room was an older man seated at a messy desk. Without hesitation, she introduced herself to him.

"I see, Mrs. Wood. Welcome. I'm Bud Rhodes. Oscar left you an envelope along with the house keys. He said he included notes about his ostrich operation." Bud pawed through a pile on his desk, found the envelope and handed it to her across the counter.

She stared at it for a moment. "I assumed Mr. Martin would walk me through everything," she said slowly.

"Sorry. I thought you knew he'd moved to Hawaii." The Realtor laughed at the oversight. "Oscar employed a local man by the name of Don Winkleman to help with the birds. I reckon he's been handling things since Oscar skedaddled."

"I see. I hope his notes are detailed…" She opened the envelope but couldn't focus on all the paperwork she was seeing. "This business is all new to me. Everything here is new to me."

"Well, now, we've got a right, nice little town. What you see here is our commercial district. You and the little lady," he said, smiling down at Andee, "need to visit our museum. It dates back to the 1916 raid by Pancho Villa. We've even got artifacts from one of the original Harvey Houses that catered to transcontinental railway travelers. It's open now, if you'd like to take a tour."

"I'm afraid I can't." Jenna glanced at her watch. "I'm to meet our moving van at the house right about now."

She was exhausted from the long drive and the heat. And admittedly unsettled by the news that Oscar Martin was gone and hadn't told her he'd be leaving and she'd be plunged into ranching straightaway. Thank heaven, he'd left her with someone to help.

"No problem. I'll mark where you're going on this map. Your property isn't too far off the main highway. It's about four miles out of town."

"And there's a rental home?" she suddenly thought to ask. If Oscar Martin hadn't told her he was leaving, what else hadn't he told

her? "Here in town, correct? And it's occupied?"

"Yes."

Well, that was a relief, anyway.

"Belonged to Oscar's great-aunt," Bud
continued. "When she passed on, he elected
to keep it for added income. The house sits
about here." He pointed to a square on the
map. "The address is on the deeds in your
packet." He drew an X approximately two
blocks into the square. "It's currently rented
by a nice young fella who lived here as a
boy. He returned a few months ago to open
a business."

Bud stood and went to the window to peer
out.

"I 'spect you just missed him. Before you
came in, I saw his pickup parked outside
the bank."

Relieved to hear that her renter was nice,
Jenna thanked the Realtor for his help and
guided Andee out.

"Mommy, I'm hot," Andee complained as
Jenna unlocked the SUV.

It was a good thing Jenna had stocked a
cooler with ice and water at the motel that
morning. She opened a bottle and passed it

to the girl. "We need to remember to drink more, sweetie. It's much drier here."

"Why?"

"I suppose because there's no ocean nearby."

Andee accepted that answer and buckled herself into her kid seat in the back.

After a brief check of the map, Jenna set out.

It took her less than fifteen minutes to find the rutted lane leading to the ranch.

Her first glimpse of the rambling two-story house was a letdown. It wasn't as white as it had looked in the photos. The porch didn't run all the way across the front. And the evergreens, maybe spruce, which she had thought shaded the house, were brown. Covered in dust, she guessed, squinting against the hot wind blowing the dust through her open window.

She shut the window and climbed out of the SUV, taking in the tufts of grass in the yard as she opened Andee's door. She couldn't really call the grass a lawn.

She had wanted so much for this life-changing move to New Mexico to be exactly what she and her daughter needed. Her family had told her that she didn't know what she was doing. And she'd blithely argued that she'd done her research.

Nothing in her research had prepared her for what she was seeing now. And maybe that was why the previous owner had left town on the quiet.

There was more "lawn" evident in some of the pens that ran parallel to the highway, which was separated from her property by a strip of land and a perimeter road Jenna hoped didn't get much traffic.

Groups of gangly birds were huddled under canvas-topped awnings. Since the dry breeze took her breath away, Jenna didn't blame the ostriches for seeking the least little bit of shade. If Oscar Martin had a manager, there was no sign of him—or any living human being, for that matter.

She helped Andee down and they went into the house, where a second wave of fatigue swept over Jenna. It was only marginally cooler inside, and yet the inspector she'd hired through the Realtor had said the house had swamp coolers. Of course, she knew swamp coolers weren't air conditioners and they worked better if a couple of windows were cracked open. It was at least reassuring that she could hear the sound of a motor running somewhere.

She had promised to call Melody the minute they arrived. But knowing that her sister and Rob insisted she was making a bad decision—and worried they were right—she decided to wait until she was settled in.

She glanced out the living room window and saw the moving van lumbering toward the house.

Good. A reprieve.

After telling the movers where she wanted her furniture and boxes to go, she and Andee went to unload the SUV. On her second trip, while her daughter remained inside unpacking her stuffed animals, the drone of an airplane directly overhead made Jenna pause. Unable to shade her eyes because she had both arms filled with clothes on hangers, she squinted to scan the sky.

She was surprised to see a small red-and-white plane flying incredibly low. So low, her heart skipped a beat. It swooped over the ostrich pens and for a moment blocked the sun, casting a hulking shadow.

Tearing her eyes from the plane, Jenna saw spindly-legged birds bolt from under the canopies and run awkwardly to the far end of the enclosure. The plane's shadow followed, causing birds to bump into fences and one another. Then the plane made a right turn and headed for a low rise Jenna thought probably marked the edge of her property.

She held her breath and waited for the sound of a crash. Nothing.

"Mom," Andee called from the doorway.

"I'll be there in a minute, honey."

At the fence, she had no idea what she should do to settle the agitated flock. Thankfully, before she could come up with a plan, they calmed themselves and wandered back to the shade.

Since she hadn't heard a boom, Jenna assumed the plane must have landed. She had no idea she'd bought property near an airport. That very notion unnerved her.

"Mommy, are the ostriches okay?" Andee asked, appearing at her side.

"I think so." Turning to go into the house, Jenna muttered, "That plane shouldn't have flown so low."

She watched her daughter carefully after that close encounter with the small plane.

She knew neighbors on base had discussed Andrew's plane crash around their kids. And even though Andrew had been gone too much to be a hands-on dad, their little girl had always tagged after him when he was home. And he'd taken her to see his plane. Flying had been his life. He'd even bought her picture books of planes.

But since Andrew had come and gone so often, Jenna was aware that Andee hadn't yet fully comprehend his death.

Up to now they'd only casually mentioned that Andrew was in heaven. But Andee was a bright child and Jenna's mom had said there would be an appropriate opening to discuss what death meant.

This wasn't the time, though, Jenna decided.

To distract them both, she toured Andee through the rest of the four-bedroom, two-bath house while two of the movers set up their beds.

The wood floors in the living room needed waxing, Jenna noted. And hot as it was, Jenna couldn't imagine ever needing the beautiful old fireplace at one end of the room. But when she expressed that thought, the youngest of the three movers laughed.

"Nights in the desert can be brutally cold. I grew up in New Mexico," he added as if to prove his point.

The kitchen was outdated but clean, its cupboards painted a sea-foam green. Jenna imagined she'd like them better in white. But she also knew it'd take time to put her stamp on the place.

After the movers left, she dug out the linens to make up Andee's bed.

She wished she'd thought to note the call letters painted on the underside of that plane. Even if there was an airport in the vicinity, the plane had flown dangerously low. If the pilot had violated some local flight ordinance, she should report the incident.

The plane could belong to a local rancher. She knew it wasn't uncommon for ranch owners to fly private aircraft. If that was the case, perhaps he—or she—would respond to a neighborly request to not swoop so low over her pens.

Martin's ranch manager might shed some light on the matter. Where was he? He obviously didn't live on-site. Later she would sit and read Martin's notes. It would suit her if the helper only worked part-time. She hadn't factored in the cost of hired help.

"There, Andee, your bedroom looks put together. Would you like to help me make up my bed?"

"Mommy, I wish there wasn't a bathroom between our bedrooms. You're too far away," she said as she scooped up Cubby Bear.

"Honey, you'll be fine sleeping in here. We'll leave both connecting doors open. You'll have your animals and dolls to keep you company."

Andee's shoulders slumped.

Jenna worried about how clingy she'd become since the funeral. "Tell you what. I need to phone Auntie Melody to let her know we arrived. Would you like to talk to her a minute?"

"No, it's okay." Andee wrapped her arms tightly around her much-loved bear and trailed her mother into her bedroom.

Jenna made her bed, then sat on it and punched her sister's speed-dial number on her cell phone. She kept the call brief, putting a rosy spin on everything. She might have broken down if she'd heard the hint of an "I told you so."

"Our next step," she told Andee after ending the call, "is lining kitchen cabinets with the pretty contact paper I brought. Do you want to help peel the backing off after I measure and cut?"

"I guess so. Can we eat first? I'm hungry."

"Sure. I'll fix cheese sandwiches from stuff in the cooler and slice an apple for dessert. Tomorrow we'll find a store and shop to fill our refrigerator."

"Mommy, why isn't our house near other houses like where we used to live?"

"This is a ranch and we need more land to raise birds as big as the ostriches."

"Where are houses with other kids?"

That question stopped Jenna. She cleared her throat. "Soon we'll hunt up the school where you'll go in September. And I saw a park on the map the Realtor gave me. I'll bet kids play there."

That seemed to satisfy Andee, but it made Jenna wonder why she hadn't given more thought to how isolated they'd actually be living here.

*No, we'll be fine. Pioneer women survived in much more isolated conditions.*

They ate a light lunch, then lined the cupboards, a chore that took most of the afternoon. "Andee," Jenna said as she pressed down the last piece of contact paper, "I need to look over Mr. Martin's notes on how to care for ostriches. While I do that, why don't you color?"

The girl ran to her room and came straight back with two picture books.

Jenna understood that Andee didn't want to be out of her sight given that she'd left the child with her grandparents for a week after the funeral while she'd visited the ostrich farm in Georgia.

A farm, she might add, that looked much more prosperous than this one.

Then they'd moved in with Rob and Melody, and Jenna had hoped things would settle.

Stifling a sigh, she opened the envelope and started to read.

There were instructions about gathering eggs every other day and choosing some to put in incubators for hatching, similar instructions to those she'd gotten from the Georgia couple. She knew that eggs not sold to a wholesaler stayed in the incubators for forty-two days.

It seemed straightforward. It was as she'd told Melody: raising ostriches wasn't difficult.

Oscar Martin apparently had derived income from four markets: the sale of eggs, feathers, meat and leather. The last two involved aspects of the business that didn't appeal to Jenna. But it looked as if the manager was used to handling the meat and leather production for Martin. And it didn't seem as if the man's salary would break the budget Jenna had set up for herself.

"Before the sun sets, Andee, I want to inspect the pens, the hatchery and get a closer look at our ostriches. Would you like to come along?"

Nodding, the child closed her book, slid off the kitchen chair, picked up her bear and then reached for her mom's hand.

"Oh, nice," Jenna said as they left the porch. "There's a slight breeze. It's still hot, but that gives us some relief."

"Ostriches are funny-looking," Andee announced. "But they have pretty eyes," she added, stopping to stare at the three birds that had ventured close to the fence. "They kinda look like Big Bird."

"They do at that. Look at their long eyelashes." Jenna pointed to one peering at them over the fence. "Each adult eats about three pounds of food a day," she said, consulting the notes she'd brought with her.

"What do they eat?" Andee asked. She shifted her stuffed bear.

"Um, mostly grass. I suppose that's why it's much greener in the pens than in the yard around the house. We'll be sowing grass seed in the empty pens, which explains why there are so many empty ones. When the grass comes up, we'll move the birds and reseed the pen they were in."

Jenna opened the door to one of several sheds that were really small barns. "Good, these bins are labeled. I see the grass is supplemented with alfalfa and corn that has vitamins mixed in it."

"What's supple…supple… What you said?"

"*Supplement* means 'added to.' Like we eat salad with our meat and potatoes. And I give you chewable vitamins as a supplement." They left the shed and turned to the next page of notes. "The man who owned these birds said they do best living outside in the fresh air. But they need exercise. Each pen is big so they can run around."

Andee ventured closer to the pen of milling birds. "I like being outside, too. Maybe I can play with them, Mommy."

"Well, we will have to see about that. Perhaps you can pet some of the babies. I saw eggs under the lights in the incubators, but it doesn't look like we have any smaller than some juniors in that pen farthest from the house."

As she finished speaking, a small plane rose out of the direction where the earlier plane had disappeared. This one climbed higher and didn't fly directly over them. Even so, she knew the noise of an engine winding up could put some of the birds in a flap.

Jenna watched the plane until it became a speck in the distance. The Georgia couple had told her that ostriches were excitable. And Martin, too, had indicated in his notes that being overwrought could lead to disrupted egg production.

Like it or not, Jenna decided, first thing tomorrow she needed to locate where the planes were based and register a complaint.

THE NEXT MORNING, electing to breakfast at the café she'd seen in town, Jenna gave the waitress their orders for pancake combos and then casually added, "We're new to the area. Yesterday I saw a couple of small planes in the air, but I don't see an airport on the map my Realtor gave me."

The waitress paused. "Airport? There's none closer than El Paso. Oh, wait. I almost forgot, one of our hometown boys recently moved back and has reopened a defunct private airpark about twenty minutes out of town." She popped her gum and stabbed a finger in the direction of Jenna's ranch.

Later, after their breakfast was paid for, Jenna managed to extract from her the name of the road to the airpark. They buckled in and set off.

The road to the airpark was gravel and littered with potholes. After she hit a particularly bone-jarring dip, she muttered a prayer that she wouldn't blow a tire or break an axle on the Cherokee.

Her sister had been right about that, too. Her old car wouldn't have survived this treacherous drive.

At last she topped a small rise and looked down on a weather-beaten facility. Definitely the airpark, because runways marked by reflectors fanned out from the opening of a low-slung multiplane hangar.

Slowing, Jenna saw a plane parked outside what might be an office. She braked when she caught sight of a man standing on a ladder, his head buried inside the open airplane engine.

Setting her emergency brake, she fought an unexpected kick to her stomach. It shook her to see the lean man in an olive-drab military jumpsuit, the type Andrew and his fellow flyers wore.

She fumbled with the key as she shut off the motor, grappling with her feelings.

Andee unfastened herself, threw open the back door and raced toward the ladder yelling, "Daddy! Daddy! Daddy!"

"No, no, sweetheart." Scrambling out, Jenna registered the shock on the mechanic's face as he straightened, dropped a tool and nearly toppled off his tall perch.

Jenna caught up with Andee just short of the ladder. She dropped to her knees, arms encircling her daughter even as her heart spiraled.

The blond stranger's short-cropped, trying-to-curl hair didn't resemble Andrew's dark buzz cut. But he had those clear blue eyes—flyer's eyes. Eyes the exact shade of a perfect sky for flying. It was the attribute that had first attracted Jenna to Andrew.

As the stranger descended the ladder, Jenna controlled her fast-beating heart as she cradled Andee, who by then had discovered her mistake and had begun to sob.

"Shh, sweetie. Mommy's right here." Even as Jenna's gaze lit on the stranger's scuffed boots, she heard his taut voice above her.

"Lady, I don't even know you."

Moving her inspection up his long legs, past narrow hips to a wider chest, she mumbled, "I'm so sorry. It's your flight suit. My husband was an Air Force pilot. Andee's barely six. I'm afraid she hasn't fully grasped that her daddy's…uh, in heaven."

Jenna hugged the child tighter and kissed the top of her curls. She saw the man yank a red rag from his back pocket and wipe his greasy hands. And in the moment before he took a step back, she thought she saw those gorgeous blue eyes cloud with pain.

# CHAPTER TWO

FLYNN'S LEGS STILL felt shaky from his near slip off the ladder. His bad leg had buckled when the kid had run toward him calling "Daddy" as if she meant it. That had more than rattled him. Now, though, looking at the attractive woman who'd announced she was an Air Force widow brought back memories he'd wanted to forget.

Such as the duty visit he'd paid to his best friend's pregnant widow after he'd gotten out of the hospital. Chip's widow had wept throughout his twenty-minute stopover even while she'd demanded to know how he'd survived the crash when her husband had come home in a casket.

Yes, Chip had been the pilot assigned to fly that mission. Also true, Flynn knew his best friend hadn't slept well the night before. Maybe the outcome would have turned out the same if Flynn had volunteered to fly. But maybe it wouldn't have. And that continued to haunt him.

Now this woman and child brought everything hurtling back. What did she want? Flynn hoped it wasn't flying lessons. He didn't think he could teach a service brother's widow to fly.

"Is she okay?" he nervously asked the woman who stood once the little girl's crying had tapered off.

"She's better. The concept of permanent loss is difficult for a child to grasp," the woman said, leaning over to blot the child's tearstained cheeks with a tissue she'd pulled out of her blue jeans.

He found himself mesmerized by the tender mother-and-child moment.

Flynn hadn't let himself fall for any woman since the one he'd figured he'd marry had dumped him. Saundra had made it clear that she'd expected him to stay in the military until he made full colonel and could provide her a better lifestyle than…well…than the one he wanted.

"You know," he said, wading through his memories, "the concept of permanent loss isn't easy for anyone." When the woman didn't respond, he quickly added, "My name is Flynn Sutton. I own this airpark, such as it is. What can I do for you?"

"I'm Jenna Wood. This is my daughter, Andee. I own the ostrich ranch beyond those hills." She pointed and Flynn turned to look over his shoulder.

"Really?" he said. "I know a guy who raises ostriches somewhere over there. Well... we aren't actually friends, more like we were introduced. I've never visited his ranch," he said, gesturing with a hand.

"This whole county was mostly small farms when I was a kid. I left to join the Air Force and have only recently returned. Nearly all of my daylight hours have been spent clearing runways and readying hangars to house planes. I plan to teach flying, but for now I'm tinkering with my planes and renting out hangar space..." He caught himself babbling and paused. "Uh, do you own a small plane? Or...is it lessons you're after? I won't be offering classes for a while."

"Oh, no to both. I'm here because a plane flew far too low over my pens yesterday. It scattered my flock, and I worry that if it happens again some of them could be injured.

I came to ask if planes could take off and land from a different direction so as not to frighten my birds."

Flynn frowned. "If your husband was a pilot, surely you know planes take off and land with prevailing winds. Anyway, this airpark had the runways already set when I bought it. But I'm only set up for daytime flying… Although, eventually I'll install lights so my customers can take off or land at night, but—" Once again Flynn found himself running off at the mouth. "What I'm saying is, the lane directions are what they are." He gave an offhand shrug.

Jenna filtered her fingers through Andee's hair. The girl continued to cling so tightly to Jenna's leg, she couldn't have left if she'd been ready to give up and go.

"Could you at least ask your customers to not buzz my pens?"

Flynn spread his hands. "Sorry, I only rent to them. I've no say over where or how they fly."

Pursing her lips, Jenna unwound Andee's arms. "Then thanks for nothing, Mr. Sutton. The way you feel about planes, you may want to tell the plane owners that I fully intend to check to see if they're breaking any city ordinances."

Flynn started to say he doubted her ranch would be zoned in the city, but the woman had grasped her daughter's hand and was prepared to leave.

Just then his dog loped out from the closest hangar. And after giving a couple of excited barks, the part sheep dog, part no-name breed bounded up to the kid and licked the lingering trail of tears off her face.

The woman shrieked and attempted to shield the girl. To no avail, it turned out, since the kid flung her arms around his mutt, instantly all giggles.

"It's okay, don't panic," Flynn assured the woman. "I hoped when Beezer adopted me that clients and visitors might think he's a guard dog. Really he's a cupcake."

"Mommy, he likes me." Andee petted the dog's shaggy gray-and-cream-splotched fur.

"I see that, honey. But...we need to go now. Please tell him goodbye." Jenna shook out the tissue again and this time wiped the slobber off her daughter's chin.

"'Kay." The girl clutched the animal's ears

and pressed a kiss on his black nose. When she straightened, she resisted her mother long enough to offer Flynn a shy smile and a hesitant wave.

He lifted his hand in response and returned her smile. He loved kids. On his leaves he'd spent as much time as he could with his sister's two boys. Really, kids had always figured in his future. A major reason why it was as well he and Saundra had split up.

Man, he needed to forget her. As he kept Beezer from following the cute little girl and her very pretty mother, he could've kicked himself for continuing to go back to Saundra.

Beezer rubbed against Flynn's good leg and whined. "I know, boy. You like people. Sorry, fella, you're stuck with me."

After the Jeep Cherokee had driven a ways away, Flynn released his grip on the dog's collar and briskly rubbed his furry sides. "Remember who found your skinny bones skulking around the hangar and took you in and fed you so that your ribs no longer stand out, you ungrateful mutt."

He stood and looked after the SUV. "Don't be swayed by a pretty face."

IT HADN'T ESCAPED Jenna's attention as she'd helped strap Andee into her car seat that the airpark owner's smile carved a dent in his right cheek that looked suspiciously like a dimple. She was a sucker for dimples. And military men had a way of turning the heads of females in her family, regardless of age. As her six-year-old had just proved.

Here she'd moved them across the country to get away from uniformed airmen only to find a hot-looking pilot owned a business a few hills removed from her new home.

Clamping her back teeth together, Jenna got in and drove off, ignoring how Andee kept waving.

"Mommy, why don't we have a dog?" Andee asked once the airpark disappeared behind them in a ruffle of dust.

Jenna tilted the rearview mirror so she could see her daughter better. "Well, mostly we lived in apartments," she said, not wanting to tell Andee that her father had repeatedly vetoed the suggestion of adopting a dog or a cat. Andrew had always been something of a neat freak. But he'd gotten more obsessive on his last few rotations home between tours.

"We don't live in a 'partment now," Andee responded.

"No, but I'm not sure if the ostriches would react well to a dog running around."

"What if he didn't run around? I could keep him inside the house with me."

Jenna frowned and realized she wasn't going to win this argument with logic. "You haven't even seen baby ostriches yet. I'm counting on your help feeding the babies after they pop out of their eggs."

"What will I feed them? We don't have any milk or anything in our 'frigerator."

"It so happens I see a grocery store in that strip mall across the street from the next stoplight. We'll go there and buy some groceries—for us, not for the birds. Mr. Martin, the man who used to own our birds, left their food in one of the sheds, remember?

"Ostriches don't eat people food," Jenna reiterated after she parked and helped Andee out.

"This isn't like our old store," Andee said, standing inside the door as her mother found a grocery cart.

"We'll probably have to get used to new brands, but the food will be the same. Besides milk, what can you think of that we need to get?"

"Pizza and pasketti."

"Oh, you funny girl. You'd eat those seven days a week if I'd let you."

"I like soup and cheese sandwiches, too, Mommy."

"That you do. Here's the soup aisle. It's a good place to start."

Jenna added up prices as they meandered the aisles. She hadn't told her family, but she'd had to pay cash for the ranch. It was a shock to learn that she didn't have a credit rating even though with Andrew gone so much she'd been the one to handle their budgets. She'd never questioned that their on-base housing and utilities had been in his name.

Before his death she hadn't given much thought to what went on behind the scenes in banking. They'd had a joint credit card.

After Andrew's death she'd had to apply for one in her name. The bank had issued her a debit card, which she'd needed to watch closely, since Andrew's benefits had been frozen until the completion of the investigation.

Before their marriage, she'd lived with her parents. After, Andrew had been the sole breadwinner.

Now it was all up to her.

Andee, who had wandered ahead in the aisle, suddenly ran back and plopped a box in the basket.

"Whoa, there. What are you getting, sweetheart?" Jenna picked it up and was surprised to see it was a supersized box of dog biscuits. "Honey, we don't need this. I said we might not be able to get a dog because of the ostriches. Run and put this back on the shelf, please."

Andee pouted. "But I can feed Beezer when he comes to visit me."

"Uh, honey...I know you liked Beezer a lot, but I don't want you to get your hopes up. We don't really know his owner. I can't think of any reason why we'll see him again. Put the dog treats back. I promise I'll ask Mr. Martin, the man who owned the ranch, if having a dog would scare the ostriches."

The girl clutched the box that bore the face of an almost dead ringer for the gray-and-cream-splotched dog she'd taken such a shine to. Then, long-faced, she dragged her feet back down the aisle, leaving her mother once again irritated over the unexpected consequences of her useless meeting with Flynn Sutton.

IT DIDN'T TAKE long to reach her card's limit and pack the back of the SUV with groceries.

In short order they reached the ranch. That brought a smile to Jenna's face—the very fact nothing in this town—even split in two by a major highway—was more than a dozen minutes from home. Most bases they'd lived on were huge and had taken longer than this to navigate from one end to the other.

Locked in thought, it took Jenna a few moments to register that a silver pickup with a skewed back bumper sat in the spot outside her home where she intended to park. She slowed as she noticed a man emerge from one of her sheds.

She pulled around the pickup, stopped and released her seat belt. She heard Andee doing the same. "Sweetie, stay in your seat for a minute. There's a man, a stranger, over by the ostrich pens. He's probably the manager the Realtor mentioned. However, I need to have a word with him to be sure."

"Okay." Andee leaned forward and pressed her nose against the side window. "Does he have a dog?"

"None that I see," Jenna muttered. "If he is the interim manager, I'll ask if he knows of any problems with us getting you a dog."

"Yay. I hope he says it's okay." Andee settled back to slurp the chocolate milk they'd splurged on.

Jenna saw the guy pull a ball cap from his back pocket as she closed the gap between them. He adjusted it to shade his eyes from the midday sun and leaned on a pitchfork he'd carried out of the shed.

Stopping short, Jenna gave her name. "I'm the new owner," she added. "I assume you're the man Bud Rhodes said was taking care of the ostriches in his absence."

"Yep. Don Winkleman. I didn't come by yesterday because Oscar said you were due in. I expected to hear from you."

"I didn't know your schedule."

"Been working some every day for two years. I wanted to buy the place, but Oscar needed all his money up front and I wasn't able to get 100 percent financing. You'll pardon me if I say you don't look like a rancher."

Jenna chuckled. "I'm still getting moved in. I have gloves and boots, so I'm sure I'll look the part of a rancher soon."

"Still, all the trappings don't make you a rancher." Don spat off to his right and wiped his mouth with a blue kerchief he pulled from a pocket in his overalls.

She couldn't say she liked this guy's tone.

He set the pitchfork against the shed. "I manage the place. That's worth more money." He abruptly named a figure substantially higher than what Oscar Martin had put in his notes.

The new amount he requested bowled her over. But Jenna refused to let his directness cow her. She figured the amount he'd named was for full management. She'd already planned that by working with him she'd soon be able to cut some of his current part-time hours. But she wasn't about to share that idea with him now.

"I'm not prepared to pay more than Mr. Martin was paying you."

"Sorry, that's what my services are worth, little lady. It's more than fair."

*Little lady?*

Jenna studied his iron jaw. He thought he

had her over a barrel. Maybe because she was new to the area or maybe because she was a woman. Either way his demand nettled Jenna. "Like I said, Mr. Winkleman, if you want to continue working for me, at the moment I'll match what Mr. Martin paid you. At some future date I foresee needing less hours, though."

"That's not acceptable."

"Well, you're free, of course, to quit."

The man appeared shocked, then his face hardened and he leaned toward her. "Nobody around knows this business like I do. You'll regret letting me go."

Still smarting from her failure to make any headway at the airpark, Winkleman's attitude left Jenna doubly resolved to stand firm. "Please go. Tomorrow I'll hire your replacement and drop off a check with Bud Rhodes for the hours you worked today."

Winkleman took another step toward her and fisted his hands at his sides. "You won't find anyone in town capable of filling my shoes. Soon enough you'll come begging and it'll cost you even more to get me back."

Andee had silently left the SUV, made her

way over and was now clinging to Jenna's shirttail.

Worried that she may have been foolish to provoke this man she knew nothing about, Jenna deliberately set Andee behind her.

She'd never been more relieved to see a vehicle pull into her lane than at this moment. Whoever drove the newer blue pickup, their timing couldn't have been better.

The three watched as it drove up and stopped adjacent to the Cherokee. Only then did it cross her mind that the newcomer could be a friend of Don Winkleman's. Just in case, she eased her cell phone out of her pocket and prepared to dial 9-1-1.

*What if this area doesn't operate on 9-1-1?*

Stuck between a glowering Winkleman and the blue pickup, Jenna's heart pounded.

The door opened and Flynn Sutton, the airpark owner, emerged.

Andee let out a squeal. "Mommy, Mommy, look! Beezer did come to visit me. You said he wouldn't, but I knew he would."

Andee nearly mowed Flynn down in her haste to meet his seemingly equally excited dog.

"So it is you," Flynn said, taking off his

mirrored sunglasses as he approached Jenna. "I figured it had to be," he muttered. "After you left I received a fax from my landlord. Oscar Martin said he'd sold everything and now I owe my rent to the woman who bought him out."

"You? You rent the house in town?" Jenna's jaw went slack.

Flynn ran a hand over his close-cropped hair. "Seems so," he said. Then, as if seeing the other man for the first time, Flynn glanced from him to Jenna and asked, "Is there a problem here?"

She ran an eye over the lean yet muscular pilot who no doubt would come to her rescue if she needed help. But she hadn't come here to rely on another man.

She'd gone from relying on her dad, to relying on Andrew, to relying on Rob and Melody. A single mother at thirty-one, it was time she took care of herself.

"No problem," she said. "Mr. Winkleman was just leaving."

"That I am." Stalking to his pickup, he yanked open the door and vaulted inside. "You owe me half a day's wages!"

He slammed the door, started the pickup

with a roar and cut the wheels in such a tight turn, he scattered sand in his wake.

Flynn reached out to shield Andee and Beezer from flying dirt.

Sputtering in indignation, Jenna rushed to help. "Andee, honey, are you okay? That was uncalled for," she said, using both hands to dust off Beezer's shaggy fur.

"What was that about?" Flynn asked, staring after the truck.

She shrugged. "He worked for Mr. Martin and I let him go. I expect he was blowing steam. Is there something you needed other than to introduce yourself?"

Flynn twisted his lips to one side. "I hate to start our business dealings with a complaint…"

She suppressed a groan. Could this day get much worse?

"But when I went home for lunch, my air conditioner was making funny noises. Before I finished eating, it quit. The house is small, so it didn't take long to feel like an oven inside. I climbed up on the roof to take a look at the unit—"

"You what? You can't just… I mean, I would be liable if—"

"I know about all there is to know about an airplane, but I'm afraid I know nothing about air conditioners. It's leaking. I couldn't tell from where."

A knot balled in Jenna's stomach. Because she'd had to deplete her savings to buy out Oscar Martin, and because Andrew's death benefits were being held up, she was short of working capital. Everything had cost more than she'd budgeted. The property. The insurance. The Jeep. Even groceries. The last thing she needed after her unsettling encounter with Don Winkleman was another costly problem.

Tugging on her bottom lip, she organized her thoughts. "I'm not familiar with any of the reputable businesses in town. I guess I can check with my Realtor. Do you know a repair service that can send someone to take a look at it?"

"I do."

"Wonderful. If you don't mind calling them, since you'll no doubt need to arrange to be home to let them inside, I'd appreciate it."

She took the grocery receipt out of her

pocket, ripped off one end and jotted her cell number on the back.

"Now, I really have to put my groceries away. And with Winkleman gone, I have chores that need doing." She struggled a moment with panic, realizing chores she'd never done before and repairing things like Sutton's air conditioner were suddenly all on her. "If you'll ask the repair person to call me with an estimate, I'm sure we can get you fixed up ASAP," she said, not feeling confident at all.

Flynn took the paper and tucked it into a side pocket in his camo pants.

She tried not to think how fine he looked in the T-shirt and pants. How well toned.

He opened the door to his truck and snapped his fingers at the dog. "Come on, Beezer, we gotta go."

Plainly, Andee was reluctant to release her grip on the big dog. "When can Beezer come to visit again?" she asked. "I wanted Mommy to buy him some doggy bones at the store. She made me put them back 'cause she said Beezer wouldn't come to our house." Her tone was decidedly accusatory.

Jenna averted her eyes from the scene as

her daughter finally let go of Flynn's pet and the dog leaped into the pickup.

"Oh, wait," she said as Flynn started to join his pet. "It's silly since I own the house, and somewhere in the stuff I got from Mr. Rhodes is the address. I really should make time to drive by and have a look at it."

"Sure thing." Flynn reached into his glove box. He plucked out a business card, turned it over and wrote his address. "It's a doll-house compared to this place," he said, handing Jenna the card. Their fingers brushed and they both pulled back so fast the card fluttered to the ground.

Flynn scooped it up. He continued to eye her home as he extended the card by its edge. "Your place is big for two people. It's pretty remote, too. But, hey, I guess Oscar lived here alone."

In Jenna's estimation he could have kept those comments about her home being re-mote to himself. After all, she was still somewhat disturbed by Don Winkleman's attitude.

"It's more space than Andee and I are used to," she said, tucking her daughter against her right thigh. "We're going to be happy here, aren't we, munchkin?" She ran a finger down Andee's dusty nose.

"We've got lots of room for Beezer or a dog like him," the girl announced, causing Jenna to blush.

Flynn laughed. "G'bye." He again headed for his pickup and it was the first time Jenna noticed he walked with a limp. She wondered what his story was.

She watched as he got into his pickup and shoved the dog over. He closed the door and rolled down the window, waving as he made a slower turnaround than the one Winkleman had.

Beezer leaned around his master, stuck his big head out the window and barked, his ears flapping.

At the sound of her daughter's joyous response, Jenna vowed to call Oscar Martin that night to ask if a dog might scare the birds.

## CHAPTER THREE

"DO YOU THINK Beezer can have a sleepover with me sometime?" Andee sounded hopeful as she peered up at Jenna.

"Probably not, honey. I don't think dogs understand what's enjoyable about a sleepover. Not like kids do. Hey, we have groceries to take into the house." Jenna went to the Cherokee and lifted out two bags. "Will you grab the milk, please?"

"Okay." The girl kicked at the dust on the way to the vehicle.

"I know our new home doesn't have kids nearby to play with. But I'm sure you'll like helping out with the ostriches."

"What can I do with them? They're way bigger than me."

Jenna glanced at her daughter's long face as she set one bag down and unlocked the door. "It takes a few weeks for chicks to hatch in the incubator. Tonight I'll study up on how many chicks it's advisable to add to our flock."

"I want lots."

"We can't add more than the land will support." Jenna set her bags on the counter, took the milk jugs from Andee and placed them in the fridge. "Mr. Martin's notes say chicks grow fast. He said it takes an eighth of an acre to sustain an adult bird. That's why we'll sell most of our eggs."

"I'm hungry. Can I have a peanut-butter-and-jelly sandwich?"

"I'll fix us both one right after I bring in the rest of the groceries."

When she returned with the remaining bags, Andee was sitting at the kitchen table snuggling Cubby Bear. She'd gone back into her shell.

As Jenna stored the things she'd bought, she contemplated checking in town to see if the school or library offered summer classes for kids. Swimming, maybe, or little theater.

Before Andrew's investigation, Andee and her former school friends had loved to dress up and play make-believe.

As if associating with Colonel Wood's daughter would somehow rub off on their kids.

After she folded the last empty bag, Jenna got down plates and opened the bread. In the middle of spreading peanut butter, Andee suddenly said, "Can Daddy see us here in our new place?"

Jenna fumbled the knife and it clattered against the plate. "See us how?"

"My Sunday school teacher said Daddy could look down and see me from heaven. She said heaven is up above the clouds. Here, there aren't many clouds." Andee's little face crinkled, worry plain in her eyes.

Jenna carried their plates and the jar of jam to the table. Sitting, she slowly spread strawberry jam on the slices of bread that weren't covered with peanut butter. Still struggling in her own mind, she cut one sandwich in two and slid it across to Andee.

She'd had a hard time wrapping her head around the fact that Andrew had flown extensively in war zones and returned in one piece, only to die practically in his own backyard in a senseless, controversial accident.

She couldn't—wouldn't burden Andee with her own uncertainties.

"Heaven is a huge place, and it's...everywhere. Do you remember when we drove a long way from home to see a rocket launch?"

Andee nodded. "It went up and up and up, and disappeared."

"That's right, the rocket went all the way to the moon, but it still didn't reach heaven. Do you remember how Grandma said he's with you every time you think about him?"

"Uh-huh." Andee stared at her sandwich a moment longer. "Do we get milk to drink?" she asked, placing her bear in an empty chair before she picked up half of her sandwich and took a bite.

More than happy to change the subject, Jenna jumped up, took down glasses and poured each of them a glass of milk.

"What was that bad man doing here before Beezer came to visit?"

Jenna swallowed what she was chewing, then chased it with milk. "I don't think he's bad, Andee. He wasn't happy. He worked for the man I bought the ranch from, but he wanted me to pay him more for doing the job he'd been doing. I didn't—don't think that's right. I told him no."

"So is that why he got mad and left? What if he comes back?"

"Don't you worry, okay? Mr. Winkleman thinks I can't do without his help. Tomorrow, we'll go into town and find someone else.

"If you're finished with your sandwich, let's stack these plates in the sink and go see what he was doing with the ostriches. I'll bet it's something you and I can handle."

"Okay." Andee slid off her chair and carried her plate to the counter. She went back and collected Cubby Bear, then waited for her mom by the kitchen door.

Jenna took off her earrings, tied back her hair, got out one of three pairs of work gloves she'd bought and led the way to the pens.

"I saw Mr. Winkleman set down this plastic bag when he came out of the shed. Shall we see what's in it?"

Andee trudged not so enthusiastically after her mom. She held her bear tight to her chest.

"Oh," Jenna exclaimed, "the bag is filled with ostrich feathers."

Peering into the bag, Andee asked, "Do the feathers fall off?"

"Some do. Mr. Martin used to only take

the feathers during molting season—when they fall off—so we don't have to hurt the birds to get them. The sale of feathers is one thing that makes raising ostriches profitable. That means, what pays us money," she added because she saw Andee open her mouth.

Instead the girl asked, "Who wants feathers? What good are they?" She picked one out of the bag and studied it. "It's big."

"Ostrich feathers are the only feathers that naturally absorb dust instead of pushing it away. Hmm, I wonder if my feather duster is ostrich... I remember an article I read said some car manufactures like ostrich feathers for the final dusting before they paint a car.

"Stay with the bag for a minute, Andee. I'll go inside and get his notes."

"Will you come right back?"

"Yes, silly. And I'll leave the door open so you can see me."

Andee nodded.

Because Andee acted so uneasy, Jenna whipped into the kitchen and grabbed up the folder of notes. She was out of breath after running back. "Okay, so that didn't take long, did it? But, sweetheart, I can't have you worrying any time I'm out of sight. You used to go out to play catch or to ride Brittany's bike."

"At our old house there wasn't so much nothing," Andee said, sweeping her arm in an arc that encompassed the desert land beyond the ranch.

"That's the difference between city living and country living." Jenna knelt and opened the folder of notes.

"What does it say about the feathers, Mommy?"

"It says the ostrich feathers are soft because the birds don't fly. They use their feathers to warm them on cold nights and to shade the chicks we'll return to the pens."

"So, taking the feathers really doesn't hurt them?"

"No. It's like cutting our fingernails and toenails. The loose feathers can safely be plucked." Jenna gazed through the fence at the tall, gangly birds. "We'll have to blindfold them, though, to help keep them calm."

"My teacher used one at Tessa's birthday party when we pinned the tail on the donkey."

"The very same... Maybe I was too hasty in firing Mr. Winkleman," Jenna muttered.

"I suspect there's an art to plucking feathers."

"Is that the blindfold?" Andee asked, pointing to what looked like a black silk scarf draped over the doorknob of the small shed.

"Sharp eyes. I didn't notice it hanging there." Rising, Jenna walked over and picked the item up. "I bet you're right, Andee. This is soft. It's folded and sewn so it can be tied."

"I'm not big enough to help."

"No, you're not." Hauling in a deep breath, Jenna slowly let it out. "I sank all of our money into this operation. I need to buck up and do this."

Just as she made the proclamation, the same airplane she'd seen and complained about to Flynn Sutton appeared over the row of hills and climbed slowly and noisily as it passed over the ostrich pens like a giant predator. As before, the birds ran in circles when the plane momentarily blocked the sun.

Squinting, Andee tipped her head back. "Is that Mr. Flynn? Do you think Beezer is with him?"

Jenna, who'd held her breath as she'd watched her flock scatter in disarray, didn't answer until Andee pressed her again. "I don't think it's his plane, sweetheart. And Flynn is his first name. Anyway, I doubt his dog flies with him."

"Why not?"

"I don't know. That was me guessing. On the other hand, dogs love to ride in cars... I just wish the pilot would stop flying right over our pens. Listen, I'm going to attempt to gather feathers. If you come stand by this fence, you can see into the small pen. I'll shoo three or four birds in and see if I can blindfold them one at a time. But don't you laugh if I mess up," Jenna ordered, grinning at her daughter.

Andee didn't laugh; she grew solemn. "What if they bite you, Mommy?"

"Then I'll turn them loose and definitely hire someone tomorrow to take Mr. Winkleman's place."

Nervous, Jenna took the blindfold and marched into the big pen. Opening the gate to the smaller one, she waved the blindfold and cornered four ostriches. As if they knew the drill, the birds high-stepped into the small enclosure. Feeling a tad smug, Jenna smiled to herself—until she saw it was a bin of cracked corn clipped to a rail of the fence that had enticed the ostriches.

After three tries, she managed to tie the silk scarf around one bird's eyes. It stood still enough for her to move to its back. She gingerly tested a few of the longer feathers. One slipped right out. Afraid of hurting the bird, she worked slowly across the tail until the ostrich grew antsy and began digging its claws into the sandy soil. She only had a dozen or so feathers in her bag. All the same, she untied the blindfold and caught the next bird.

"Are you getting lots of feathers?" Andee called.

"Not so many," Jenna said. "If Mommy doesn't get better at this, we won't be supporting ourselves on feathers."

The second ostrich was larger and she was more successful. Developing a rhythm, Jenna moved to bird number three. She'd barely tied the blindfold when her cell phone rang to the tune of "Bolero" she'd programmed into it. The penned ostriches hissed and bolted at the raucous noise.

Clamping her teeth together, Jenna yanked off one glove and fumbled the phone out of her pocket. "Hello?" she said loudly, fully prepared to tell her sister she'd have to call her back, because who else would phone her?

Before the caller responded, Andee let out a shrill scream, ending in a wail.

"Mommeee! Momm…eee! That bad bird took Cubby Bear."

Jenna could see Andee shake the fence as she climbed up the rails and extended her arms toward a strutting ostrich that indeed had the stuffed bear by an ear. The bird vigorously shook the toy from side to side.

She hurriedly stripped the blindfold off bird three and hollered, "Stop! Drop that this instant. Oh, for Pete's sake."

Scrambling out of the pen, she waved the phone she forgot she had in her hand. Keeping her quarry in sight, she plowed a path through a flock of birds that had begun to chatter.

"Is everything all right?" Jenna heard a disembodied masculine voice waft from her phone.

"Who is this?" she demanded, bringing the phone to her ear, chasing the ostrich that still had a grip on Cubby.

The child's wailing had risen to a siren's pitch.

"It's Flynn. I repeat, is everything all right?"

"No, it's not," Jenna said. "An ostrich has Cubby, and Andee is throwing a fit. Whatever you need, you'll have to call me later."

"Uh, sure. Can I help?"

Jenna stuck the phone back into her pocket without answering. She waved her arms at the offending bird.

"Andee, please hush! Your crying is making trapping him harder."

Of course she didn't stop crying; she wanted her toy. However, she did cut the decibel level enough for Jenna to slow the ostrich, who ran in circles around her. She discovered that an ostrich could cover a lot of ground on those long, spindly legs.

Wishing she had brought some of the cracked corn with her, she took a calming breath and figured out a way to cordon off the thieving bird. Having foiled his escape route, she swatted his scrawny neck with a glove. The ostrich swung around to peck her, dropping the bear. Triumphant, Jenna grabbed Cubby by a leg—but not before the ostrich drilled her left arm with its beak.

Trying not to react—sure her shirt had a

hole and afraid her arm was bleeding—she hurried out the gate.

Andee ran to her, arms outstretched.

As Jenna looked for any damage to the bear and herself, she decided this was not a good beginning to ostrich ranching.

Her phone rang again. Once more the birds closest to the fence stampeded for a canopy.

"Yes? Hello?" Jenna did her best to keep her voice calm.

"It's Flynn Sutton again. What in blazes is going on over there? I'm at the airpark. Do you and the kid need help?"

"No, but thanks for asking." Jenna sagged against the metal fence rails. "It's a long story and I won't bore you with details. I'm sure you didn't call to check on my well-being—the first time."

"Uh, no. I called because the air-conditioning guy can check out the unit today. I have an appointment in town at four that I expect will take about an hour. He said he'd stop by at five. But he thought since you own the place, it'd be a good idea if you were there."

Jenna looked at her watch. It was three forty-five. She didn't know where the day had gone. She had maybe a hundred feathers for her effort. Andee had Cubby in a body-lock—but she'd retreated to the side of the shed, where she now huddled, looking anxious.

"That was a mighty sigh," Flynn said. "Look, if it's inconvenient for you to get away, I'll make that clear. I'll have the repair guy write an estimate. But if you don't mind, I'll drop it by this evening. I'd like to have it fixed ASAP. I don't relish sleeping in an oven."

"My problems aren't yours, but your problem with the air conditioner is mine. I'll clean up and be there at five. Maybe it'll be something the repairman can fix today."

"I hope so. Thanks. If I'm not right there on the dot, the repairman's name is J. D. Fuller. He should be in a panel truck marked with Hometown Electric."

"All right. Goodbye." Jenna slid the phone back into her jeans. Happy that blood wasn't running down her arm, she returned to the pen long enough to retrieve the blindfold she'd dropped. Darting past the curious birds, she latched the gate and crossed the dusty yard to where Andee hovered.

"Is Cubby okay?" Bending, Jenna inspected the brown bear that had been Andee's favorite toy since he'd been a present for her second birthday. Jenna had done the birthday shopping because, as usual, Andrew had been away. But he'd surprised them by coming home in time, so Jenna had let him give their daughter the bear. From then on Andee associated the stuffed animal with having her daddy home.

Since the funeral, the bear had been her constant companion.

"I thought his ear would be ripped off." Andee inspected the ear, wet from ostrich spit.

Jenna sponged it dry with a tissue. "I imagine the bird was attracted to the red satin bow around Cubby's neck. Maybe you didn't hear us the day Auntie Melody, Uncle Rob and I discussed how ostriches are attracted to shiny things. That's why I took off my earrings earlier. The bird wasn't being mean, Andee. Just curious."

"It scared me."

"I know, sweetie. You scared me when you screamed." She gathered her daughter, bear and all, in her arms and trudged to the house. "That was Mr. Sutton on the phone.

We're going to change clothes and meet him at his place."

"I get to see Beezer again! I wish he was mine."

This time Jenna recognized when she sighed. Flynn Sutton's dog was another problem.

Inside the house, Andee set her stuffed toy in a kitchen chair. "Are we going to dress up in dresses to go see Mr. Flynn?"

"No. No, of course not." Jenna tucked her gloves in a drawer. "You probably don't even need to change. I was in the dirty pens. I need to shower."

"We always wore dresses when we went to get Daddy at the airport."

"Yes, well…Mr. Sutton is not Daddy," Jenna said through her clogged throat as she headed for her bedroom.

"I want to call him Mr. Flynn, or Flynn, 'cause I like that name better."

"Maybe he won't mind, Andee." She stepped into the shower and turned it on. She took the time to wash her hair.

Chasing ostriches around was hot work. Maybe she should have agreed to pay Don Winkleman more.

Rob and Melody's skepticism about her ability to make a go of the ranch was proving valid.

She vowed, as she dressed, that she'd do whatever it took.

She felt refreshed and upbeat by the time they left the house.

"It's hot inside the car, Mommy."

"I've turned on the air. It should cool down soon." As she adjusted the vents, Jenna felt compassion for Flynn Sutton's predicament with his home air conditioner. She hoped the repairman could offer an easy fix.

"Do you know where Mr. Flynn lives?"

"I have the address," Jenna said, turning off the main street and driving in the direction the Realtor had marked on the map. The residential area didn't look overly prosperous. Not that the homes were in decay, but they were far from being as elegant as the residential areas in Florida and Maryland.

"There. It's that cream house with the dark green shutters."

"I don't see Beezer."

Jenna rechecked the address on the back of Flynn's business card. It was the right house. "It's just five o'clock. Apparently we've beaten the repairman and Flynn."

"Ah, you didn't call him Mr. Sutton, either."

Jenna frowned and parked at the curb. Oddly, in spite of counseling Andee on what to call him, she'd begun to think of him as Flynn, too. "He is renting from us, honey, so we'll probably be on friendly terms."

A panel truck with the Hometown Electric logo splashed across the side pulled to a stop behind Jenna. She got out of the Cherokee and put on her sunglasses.

"Mr. Fuller?" She extended her hand to the young man, who'd also gotten out.

"Ms. Wood, I guess?" He grinned and briefly touched Jenna's hand. "Flynn said he might be detained. I'll just run up a ladder and have a look at the unit."

"Fine, we'll wait under that tree." Even now she felt a trickle of sweat under her bra.

J. D. Fuller was on the roof by the time Jenna saw Flynn's pickup round the corner. He pulled into the driveway and sprang out of his truck, removing his sunglasses as he greeted her. He wore gray pants and a pale blue short-sleeved shirt that matched the color of his eyes.

He looked as handsome in civilian dress as he did in a flight suit. Better, maybe, she thought grudgingly.

She wished she hadn't changed into her worn jeans.

Beezer leaped from the pickup, zeroing in on Andee, who greeted him with a big hug.

"Those two are quite a pair." Flynn smiled at Jenna. "Have you been here long? Any verdict from J.D.?" He squinted up to the top of the roof.

"No, but he's only been up there a few minutes. I've heard some banging around."

"I'd open up and let you inside, but in this five-o'clock heat it's probably cooler out here." Flynn put his sunglasses back on.

"That's okay. I'm pleasantly surprised to see this home is among the nicer ones on the block. And you have flowers along the front. That's more than I have."

"Yeah, I even have a nice patch of grass out back. Oscar said the couple who rented before me loved to garden.

"There, looks like J.D. is finished his inspection." Flynn moved toward the ladder and Jenna took in his limp again.

The repairman stepped to the ground and adjusted his baseball cap. Waggling his clipboard, he beckoned Jenna closer.

She didn't like the deep grooves between J.D.'s eyebrows.

"The compressor is shot," he said.

That didn't sound good. She could see the two men share a look.

"What does that mean in the way of repairs?" Jenna asked.

"It means you need a new air conditioner. As old as this unit is, it's more costly to replace a compressor than to buy a new unit with a current SEER factor."

Jenna glanced between the two, silently asking for more explanation.

Flynn undid his top button to open his collar and rubbed his neck as he hooked his sunglasses on the shirt. "SEER stands for Seasonal Energy Efficiency Ratio. New regulations come out every few years."

"I see. But this house passed inspection a few weeks ago," she said. "Shouldn't I have known about this issue then?"

J.D. shook his head. "When these suck-ers go, they go fast, often without warning. I maintained this for Mrs. Wilson. It operated fine. Now, poof, it's shot."

Taking a deep breath, Jenna pinched the bridge of her nose.

"I have brochures in the truck on the types we handle. Any of them could be installed as soon as possible." J.D. ripped the sheet off his clipboard and passed it to Jenna. He loped off to the open back of his panel truck, where she heard him rummaging around.

"This is a bummer," Flynn murmured, eyeing Jenna.

J.D. jogged back and gave Jenna three brochures. "The cheapest we recommend is $5,500 on up to $12,000. For a house this size I suggest the one at $8,000. It's a workhorse and over the long haul will give you the best bang for your buck."

All Jenna could think was that $8,000 was way more than a buck. Way more than she had in the savings account. "Is there such a thing as buying used?" she asked hesitantly.

The repairman looked sympathetic. "No."

Not looking at Flynn, she paced back and forth, trying to figure out what to do. "The truth is I can't afford any of these air conditioners at the moment. I'll need to arrange for a bank loan, and I worry that since I'm new in town that may take time."

The men didn't respond. Flynn ran a hand through his cropped blond hair. "My rent's paid up for this month. To be honest, I've sunk so much into the airpark I'm sort of strapped for cash, so I'm not in a position to front you the money and take it out in rent."

Jenna glanced at Andee, who sat beneath the tree pretending to read to the dog.

Turning her gaze on Flynn, Jenna took a deep breath and said in a rush, "All I can think to do is to temporarily offer my upstairs. It's vacant. Two bedrooms with a full bath. One room has a double bed and dresser and a TV. The movers hooked up cable. The second room has a daybed, a nightstand and bookcase. As for kitchen privileges, I can make room in a cupboard and the fridge. We can set a timetable so we don't trip over each other."

Flynn scrutinized Jenna for the longest time, then his dog. Even though Beezer sat in the shade, he was panting hard from the heat. "It isn't ideal," Flynn muttered darkly. "I'll give you a month to square things with the AC. Just so we're clear, there's no need to get chummy because we're sharing a house."

Jenna's mouth dropped open, then snapped shut. She sensed heat rising to her cheeks and was sure of it when J.D. said, "My card's stapled to those brochures. Call when you decide which unit you'd like." He left in a hurry.

Jenna clutched the brochures, locked in a glaring match with her renter.

## CHAPTER FOUR

"Look, the thing is…I don't keep regular hours," Flynn said, grasping at straws. Of course he couldn't admit he didn't want to live with her, but it sure didn't look as if he had another choice.

He should have known he couldn't trust this woman to keep a simple business contract; he paid rent, he got a decent roof over his head…and air conditioning.

And now, burned by another woman who couldn't keep a commitment.

He'd given Saundra an engagement ring shortly before he'd gone on his last tour abroad. She was to live in his apartment while he was gone and they'd get married as soon as he came home. His family had been ecstatic. Only, things changed drastically when he returned home broken, needing a new knee and months of rehab. Saundra wasn't meant to play nursemaid—not that he'd asked her to—and hadn't dealt well with his decision to leave the military, either.

"I haven't established a routine yet," Jenna said, plainly putting the brakes on her own irritation. "Believe me, this isn't an arrangement I'd opt for if I could see another choice. I spent part of today insisting to Andee that Beezer could not come to our house for a sleepover."

That triggered a full-bodied laugh from Flynn.

"It's not as if we're going to be *roommates*," she was quick to add.

Flynn lifted an eyebrow before dropping his sunglasses to cover his amusement. He guessed Jenna Wood had stronger objections to this forced situation than he did.

What was there about him that she found so objectionable? Shouldn't he be relieved? Well, he wasn't. And that gave him pause, which killed his sense of humor.

He cleared his throat. "The bank is already closed today. I hope you plan to see about that loan first thing tomorrow morning."

"I do, so don't lose sleep over it." Jenna put on her own sunglasses. "Andee, bring your book, honey. We're finished here."

"Beezer likes *The Very Hungry Caterpillar*. I told him next time I'll read *Goodnight Moon*." Andee hugged the dog, then skipped to the car. The dog shook himself and ambled after her.

"I bet those two will be happy," Flynn muttered.

"Undoubtedly," Jenna snapped. "I certainly hope Beezer doesn't scare my ostriches like the low-flying aircraft from your airpark."

"I did mention your concern to the pilot," Flynn said.

"You did? When? I'm sure the same plane scattered my birds again today. It was noon or a tad later."

"Hmm. I spoke with him when he showed up to fly today. It was right before I went home for lunch."

"Thanks for saying something, even if he apparently didn't pay attention. Yesterday you didn't sound as if you'd involve yourself."

"It's not my place to. But, like I said, the opportunity presented itself."

"He's probably dropped down on my list of problems anyway." Jenna frowned. "I really should buy two air conditioners. My house is only equipped with a swamp cooler. I prefer AC. It cools better."

"Maybe if you crack open a window it'll work better."

Jenna studied Flynn pensively. "I'm not keen on leaving windows open at night. Especially not downstairs, where Andee and I sleep."

"Ah. Well, installing security screens on the lower level might be cheaper than buying a new air conditioner big enough to cool your house. There are bound to be drafts."

"Mommy," Andee called. "I thought you said we had to go. The car is hot."

"I'm coming."

"Did you ask if I can call him Mr. Flynn?"

Flynn glanced between the pair. "You can both call me Flynn." He lowered his voice. "It seems easier if we use first names, considering…" He hesitated. "Will it be less confusing if I bring my stuff over tonight after she's in bed?"

"So she can wake up and find you there in the morning? Not that she goes upstairs. I'll make it plain she's not to bother you. The dog is a different matter. Keeping her from loving on him will be hopelessly impossible." She frowned. "Like I need this aggravation."

"I'd check into one of the motels, but neither allows pets."

"Well, maybe we'll laugh about it once it's over."

"I really doubt that."

Jenna stiffened. "Of course not. What was I thinking? I'll check to be sure you have bedding and towels upstairs. Beyond that, I've no desire to run a motel. The rooms don't come with maid service." She turned and marched to her vehicle.

Flynn pinched the bridge of his nose. He'd set her off again.

The dog gave a woof as Jenna got in the SUV.

"Beezer, come here, boy. Let Andee go. Come on, you traitor."

The dog finally came to him as Jenna drove off, and butted his thigh. "Hey, careful, buddy." He stepped out of Beezer's reach. "Keep your paws crossed that my stupid blood pressure will be normal tomorrow. I need the VA doc to approve my flight physical. I want to start advertising those flying lessons… Maybe get Travis Hines signed up for a refresher course."

"Did the man fix Mr. Flynn's air conditioner?"

Jenna tilted the rearview mirror just enough to see Andee. She had thought to wait until their evening meal to break the news concerning their houseguests. But this was the perfect opening. "The house needs a new one."

"Why?"

"The old one broke and won't cool the house now."

"Beezer was hot sitting with me in the shade. Will living in a hot house make him sick?"

"Honey, Flynn rents that house from me, so getting a new air conditioner is up to me. Since it will take a while to arrange to get one, I invited him to stay upstairs at our house."

"And Beezer?"

Jenna sighed. "Yes, Beezer, too."

Andee clapped. "I hope it takes a long, long time to get a new air conditioner. I want Beezer to stay with us forever."

"That's not even a remote possibility. And

Mr. Flynn needs his privacy while he's at our house. Understood?"

"What's pri...va...cy?" Andee dragged out the word.

Jenna slowed to turn off the highway onto their lane. She didn't answer at once, because suddenly, talking about inviting a man she hardly knew to move into the house with them gave her pause. What did she really know about him?

"Mommy? You didn't answer."

She stopped outside the house and turned around. "Privacy means leaving someone alone."

Andee scowled at her from between stuffed-animal ears.

Jenna recognized the stubborn streak she'd run up against before. "The upstairs is off-limits to us. Just like Auntie Melody and Uncle Rob's bedroom suite was when we lived with them."

"They didn't have a dog. I bet Beezer will want to come down and play with me."

So much hopefulness shone through that statement, Jenna sighed and gathered up her purse. Andee had weathered so many disruptions in her life of late, Jenna felt guilty for that.

Maybe the bank would grant her a loan tomorrow and Flynn Sutton and his dog would be gone within the week.

"Let's go in. I'll fix spaghetti and a salad for dinner. How's that?"

Andee tried to hold on to her frown, but spaghetti was her favorite and she shot inside. Jenna employed bribes judiciously, but this was one time she didn't feel bad about in the least.

As Jenna prepared the meal, she took a moment to phone Oscar Martin in Hawaii.

"Mr. Martin, this is Jenna Wood. I bought your property in New Mexico."

"Right. How are you getting along? I hope my notes make sense."

"They're very detailed. Thank you. I hadn't realized you would already be gone when I arrived—that was a bit of a surprise."

"Yeah, about that. I should've let you know, sorry, but I had an opportunity come up that…wouldn't wait. Couldn't have really told you much more about the birds than are in those notes, though."

"It's…fine. We'll figure it out. I'm afraid

I had to let your manager go, which hasn't helped matters."

"What? What did he do this time?"

"This time? So he's... Never mind. He's gone now. He demanded more money, which I didn't have to pay him. Got a little heavy-handed about it, and I'm relieved to be rid of him."

"Well, he always did have a temper."

"I'm calling because my daughter would like to get a dog. Do you know if that poses a problem for the birds?"

"Well, I never had one. But lots of times folks driving past on the highway stopped in to see the birds—ostriches aren't your every-day sight in New Mexico—and often they had kids and dogs. Little yappers disturbed the birds. I think I put in the notes that noises give them a fright. I suppose there are dogs that don't bark much."

"Yes," Jenna murmured, her thoughts on a big, lumpy dog that barked whenever he saw Andee and airplanes that swooped overhead. "Well, thank you for sparing the time to chat with me. I hope you're enjoying retirement."

"Living by the ocean is great. I do miss the ranch, though. You enjoy the place. And

sorry Winkleman didn't work out. Don't hesitate to call if you have other questions."

Certainly some surged to the fore. But
they were all impossible for the man to help
with from so far away. "Thanks."

Jenna hung up after he said goodbye.

She guessed she'd see how much Beezer
barked.

JENNA SAT AT the kitchen table after dinner
studying Oscar Martin's notes. Andee sat
across the table putting together her second
puzzle.

"I don't know, Andee," Jenna said for the
umpteenth time. "Relax. Beezer and Flynn
will get here when they get here."

"That doesn't say when. Where will the
hands on the clock be when they come?"

Her uncle Rob had begun teaching Andee
how to tell time. She did pretty well for six,
Jenna thought, glancing up at the cat-shaped
kitchen clock. "Can you tell me what time
it is now?"

"Um. The little hand is on seven. And the
big hand is on six," Andee said, pointing.
"I don't get the between numbers. It's after
seven, but it's before my bedtime."

Jenna was about to explain again how the minutes worked when she heard a vehicle pull to a stop outside.

Andee saw the splash of headlights on the wall. "It's them. They're here. They're here!" she shouted, scrambling off her chair to dash and open the door.

"Wait!" Jenna jumped up, spilling her coffee and almost knocking over her chair. "Andee, we need to look out the window to see who's coming before we open the door."

Andee blinked. "Who else would come? We don't know anybody here 'cept Flynn and Beezer."

By now Beezer had both paws on Andee's shoulders and was licking her face. The girl giggled and the sound swept aside most of Jenna's lingering reservations.

"Do you need help bringing in your stuff?" she called to the man sliding two boxes and a large canvas duffel bag over the tailgate of his canopied pickup bed.

"I've got it, but thanks. One box stays in the kitchen. The other has Beezer's food and bowls. You decide if you want those to go upstairs. The duffel goes to wherever I'll be…uh, living."

"There's a laundry room off the kitchen. It has a tiled floor and a back door leading outside. I assume you take Beezer out after he eats and drinks. That would be handiest. But the upstairs bath is also tiled."

"If Beezer ate down here, I could help feed him," Andee piped up.

"Shh, honey. It's up to his owner."

Flynn staggered in juggling the duffel and boxes. He adroitly stepped around the girl and dog while also avoiding contact with Jenna, who held open the screen door. "The top box is my groceries," he said. "A few items need refrigeration. Just set the box on the counter if you will. I'll unpack it after I store my other stuff."

Jenna relieved him of the top box. Even though he said he'd unpack it, she took out the items that sat on top, making room in the fridge on a lower shelf. As she shut the door, she realized Andee and the dog had begun to chase after a well-chewed rubber ball that Beezer must have carried inside.

"Sorry," Flynn said. "That's his outside toy."

"Isn't Beezer smart?" Andee squealed. "He can catch the ball when it bounces high."

"Did you hear Mr. Sutton say that isn't an indoor toy?"

"Hey, if we're gonna all live under one roof, you've gotta call me Flynn. Otherwise I'll always be looking around for my dad."

His cell phone rang. He set down the items he held to take out his phone. "Speak of the devil," he muttered. "Excuse me a minute. Although it's gonna be my mom calling, not my dad."

Spinning to present his back to Jenna, he put the phone to his ear. "'Lo, Mom. I knew it was you…Uh, that's my landlady's little girl. She's playing with Beezer. Can I call you back later?…What? No…You've totally misunderstood. I'm not moving in with my landlady…Well, I am, but my room is up-stairs. Just bringing in my gear."

Jenna noted the stiff set of Flynn's shoulders.

"Mom…I explained that the air conditioner on my rental blew its compressor. I'm only bunking in her spare room until it's fixed… I let you know so you won't leave messages on my house phone. Just call my cell."

Sensing his mounting frustration, Jenna crossed to quiet her noisy daughter. "Andee, please sit and play quietly with Beezer. Flynn is trying to talk on the phone."

Andee's laughter faded in time for Jenna to hear Flynn all but shout at his caller, "What difference does it make how old...? Lonnie, put Mom back on...It doesn't matter...Yes...Six, I think...I'm hanging up now. Stop laughing. Goodbye."

He smacked the face of his smartphone and jammed it into his pocket.

He turned almost sheepishly. "Ah, that was awkward. Sorry, but I happen to be cursed with an interfering family."

"Frankly, I'm glad to know it. I started to have second thoughts about inviting a man I knew so little about to stay in our home."

Flynn gave a low chuckle. "That's rich. I had similar reservations. FYI, I have a meddling mom, an easygoing dad, a nosy older sister with a somewhat nosy husband, and two oblivious boys. They're eight and ten, and think I'm cool. The whole batch lives in Abilene. What about your family?"

"A sister and brother-in-law in Maryland—they meddle, too. My parents live in an expat community in Costa Rica. When my dad retired from the Army, my parents decided to live where their money would last longer. They spent two weeks with me when Andrew, uh—" She broke off abruptly and sucked in her lower lip as she glanced at her daughter.

"Gotcha. Enough about our families. I should take this duffel to where you want me to bunk." Flynn hoisted it.

"Through that arch is the living room. The stairs are on the left. This house has a front entrance into the living room, but it seems easier to come in through the kitchen."

"Makes sense to me." He started for the arch, limping.

"I hope navigating the stairs won't be too hard on your leg."

He paused. "It's a war injury. On the mend. Climbing stairs will be good therapy."

"Sorry, I wasn't being nosy."

"It's okay." Flynn ran a hand up and down his thigh.

Jenna thought he sounded terse and wished she hadn't drawn attention to his limp. To make amends, she picked up the box he'd left behind. "While you store your personal belongings upstairs, I'll set up Beezer's food bowls in the laundry room."

Andee, who had been sitting quietly with the dog's head in her lap, sprang up from the floor. "I'll help. I'll fill his water bowl, okay?"

Jenna was grateful when Flynn disappeared and she could relax. She set out a rubber mat that fit nicely in the empty space beside the dryer. "Here." She handed Andee a ceramic bowl that had *Water* painted in blue letters on its side. A matching bowl said *Food*. Having never had a dog, Jenna wasn't sure if she should fill the food dish with the kibble Flynn had brought or not.

Andee carefully set down the bowl of water. Beezer crowded in and immediately began lapping it up. "He's thirsty," the girl announced as she poked her nose into the box. "Hey, Flynn didn't bring any treats. We should've bought those, Mommy."

Jenna started to say maybe Beezer wasn't supposed to have treats, but she was interrupted by Flynn walking in, carrying a leash.

"I'm going to take Beezer for a walk."

"I wanna go, too," Andee said.

"It's your bedtime. Go in now to brush your teeth and get ready for bed. I'll come in soon and read a story. So choose a book."

The girl pouted, but Jenna remained firm. To Flynn, she said, "I don't know where you plan to walk, but I hope Beezer doesn't bark and scare the ostriches."

"I figured we'd go out to the end of your driveway and back. I wish I could take him for a run out on the desert." He tapped his thigh. "Do you run?"

She laughed and shook her head, but then wondered if he was angling for her to exercise his dog. "I'm not big on working out," she said.

"Really?" Flynn made a slow inspection of her as she stood in the laundry doorway. "How do you stay in such great shape?"

"Motherhood," she said drily. "Before you go, let me give you keys to the doors."

He followed her as she ducked back into the kitchen and took two keys off a wall rack. "I have extras for the kitchen door and for the one going out through the laundry room. I seem to have only one for the front entry."

Flynn took them. "These are plenty."

Feeling tension creep in again, Jenna opened an upper cupboard. "Earlier, I cleared this cupboard for you while you're here. Feel free to use any of the dishes or silverware. It's in this drawer." She tapped the knob.

"Okay. I'll take care of myself. Don't let me wreck your routine. Ignore that I'm even here," Flynn said.

Jenna thought that was highly unlikely. Already her nerves reacted involuntarily each time they were alone together. As now.

"I have an appointment at the VA tomorrow," Flynn said. "On the road to Albuquerque. I never know how long I'll have to wait, so if sometimes I roll in late, don't think I'm not coming in." He clipped the leash onto Beezer's collar.

"Do you take the dog to your doctor appointments?"

"Oh, sure. Staff there love him."

"Andee and I are pretty casual about when we eat, too. But you can use the kitchen whenever you want."

"Uh, tonight, after I come back from the walk, I figure I'll go upstairs and watch TV awhile before I hit the sack. So I won't disrupt your evening."

"When you come in, please turn out the lights."

Flynn nodded and left through the kitchen

door. Jenna heard the lock turn and let out a wobbly breath. Hurriedly she swept up the folder of notes and went to the living room.

"Can Beezer sleep in my room?"

"No. He's gone with Flynn on a walk. Let me drop this in my room and I'll be back to read to you. While we're in town tomorrow, we should sign up for library cards. Maybe they'll have a story time so you can meet some local kids."

"I'd rather stay home and play with Beezer."

Jenna rubbed away a frown. Was it only this morning that plucking ostrich feathers had been her biggest problem?

FLYNN WOKE UP and crawled out of bed. He'd slept better than expected in a new, unfamiliar bed. Sometimes his knee and leg ached so badly they didn't let him sleep. He peered around the room for Beezer, who'd been stretched out on the bedside rug when he'd turned out the lamp.

The door was ajar. He was sure it'd been shut last night.

The morning light drew him to the window. Jenna Wood, in cutoffs and a tank top, was dragging a hose over to fill water troughs in the ostrich pens. She was oblivious to being spied upon.

Flynn idly scratched his chest. He probably should feel guilty, but he didn't. He stayed at the window until she'd shut off the water and commenced filling bins clipped to the fence with dry feed. His own stomach reminded him it was breakfast time. He smoothed the bedcovers, gathered some clean clothes and went in to shower.

Refreshed and dressed, Flynn found Beezer in the kitchen with Andee Wood. So, had the girl sneaked upstairs and let him out of the room, or had Beezer figured out how to open the door? It wouldn't be the first time for the accomplished escape artist.

"Good morning," Flynn said, crossing the room to the cupboard Jenna had assigned him. He moved things around on the three shelves, but didn't see his cereal. That was when he saw his box already on the table in front of a stuffed brown bear. Andee slurped from a big bowl filled with his Froot Loops. And Beezer, the mooch, ate the same from an even bigger bowl tucked under the table.

Flynn picked up the box and shook it.

"It's all gone." Andee wiped her milky

lips on the sleeve of her robe. She stared up with huge blue eyes that Flynn realized were much lighter in color than her mother's.

"I see the box is empty," he said. "Beezer has dog food, you know."

"But he really wanted Froot Loops today. See, he ate his breakfast all up."

Even as the big dog licked milk off his chops, he put a paw on the girl's leg and eyed her bowl. Flynn decided this situation would be better handled by Jenna. "Okay, Beezer is coming with me. I saw your mom out by the ostrich pens. I'll tell her goodbye and let her know you're up."

The girl just blinked, so Flynn grasped Beezer by his collar and they went out the kitchen door.

He put the dog in his pickup and strode across the yard to where Jenna appeared to be pulling feathers from an ostrich. "I'm leaving," Flynn called. "Andee's up."

Spinning, Jenna set the plastic bag she held outside the fence. She turned back a moment to remove a scarf from around the bird's head. "Thanks for letting me know. I'll go check on her. When I peeked in on her this morning, your dog was sharing her bed."

"Is that right? He was lying on the rug next to my bed when I fell asleep. Another thing… Andee emptied my box of cereal this morning. What she didn't eat, she fed to the mooch."

Jenna's mouth opened. "Oh, I apologize. I'll certainly speak to her. Let me wash up and I'll fix you something. Scrambled eggs and toast, or French toast?"

"Not necessary. I'll grab something at the café." He paused. "I'm afraid to think what it says about me that during my lengthy sojourns in war zones, what I missed most was the breakfast cereals I ate as a kid. I brought Froot Loops. It could as easily have been a giant box of Cocoa Puffs."

The woman clearly thought he was ratting her kid out because he was possessive of the cereal. He cleared his throat. "A bowl the size Andee fed Beezer isn't good for him. The chocolate…" he explained.

"I understand. She'd never mean to hurt him. I'll take care of this, and I'll replace your cereal."

"Now you're making me feel like a jerk. If you'd like, I'll talk to her about some people food being bad for dogs."

"That would crush her, coming from you. I'll do it. I need her to learn right from wrong."

"He was a stray. I ran ads for weeks trying to find his owner. As fast as he took to Andee, he may well have come from a home with kids."

"Hmm. That would explain his instant bonding." She smiled.

Flynn felt that smile clear to his toes. "I, um, have to run."

Jenna shaded her eyes with a hand. He didn't run, but certainly left as fast as he could manage on a bum leg.

The man was a dichotomy. Gruff one day and kind and humble the next.

Andrew would never have offered to explain to Andee about the food. He had always left everything like that up to her. Andrew had been self-disciplined and expected it of others. Yet early in their relationship he'd known how to have fun. He'd grown more intolerant with each added duty tour abroad.

Truthfully, sometimes she'd been glad to have him leave.

Why did that come to mind now?

# CHAPTER FIVE

JENNA WENT INSIDE, not looking forward to the talk she needed to have with Andee. As it turned out, she saw at once by her guilty expression that her daughter knew she'd done something wrong.

"I ate all of Flynn's cereal. That wasn't nice, was it? I bet he's mad, huh?"

"You should have asked and not just helped yourself to something you knew didn't belong to us. As for Flynn being mad, he was more concerned that you fed Beezer so much cereal. Some people food is really bad for dogs, honey."

"Oh, no. Will Beezer get sick?" Andee looked horrified.

"If Flynn had brought the chocolate cereal you love, Beezer might have. People can eat chocolate, but it's not good for dogs. So, you need to remember not to feed him our food no matter how sad-eyed he looks."

"I won't do it again. I promise." Andee hugged Jenna.

"Okay. But when you see Flynn next, you need to tell him you're sorry. I'm going to shower now, then we'll drive to town."

"Do we still have to go to the libary? Yesterday you said…" Andee's voice grew muffled as Jenna went into her bedroom and stripped off her tank top.

"My first priority has to be finding someone to help with ranch chores."

"Why?" Andee appeared in the doorway to the adjoining bathroom.

"We need the ranch to make money, sweetie. And don't ask why. Take my word for it, we just do."

JENNA PARKED THE SUV on the street near the realty office. This morning the normally quiet town seemed to bustle. Perhaps Wednesday was the day devoted to errands. It was after ten, she realized, dropping down the visor so she could do a last check of her makeup. She'd worn a skirt and sandals, and her hair was clipped at the nape of her neck. She was hoping to make a good impression.

"You look pretty, Mommy."

"Why, thank you." Jenna reached back and tickled Andee. "You look fantastic yourself. Let's go see Mr. Rhodes."

They got out of the Cherokee and Jenna took Andee's hand.

When they walked in, the Realtor glanced up from his computer. Jenna had supposed at her last visit that Mr. Rhodes was alone because his office staff had gone to lunch. Today she realized he must operate a one-man business.

"Mrs. Wood," he acknowledged as he stood to greet her. "Is everything going well with your new properties?"

"Not totally. Mr. Martin's part-time employee and I parted ways. I'm hoping you can tell me where one goes in town to hire a general laborer."

"Don Winkleman didn't stay on? He wanted very much to buy the place, but he and Oscar couldn't work a deal." He paused, possibly realizing he was giving away confidential client information. "That has nothing to do with your question."

He scratched his head.

"We don't have an employment office. There's an active American Legion Post.

Our good weather and the Post attract quite a few retired vets." He appeared to give that some thought before he added, "They don't all stick around. Some are drifters. Some would rather not work. But some would."

"Where would I find it?" she asked.

"End of the street. There's an American flag flying above the Post flag. Yes, it's probably the best place to find farm help."

"Thanks. I'll go there now."

Andee skipped along, holding her bear. A woman arranging potted plants outside a small flower shop looked up, smiled and said, "Good morning."

Returning the greeting, Jenna felt her spirits lift. Once she settled into a routine, she'd have time to make friends.

She was surprised to discover that the only door into the Legion Post opened directly into a big, dimly lit room filled with dining tables and a horseshoe-shaped bar off to her right.

Laughter drifted from a well-lit area at the back that was probably a kitchen. Two men sat at the bar. *Drinking beer before noon?* She tugged Andee tight against her and stopped well short of the bar.

"May I help you?" a man Jenna hadn't noticed behind the bar asked.

"I, uh, Bud Rhodes directed me here. I recently purchased a ranch west of town. I need someone to help with chores a few hours a day."

The man polished a section of the bar, then flung the cloth over his shoulder. "Well, come on in and see if either of these jokers is looking for work."

Jenna gingerly approached the pair and was relieved to see they were drinking coffee. Both men looked to be in their sixties. One was clean-shaven. The other had a grizzled beard and salt-and-pepper hair tied in a ponytail.

"What kind of ranch?" the guy with the ponytail asked.

"Ostriches," she said, bracing for their reaction.

The bartender was the one who laughed.

"Not interested," said the clean-shaved one. "I'm hitching to California, where a buddy of mine is camped by the ocean. I can't answer for ol' Barney here." He clapped the scruffier man's shoulder. "He tells me he's been here awhile and likes it."

"Name's Barney Fisk, ma'am. Nam vet. I don't know squat about ostriches, but I reckon I can learn." He smiled down at Andee and remarked on her bear.

Based solely on that and the fact he had kind eyes, Jenna took a paper out of her purse and jotted down her address. "I'll be home by three if you'd like to drop by and see what the job entails. The job will be four hours a day, in the morning. If that suits you, I'd need to see references."

Bobbing his head, the man tucked the paper into his shirt pocket. "Ostriches are just big turkeys, right? My pa raised turkeys in Oklahoma. I put in time wrangling those birds."

"The work's probably similar," Jenna said, feeling better knowing the man wasn't clueless about farmwork. "We'll see you later. Come on, Andee, we have another stop to make before lunch."

Out in the hot sun again, Jenna put on her sunglasses and made sure Andee did the same. "I'll unlock the car and you get your coloring book to work on while we go to the bank. It's so hot, I hope your crayons didn't melt."

"Why would they melt?" Andee asked.

"Crayons are like the cheese I put on your grilled-cheese sandwiches, which melts in the heat."

Andee laughed. But her laughter died when she found the tips of her new crayons were soft and one or two stuck together. "They're icky."

"Not too bad. I think they'll firm up in the bank's air-conditioning. We'll have to remember not to leave them in the car."

Andee's lower lip drooped. "I don't like living here. When can we go home to Auntie Melody's?"

Jenna stopped at the door to Bank of the Desert. "This is our home now. We'll adjust."

They had to.

"You and Cubby have a seat." Jenna gave Andee the coloring book and crayons and directed her to one of three chairs in the small lobby. The whole bank was minuscule compared to the one on the base.

Looking around, she didn't see a place to sign up to speak with a banker, so she went up to one of two teller windows. "I'm new in town," she told the elderly woman. "I'd like to speak to a loan officer."

"That would be Mr. Hart, our vice president. If you'll have a seat, I'll let him know you're here."

"Vice president? I only need to apply for a loan," Jenna said.

"He wears many hats," the woman—Sharon, her name tag read—responded, coming out from behind the counter to knock on a door with the gold plaque reading Franklin Hart, Jr. Vice President.

A balding man threw open the door. He had on cowboy boots and a plaid shirt with a bolo tie.

"He's not wearing any hats, Mom," Andee said loudly.

"Shh, honey. That's a figure of speech." Jenna spoke in a low voice. The banker was studying her; she hoped she still looked okay—loan-worthy. He beckoned her inside, so she reminded Andee not to stray. "I'll leave the door open so you can see me and I can see you, okay?"

Andee plopped down across from the door and opened her coloring book.

"I don't believe we've met," Franklin Hart said as he offered Jenna a straight-backed chair, then rounded his desk to pull out his. He flashed her a polished smile.

"I'm new here," she said, glancing back to make sure she could see Andee. "Jenna Wood. I bought Oscar Martin's property."

"Ah, yes. The ostrich farm." The man picked up a gold pen.

"Plus a rental home in town," Jenna added, extracting her folder from the tote. "The air-conditioner compressor quit and a local repairman for the air company said it can't be fixed, which is why I need a loan."

"Do you bank with us?"

"Not yet. My husband was in the military, so we banked on base. I want to open an account here and move my funds."

Franklin Hart opened a drawer and pulled out a stack of forms. "Where's your husband? Is he overseas?" he asked as he scribbled Jenna's name on the form.

"He's deceased." Jenna hoped her voice hadn't wobbled as she'd said it.

The banker put his pen down and looked as if he wanted to say something but was at a loss as to what that might be. A man not accustomed to expressions of sympathy, then.

She let him off the hook and opened the

folder. "I'm the sole owner of the ranch and rental, which by the way is occupied. Mr. Martin asked to be cashed out. That took most of my savings, which is why I need a six-thousand-dollar loan for the broken air conditioner."

The banker leafed through Jenna's folder. "You have no income, Mrs. Wood. No credit history in your name and no track record for your ranch."

"I…uh…" Jenna fidgeted. "I only just moved in. On page two it shows how much income Mr. Martin made each month. That will be my income."

"Maybe. Maybe not. I can't tell you how many ranchers go belly-up in their first year, and you have zero experience. Come back after you can show me a year's spreadsheet of income versus outgo."

"Next year?" Jenna squeaked. "Aren't the properties I own free and clear enough collateral?"

Mr. Hart stood, closed her folder and handed it back. "Ours is a small, independently owned bank. We've remained solvent for forty years by not accepting iffy old farms and small area homes as collateral. But I hope you'll let us serve as your personal bank."

Jenna thought his smile would have melted butter as he showed her the door.

"I'm...sorry about your husband," he said.

Her stomach was so tied up in knots, she barely managed a civil thank-you.

Where was the next closest bank? Would all loan officers see her as a poor risk? What did she own that she could sell for enough cash to buy an air conditioner so Flynn could move back to his rental?

"You were gone a long time, Mommy. Me 'n Cubby are hungry."

"Cubby and I are hungry," Jenna said automatically.

"You, too? Goody." Andee gathered her bear and coloring items.

Numb, Jenna tucked Andee's coloring book and crayons into the tote bag with her documents that apparently spelled out her lack of net worth. Not for the first time in a few short days, she found herself bordering on tears.

Outside, Andee tugged her sleeve. "That bad man drove by."

"What bad man?"

"The one you sent away from the ostriches. He doesn't like us."

Assuming Andee meant Don Winkleman, Jenna opened the café door and assured her daughter that he was no one they needed to worry about.

FLYNN SAT OUTSIDE the VA clinic nervously tapping his fingers on the steering wheel. Beezer whined and hopped over into the front seat, where he pushed his nose into Flynn's ear until Flynn rubbed his head. "You've no idea how much I want to skip this appointment, fella."

Beezer pawed at Flynn's shirt.

For about the hundredth time he checked his watch. He opened his door and the dog gave a bark as he jumped to the ground.

Pets were allowed in the waiting room. Flynn knew that some dogs had been to war and some were medical service dogs. He also knew that a few guys freaked out before their exams and their dogs calmed them down.

Flynn hadn't suffered a head injury. He didn't have PTSD. And he never used to have high blood pressure. For him, Beezer was just great company.

Unrolling Beezer's leash, Flynn clipped it to the collar. Still, he didn't rush to the door. He was fine with letting Beezer sniff bushes that lined the wide walkway. Faced with the glass door at last, Flynn sucked in a deep breath and went in.

From the number of seats filled, he figured the doctors were backed up. One other dog sat at the feet of a bearded man. That dog, a yellow Lab, rose when it saw Beezer.

"Sutton, ten o'clock appointment," Flynn told the receptionist. She was the same woman who'd checked him in both other times. A Native American with warm eyes, she smiled at Flynn and acknowledged Beezer with a dog treat.

"We're running behind," she said. "You have time to go downstairs for coffee if you'd like."

Flynn felt his anxiety building. "Thanks, but I may go out and walk around."

A woman dressed like a nurse emerged from another door. She called out a name and the man with the yellow Lab collected a cane and painstakingly got up.

Flynn took Beezer and left. He meandered a walkway bordered by cacti and stopped to look at a sculpture depicting the seals of all military designations.

The minute he set foot back in the waiting room, he felt his heart rate jack up. It was stupid. He'd faced combat missions on less adrenaline than this.

At his last visit the doc had said he'd thought a couple of pieces of shrapnel were working their way to the surface. The surgeon at Bethesda had told him it could take several years.

He sat and picked up a well-read auto mechanics magazine. Beezer dropped down at his feet and buried his nose in his paws.

Not overly interested in the magazine, Flynn's attention was drawn to a new group coming in the main door. A woman assisted a tall man who teetered on a prosthetic leg. One shirtsleeve also hung loose. The woman steadied him and tried to keep a child in check.

Something in the cut and color of her hair combined with her age reminded Flynn of Jenna. The girl was probably a year or so younger than Andee.

Beezer got up, whined plaintively and scratched at the floor.

"Easy, boy." Flynn tightened his grip on the leash. "She's a cutie, but not your new friend." As if the dog realized his mistake, he flopped down again. The couple and child made their way to empty seats across the room. The woman went up to the reception desk and presented a sheaf of papers.

Flynn's thoughts reverted to Jenna and how she'd fare hiring an employee. And at the bank. He knew Frank Hart from elementary and middle school. Before their freshman year Frank's parents had pulled him out and sent him to a private school. He used to brag that he no longer needed to associate with dumb farm kids.

If he'd had to borrow from Hart's bank, Flynn wouldn't have bought the airpark. Luckily, his loan had gone through a military credit union.

Flynn had heard Frank, now a member of the country club and all, had grown more class conscious than ever. Flynn imagined the guy fawning all over a pretty newcomer like Jenna Wood.

He tossed aside the magazine and drummed his fingers on the arm of his chair.

The owner of the yellow Lab came out

from his exam, collected his dog and left. But it seemed as though another hour passed before the harried nurse called his name.

Flynn sprang up. "Would you watch my dog?" he asked the receptionist. "His name is Beezer."

"I remember," she said and ruffled his shaggy fur. "We got along famously last time, didn't we, boy?"

Beezer raised a paw, making her laugh.

Flynn fell in behind the fast-moving nurse with squeaky-soled shoes. He heard moaning coming from one room. His throat suddenly felt bone-dry.

"Change into a gown," she said. "I'll be back to take your vital signs and set up for minor surgery. Are you having any problems?" She glanced up, pen poised over his chart.

Flynn shook his head and she disappeared before he could produce the flight-physical form he had folded in his pants' pocket. Oh, well, he'd give it to the doctor if the nurse said his blood pressure was okay. Kicking off his boots, he shed his shirt and pants.

Man, he hated these gowns. He hated everything about exams now. Once his flight status was renewed, he'd quit coming here until next licensing.

A different nurse swept in. She checked his temperature and clipped his forefinger with a pulse meter. Without a smile or a single word, she wrapped his arm with a BP cuff and donned a stethoscope. Her eyebrows drew down over the bridge of her nose and Flynn panicked, fighting to breathe.

"Are you on blood pressure medication?" she asked, unwrapping his arm.

"No. I can't take it and pass a flight physical."

She scribbled in his chart, unclipped the pulse meter and bent to remove a surgery pack from a drawer, unrolling it on the counter. "The doctor will be in shortly."

"Wait, what did it register?" Flynn called as she started to leave. He tugged at the too-tight neck of his gown.

"Too high," she said. "Dr. Warner will prescribe a med."

The door snicked shut and Flynn's body jerked. Moments later the iron-haired doctor strode in, his white coattails flapping.

"What's with your blood pressure, son? You feeling extra stressed lately?" He had

Flynn lie back, and he retook his pressure. "Still high," the doctor announced. Adjusting his glasses, he inspected Flynn's knee and thigh.

"Not until I got here," Flynn muttered, making the doctor crack a smile.

"Big, tough flyer like you afraid of me snipping out two little bits of steel?" The surgeon washed his hands, opened a pair of surgical gloves and put them on.

"No," Flynn responded haughtily.

The doctor selected a scalpel from the surgical pack on the counter. "Both pieces of shrapnel are so near to breaking through the skin, I prefer doing this without a local anesthesia. Two little cuts and they're out. Save you an extra hole in your hip from a fat lidocaine needle."

"Go for it." Flynn clenched his teeth. He was more concerned about his elevated blood pressure. He shut his eyes when the doctor snapped on a bright surgical lamp with his elbow. Flynn barely had time to suck in a breath when he felt a sting and heard metal striking a plastic basin pressed against his thigh. The doctor dabbed the spot and made a second cut. That pain was worse and it took longer before Flynn heard a second clink.

"I see one more lump. It's still too deep. Come back in four weeks. I can probably get it then. With luck that'll be the end of it."

Flynn nodded.

"Lie still. The nurse will be in to dress these spots and bring you a prescription. I want you on a BP medication. You may have essential hypertension, which can go as fast as it came on, but unless it does, you need it controlled. If you start feeling light-headed on the pills, drop by and have your pressure checked."

Flynn slid his arm out from behind his head and fell back on the table.

*Four more freaking weeks* hammered inside his splitting head.

His license ran out at the end of the month. He had to lower his blood pressure fast or he could kiss teaching goodbye.

Kiss flying goodbye.

The thought was crushing.

Moments passed and yet another nurse whipped into the room. She put on gloves, swabbed his upper thigh with something cold that brought tears to Flynn's eyes. Then she put pressure bandages on both sites. "They shouldn't bleed much. Starting tomorrow, trade these dressings for regular bandages. Use those for a couple of days, especially when you shower."

He looked up at her. "After the—"

"No, in the shower. You don't want the wounds getting wet. Oh, here's your prescription. The doctor said he explained that if the meds make you light-headed, come in. I know you fly. Dr. Warner said to have you ground yourself for now." She delivered the news with a sympathetic smile.

"Sure," Flynn said, levering his torso up on his elbows. The pain had faded somewhat.

"Your wounds look great compared to many we see." The nurse discarded the swab and recapped the bottle. "Stop at the reception desk and book a follow-up." With that she hurried out.

Flynn felt as though he'd been flattened by a steamroller.

ANDEE WAS IN her room asleep and Jenna was sitting in bed looking up banks and pawnshops on her laptop when she heard the kitchen door open. Her boarder didn't stop in the kitchen, but she heard his measured tread on the stairs and the padding footfalls of his dog.

She felt surprisingly comforted knowing man and dog were in the house for the night.

Removing her reading glasses, she set them aside with the laptop. As someone used to living alone, just her and Andee, for long stretches of Andrew's deployments, this feeling of relief ought to be alien. Especially since she'd chafed all afternoon and evening, worrying about Flynn's return and his wanting to know what had transpired at the bank. The most logical way to get the money for the new AC was to ask Melody and Rob for a loan. But their help would surely come with all sorts of pressure to give this up.

She had no idea how much Andrew had paid for her wedding rings, but the diamonds weren't small and they were set in platinum. She'd planned to give them to Andee.

The water shut off upstairs. After a few minutes all sounds ceased.

She turned off her bedside lamp.


A NOISE JOLTED Jenna awake. The room around her was black. She listened, wondering if she'd dreamed it. But no, there it was again.

It sounded like a kitchen cupboard closing. Then the fridge. Her bedside clock told her it was ten past midnight. Jenna reached for her robe and slid into her slippers. Andee had left most of her glass of milk at dinner. Maybe she'd woken up thirsty and remembered her mom had put the glass in the fridge.

She stepped into the hall and saw that the light over the sink was on.

Jenna hurried down the hall, rounded the corner and stopped dead when faced with Flynn Sutton at the sink. He was dressed only in dark blue boxers. Backlit the way he was, every sculpted muscle in his upper body stood out as if carved in stone.

"Sor...sorry to interrupt," she stammered, words sticking in her throat.

Flynn whirled from the window over the sink, spilling a glass of water and then quickly grabbing some paper towel to wipe it up. "I came down to see if you had aspirin or something. I didn't bring any with me."

Jenna jerked a thumb over her shoulder. "I have some in my bathroom medicine cabinet. Do you have a headache?"

He rubbed a hand over his thigh. "No,

I…uh… The doctor cut some shrapnel out today."

"Oh. I didn't realize you were still undergoing treatment. Wait here. I'll bring you a couple of extra-strength capsules."

Flynn started to decline, but she'd already dashed away. He set the glass on the counter and adjusted his sleep shorts. They looked as decent as if he had on swim trunks. He couldn't help noticing that Jenna wore something pink and silky that swirled around her knees.

She turned on the overhead light and set the capsules on the counter next to Flynn's glass. Her gaze lit on his bandaged leg. "Do you need a new dressing? That looks bloody."

She bent for a closer inspection and Flynn felt her warm breath on his skin. His stomach muscles tightened. "It'll be okay until morning. The nurse put on a pressure bandage… I should leave it. I'll buy some bandages and switch to them tomorrow."

Straightening, Jenna indicated by a sweep of her hand that he should take the pills. "I didn't realize you had fresh injuries."

Flynn swallowed two capsules with water, then shrugged and gestured with his glass.

"Not so fresh. It's been almost a year since our chopper was shot down. It was our bad luck to hit the ground near a land mine."

To avoid Jenna's wide eyes, he turned away and decided not to tell her how the enemy knew how to shoot down a chopper so it landed on or near a roadside bomb filled with nails, tacks and glass.

He put his glass in the dishwasher. "Don't waste sympathy on me. My best friend and another good guy didn't make it out."

Jenna clutched the front of the frilly robe she'd hastily put on. "I'm sorry," she said quietly. "I know how that is."

"Yeah, well… Listen, I didn't mean to remind you of your loss. It's late. Time to turn in again. Oh, hey, how did you make out today?"

Afraid she'd been caught watching the play of his shoulder muscles, she wished she'd gone straight back to bed after giving him the pills. "On the plus side, I hired a new part-time worker. A Vietnam vet… Barney Fisk. He's never worked with ostriches, but he came by this afternoon and he's okay with my terms. And his references checked out."

"I've run into Barney at the Legion. He's a decent guy."

"Good to know. Uh, but...the bank refused my loan request." She ran that last part of the sentence together.

Flynn leaned on the counter. "Turned you down? Why?"

"I'm not creditworthy."

"You mean you owe too much on your mortgage?"

She heaved a sigh. "I don't have a mortgage, which is why I don't have savings to draw on. The story I got is the bank doesn't lend money on farms because they're too risky."

"Farms are too risky, huh?" He shook his head. "Let me guess—Frank Hart."

She did a double-take. "Yes. How did...?"

"Knew him from when farm kids weren't beneath him."

"Well, I never had credit in my name, either. I handled our family finances, but everything was in Andrew's name. At the time I had access to everything I needed. If I had it to do over..." She let that trail.

"Don't worry," she quickly added. "Before I left my sister's I applied for my own credit card. It should arrive soon. And I have a second avenue I'm considering." She paused, trying to find the words to reassure him. "I wish I had more positive news."

He shrugged. "We're making do. Beezer's happy. Did you see he's sneaked into Andee's room again?"

"No, but I've no doubt she encouraged him. I'm fully aware you paid to have a place of your own."

"I trust you'll get it ironed out."

She bobbed her head, then motioned toward the arch. "Uh, ranch work begins early. Guess I'll get back to bed. Just shut off the light above the stove when you head upstairs." She turned off the overhead light, plunging them in shadow.

"I'll go up, too. The pills have helped already. What do we say...first one up in the morning brews coffee?"

Jenna folded her arms. "You're saying that because I already tipped my hand about getting up early. By the way, I bought you a new box of Froot Loops. And I capitulated and let Andee buy Cap'n Crunch."

"If Beezer—"

"She's promised she won't share people

food with him ever again. I'm sure she'll be a model child. Her aim is to get a dog after you guys leave."

Flynn flexed his knee, testing his bandages. "She puts me in mind of my sister's youngest son. He always thinks one step ahead."

He snapped off the stove light and moved toward the door where Jenna stood. The only light came from the glow of the moon through the kitchen window.

"Do I detect envy in your voice?" The setting felt too intimate and Jenna began to edge out of the room. "Say, are you divorced? You may have kids, for all I know."

"I don't. Came close to marriage once… I like kids. I hope to have a couple someday. I'd like my business to be making money first."

"Plans can go awry," Jenna murmured. "I hope spending time around Andee doesn't change your mind about having kids. Her favorite word of the hour is *why*. Don't let her drive you crazy." She took a few steps down the hall.

"Uh…my breakup was rough." In the dark, Flynn almost stumbled over Jenna. He put out a hand, connected with her robe and pulled back fast. "Left me leery of... I don't know what, really. If I've acted like a jerk—"

"It's okay. For the record, if Don Winkleman knows you're staying here, he'll probably think twice about giving me a hard time. If that sounds self-serving—"

Flynn lightly touched her shoulder. "I don't work far away. If he shows up and Fisk isn't around, call me."

Jenna ducked out from under his hand, but still imagined she felt the imprint. "It's not your problem." She walked on past the stairs.

"I mean it."

Her stomach reacted to his warm tone. "Andee complained to the librarian about having no friends here. Now we have one. Two, with Beezer."

She hurried to her room without looking back.

Closing her bedroom door, she leaned her head against the cool wood, shivering.

# CHAPTER SIX

FLYNN WOKE TO a room splashed with sunlight. He'd slept better than expected after his midnight rendezvous with Jenna. He stretched lazily, then realized it wasn't the sun that had woken him but rather noises outside his partially open window. Focusing, he heard shrieks followed by a woman shouting "Shoo, shoo, shoo" and "No, no, don't go that way."

He limped to the window and pulled back the curtain. The scene below had him grabbing for his pants. Ostriches were running free. They were everywhere. Staring down on his pickup, he saw a bird pecking the side mirror.

Pulling on his pants, he shrugged into a shirt, then socks and boots.

Another glance into the yard revealed several birds craning their scrawny necks to peer at their reflections in the darkened windows of Jenna's SUV. She was dashing around, yelling and snapping what he thought was a dish towel.

Every bird she herded back into the large enclosure sprinted past the covered areas to emerge from another open gate on the far side of the sheds. Jenna mustn't have known that.

He descended the stairs as rapidly as possible on his bad leg. He decided to go out through the laundry room, figuring that would put him behind the milling flock. *Wrong!* A hundred or so ostriches roamed alongside the house. Maybe twice that many wandered in the empty lot beyond the ranch's developed property.

Having no idea whatsoever how to move so many long-legged birds back into confinement, but judging Jenna had the right idea, he turned back and grabbed a bath towel out of her laundry basket.

He first checked his pickup mirrors to see they weren't broken, then waded into the melee shaking his towel like a matador wielding a cape just to get through them. He was rewarded with seeing eight or so birds charge ahead of him toward the pen.

Coming up behind Jenna, he called, "What happened out here?"

She spun around. "If I only knew." Her voice cracked. "I got up when my alarm went off and went to the kitchen to put on the coffee. I glanced out the window to admire the pink sunrise and two ostriches were looking back at me. I almost had heart failure."

"Your gates are all open. If you go close the far ones, I'll steer as many birds as I can into the main pen."

"All the gates are open? How can that be?"

"We can Monday-morning-quarterback after we get all the birds contained. Where's your employee?"

She checked her watch. "I don't know. I asked him to be here by seven. With the luck I'm having, he could've quit." She started to move off, but the kitchen door banged open.

Andee, still in her nightie and disheveled from sleep, emerged holding her bear. At her side lumbered Beezer. He gave a little yip followed by a low, excited bark.

Jenna changed direction. "Yikes! Sweetie, take Beezer back inside. We're trying to get the birds into the pens."

"Why?"

Jenna's sputtered response came too late. The dog charged down the steps and, with ears flying, began nipping at the legs of huddled ostriches. The surprised birds strutted fast into the enclosure.

"Will you look at that!" Flynn exclaimed. "Hurry and shut those far gates."

"Will he hurt them, or get hurt?" she asked as she wove through clusters of birds.

"He seems to know what he's doing," Flynn responded, watching her shut the next gate and then all the remaining open ones.

Rushing back, Jenna paused to check on Andee before she helped drive the ostriches inside. "I'm so rattled I forgot they only kick forward." She saw Flynn continue to snap a striped bath towel behind four prancing birds. But combined, their efforts were minuscule compared to the amount of ostriches the zigzagging dog brought to the pen.

"How does he know to do that?" she asked, blowing out a breath as Beezer raced off to round up another set.

"Damned if I know. Being part sheep dog, herding is his natural instinct. Hey, watch the gate. Don't let them dart out again. Open the gate when Beezer and I bring in a new batch. He's headed to the field. I saw birds at the side of the house."

"Let me go—you're limping more. You stay here and man the gate." Jenna noticed he wasn't overjoyed at being sidelined. But he did as she asked.

"Mommy, let me help!" Andee hollered from the porch.

"No, the birds are way bigger than you," Jenna said as she skirted the porch. "I know they only have two toes on each foot, but the big toe is more like a claw."

All at once an airplane rose above the foothills. Its sudden appearance stampeded birds loose in the field before the plane swooped low and flew the full length of the pens, creating panic there, too. The plane cleared the house, banked in a half circle and made a second pass, sending more birds into frenzy. Jenna stopped to watch.

Flynn gestured with both arms until the plane pulled up and flew off to the west.

"It's that same airplane that scared me 'n the ostriches the other day!" Andee shouted. "The man driving it made Beezer lose a whole bunch of birds."

"I believe it is," Jenna said, shading her

eyes to watch the red-and-white plane fade to a dot. "Andee, honey, I'd like you to go inside. Dress in the shorts and shirt I laid out on your toy chest. Then you can come back out and watch Beezer work. But stay on the porch, please."

Andee let the screen door slam shut, causing the nearby birds to flap wildly.

"Do you know that pilot?" Jenna demanded of Flynn.

"Yeah. He rents a hangar from me."

"Does he hate ostriches? Or does he get turned on by watching them panic?"

Flynn widened the gate to let the twenty or so ostriches Beezer had shepherded into the grassy pen. Closing it, Flynn stopped to pat his head. "Good dog. Go round up more birds."

Beezer bounded away to nip and nudge while steering clear of kicks aimed his way.

"Are you ignoring me because you're afraid I'll cause trouble for the pilot and lose you a client?" Jenna demanded.

"Look, he's a young guy. Cocky and immature, but I don't think he's malicious. I'll speak to him again. He may have seen birds outside the pens and flown low for a closer check. We don't know he didn't plan to report the problem to authorities."

"Oh, he wanted to be helpful. *Right*." She rolled her eyes. "I'm going to chase some out of the field. When Andee comes out, make her stay put. So far the birds haven't pecked us, but I got drilled by one the other day. I want her to like the ostriches. I want her to like the ranch."

Flynn nodded, still looking up into the sky.

It took the two of them and Beezer another hour and a half to collect all of the birds. Luckily, with the land being so flat around them, they could see when they had them all.

Breathless, Jenna called to Andee, "Come help me fill the water troughs. Afterward we'll all go in and I'll fix pancakes and eggs. Beezer gets an extra ration of his food," she said, bending to stroke the dog's heaving sides.

"I should shower and go," Flynn said.

"You need to eat," Jenna responded. "Unless you don't like pancakes and eggs."

"Oh, I like them. There aren't many foods I don't like," he said, wiping the sweat off his face.

"Okay, then. Why don't you feed Beezer and pour yourself a cup of coffee? By the way, I set a box of large bandages on the counter."

"Thanks, I appreciate that."

Jenna took Andee's hand and went to unwind the hose at the big shed.

In due time they were all seated around the kitchen table digging in to stacks of golden pancakes and a pile of scrambled eggs.

Andee asked the question that had been on Jenna's mind. "How did all the ostriches get loose?"

"That's an excellent question." Flynn frowned as he raised a forkful of eggs to his lips. "I inspected one gate latch. It looked okay. I couldn't see any way even curious birds could unlatch it. And for all four to be opened…" He shook his head, ate his mouthful and added, "It's not logical that you or Barney would've gone into all of the pens yesterday and forgot to shut every one when you came out."

Jenna picked up her coffee mug. "I did show him how to harvest feathers. As I recall we only went in and out of the pen and the inside gate to the back pen, where we released the birds we'd finished." She groaned. "Now the birds we took feathers from are mixed in with those not done."

"Do you think you should notify the sheriff?" Flynn blotted syrup off his lips with his napkin.

She gripped her cup handle and tried to ignore how tempting his lips looked. "Uh… you think it's that serious?"

"Don't you? If Beezer hadn't been so adept, or if you'd been here alone, you'd probably be rounding up birds until midnight tonight. It's pure luck that none of them stepped in gopher holes out in the field."

Jenna scraped back the hair that had fallen in her face.

"Beezer's so smart. May I give him a doggy treat?" Andee asked Flynn. "Mommy bought some at the store yesterday when we got new cereal."

"Maybe take him outside, since he tends to crunch dog biscuits all over the floor," Flynn said.

"Mommy?"

"Stay away from the pens. Tomorrow is egg collection day and we need the ostriches to calm down so they'll lay a lot."

Andee carried her plate to the sink, then ran into the laundry room, where she emerged seconds later with a large bone-shaped biscuit. Beezer padded close at her heels and barely saved his tail from getting caught in the screen door as the girl dashed out.

"He's putty in her hands," Flynn said, grinning.

Jenna let a moment pass as they listened to Andee talking to the dog. Nervously pleating her napkin, she said in a low tone, "I didn't want to bring this up with her listening, because she's already afraid of Don Winkleman. Frankly, he's the only person I can think of who might wish to cause me trouble. He did say I'd be sorry if I let him go, or something to that effect."

Flynn got up and refilled both of their cups.

"I probably shouldn't have fired him," she lamented.

He returned the pot to its burner and turned back to her. "I'll track down Winkleman in town today and grill him."

"No, don't," she said. "I mean, it's nice of you to offer, but if he is to blame, maybe letting the birds out got all the mad out of his system. Accosting him might just provoke him further."

"Maybe."

The screen door flew open. "Mr. Fisk is coming! He's pushing his big bike. Can I get a bike like the one Brittany had?"

"Not right away, honey." Jenna got up from the table and began clearing it. She set everything in the sink and ran water over the plates and silverware.

"Barney rides a bicycle out here from town?" Flynn dumped his cup in the sink.

"Barney rides a Harley," she said, turning off the coffeepot. "I asked him to shut it off and walk it in from the end of the lane." She pushed open the screen door and jogged down the porch steps, leaving Flynn to follow behind her.

"Sorry I'm late, Ms. Wood," Barney called. "I camp out and don't have an alarm. Generally the sun wakes me up, but this morning it didn't."

The news that he camped out took Jenna aback. Barney had listed an address on the makeshift employment form she'd given him. He'd put the same address on his tax-withholding slip.

"You live at a campground? Is that the address on your employment form?"

He paused before shaking his head. "I use the address for the Legion Post. But I have a bank account in the town where I mustered out of the Army. My rocking-chair money gets directly deposited there. I just...well... haven't had a permanent residence in years."

"Rocking-chair money?" Jenna slanted a questioning glance at Flynn, who had joined them.

"I think he means his social security pay," Flynn murmured as he shook hands with Barney.

"Yep. Twenty years a sergeant and what I get from the government doesn't amount to a hill of beans. But...I'm not tied down nine to five. I supplement when and where it suits me." He toed down the kickstand on his bike. "So I'd better get right to it, Ms. Wood. I'll still give you four hours today. Shall I start where I left off de-feathering birds?"

"Uh, I had a problem this morning. The gates somehow got opened. All the birds got loose. We'll have to recheck the ostriches for those already plucked. Unless you recognize those you did yesterday."

"What gates?"

"All of them," Flynn said.

"No kidding? I was careful to close and check on the ones I went in and out of. How do you reckon they got opened up?"

"We think—" A sharp jab from her elbow made Flynn stop.

"Didn't you mention needing to get ready for work?"

Flynn frowned down at her. "In fact, I have a meeting with Mayor Curtis Parker at eleven."

As he started to turn away, she was quick to ask if it was about municipal flight regulations. "That prevent planes from flying low over farmland," she added.

He avoided looking at her.

Why wouldn't he acknowledge that his tenant was going out of his way to harass the ostriches? she wondered.

"Last week the mayor contacted me about a group from Albuquerque he and the council would like to have hold a historic-airplane show here. Today he's arranging a conference call with the show owners."

Andee stopped tossing the rubber ball for

Beezer and turned to face them. "What are historic airplanes?"

"They're old planes," he explained.

Jenna frowned. "Does that mean a whole weekend of planes buzzing my ranch?"

Flynn stiffened, then slowly shrugged his shoulders, still not meeting her eyes. "Usually air shows have stunt flyers, exhibitions. I don't know if the historic planes are just for viewing or if their shows entail flights. There may be some offered."

Andee looped her arms around Beezer. "Did my daddy fly historic planes?"

"He flew fighter jets," Jenna said, still studying Flynn skeptically.

"Was his plane old? Is that why it fell out of the sky?"

"No," Jenna said quietly. "He was in an accident while he was flying. The Air Force is looking into how it happened."

The men both gave off signals of wanting to leave. "I've got to shower and change," Flynn finally said. "Barney, good seeing you. Andee, will you watch Beezer until I'm ready to go?"

She bobbed her head. Her little face pinched with concern.

Barney pointed to the pens. "I'll, ah, go get started."

"I need to clean up the kitchen," Jenna said. "Then I'll be out to help. It should be fairly easy to tell if a bird has loose feathers."

"Didn't you say tomorrow is egg collection day?" Barney asked as Flynn went into the house.

"Every other day, actually. Every two weeks they go to market. I'll phone the wholesaler Oscar Martin was contracted with. From his notes it appears his contract runs through this year."

She walked toward the pens with Barney.

"I plan to crate the remaining eggs in the morning and load them into my SUV for delivery. I hope they'll take our feathers at the same time." She opened the shed and showed Barney the egg boxes.

He eyed the stacks. "Okey-dokey," he said as he pulled a pair of gloves from his back pocket.

Jenna turned toward the house.

"Mommy, can Beezer stay with me today?"

"I think he always goes to work with Flynn."

"But if he's going to a meeting, maybe Beezer can't go."

"Well..." Jenna stalled until Flynn came out of the house. His hair was still damp from his quick shower. He'd changed into blue jeans and a black T-shirt. Both showed off his finely honed body.

Jenna felt grungy by comparison.

"Flynn, Flynn." Andee ran up to him as he slipped on his sunglasses. "Can Beezer stay and play with me today? You said you have to go to a meeting." The girl slid a hand under the dog's collar. "Beezer would rather stay here."

Flynn laughed. "Oh, he would?" The man swiveled his head toward Jenna. "What does your mother think of a dog hanging around?"

"Up to you. I made it clear to Andee that he usually goes to work with you."

"True. At the airpark he loves greeting the flyers. But I attended a council meeting once and he had to stay in an outer room. He's a people dog." Leaning down, Flynn ruffled the dog's floppy ears. "Tell you what, today he can stay. Tomorrow, though, I'm planning to fly. Beezer loves going up with me."

Andee nodded as she clung to Beezer.

As Flynn straightened and pulled out the keys to his pickup, Jenna said, "Tell Flynn thank-you, honey. He's made your day really special."

"Thank you," the little girl said. She waved when Flynn climbed into his pickup.

The dog danced a little and whined, but settled after Flynn rolled down his window and said, "Stay, Beezer, stay."

Driving off, Flynn glanced in the rearview mirror. Jenna still looked rumpled from her early-morning ostrich chase. He liked that she hadn't felt the need to do more than wash her hands and put on an apron before fixing breakfast.

Dust closed off his view, and his mind turned to Saundra. She wouldn't have chased ostriches without first putting on full makeup. Actually, Saundra wouldn't have chased ostriches.

Leaning an elbow out his open window, Flynn picked up his speed, lost in thought.

Saundra had been the daughter of a friend of one of his mom's friends, and so beautiful. She'd made him feel…something…when he'd been numbed by war. She had represented what he'd thought he was fighting for—to keep innocent people like her safe.

The Albuquerque radio station he liked blared out the newest song by The Band Perry. As he turned up the volume, he recalled that his taste in Western music had caused friction between him and Saundra.

He gave a snort.

What hadn't caused friction? Plainly, they'd had less in common than a couple should.

He couldn't blame his mom for setting him up—in fact, it had worked. His parents had been convinced he'd be better off on his next tour if he left behind someone he loved.

It was romantic to think love kept soldiers safe. Sighing, he turned down the volume. How many devoted husbands and dads had he seen die on routine missions? A lot. Too many. His best friend, Chip, for one. Flynn didn't know any guy more crazy in love or who had more looked forward to becoming a dad than Chip.

He wondered about Jenna's loss. He didn't know any details about the accident that had claimed her husband's life. Why would the Air Force still be looking into her husband's accident? Air collisions usually only took time if there was a question of wrongdoing.

A new tune began and he tapped his left thumb on the steering wheel in time to the beat. He should stick to his resolve and stay the heck out of Jenna's business.

Reaching the commercial district, he parked near the courthouse and walked to the mayor's office.

Two city council members greeted him at the door. They shook hands all around before Mayor Parker directed them inside his office.

"Let's get right to it," the portly man said, tilting forward in his chair. "If we haven't said it before, Flynn, we're all delighted to see you revitalizing what was once a thriving airfield. At the last council meeting, Dayton Hines said commercial development in a rural community like ours depends on private investors being able to land and store their corporate planes. By sponsoring this air show, our city is sure to grow."

Flynn rubbed his still-sore thigh. "I've never met Mr. Hines, although his son rents hangar space from me. Didn't you say a portion of ticket sales would be earmarked for a local charity?"

"That's right," the mayor rushed to say. "Now, son, we know you're a veteran. We don't want you to take this wrong…but the last couple of years our city park south of town has become a camp for homeless vets." The mayor bounced his pudgy fingers together. "The charity we plan to fund will buy and staff a shelter for veterans."

Glancing at the three nervous but eager faces, Flynn rubbed the back of his neck, where he could feel a prickle of tension.

"Tell me more about the show. How much of the proceeds will go to house the vets? And what's needed from my facility?"

"My contact up to now has been Dayton, but we can get the show's owner on Skype to give us particulars." The mayor buzzed for his secretary, who came in and, with a few keystrokes, set up the mayor's computer for the conference call.

The owner/promoter of the antique-plane show was congenial and a total airplane enthusiast. Flynn found himself quickly agreeing to hold the event.

They signed off and the mayor pulled out a pad. "We'll combine the air show with Pancho Villa Days. It's already set for the fourth weekend in June." He made several notes, then stood and came around his desk to clap Flynn on the back. "I have people who'll print and distribute brochures. My secretary will send out a press release. We already have a carnival booked. They can set up on the road to your airpark. The weekend will be a huge family event."

"Sounds good."

As he left the office, Flynn pictured himself taking Jenna and Andee to the carnival and air show. Providing Jenna would go…

Now, why would that be his first thought?

Sobering, he jerked open the door, stepped out into the heat and ran smack into Don Winkleman, who pulled the woman he was with out of Flynn's path.

Perhaps because Jenna was still fresh on his mind, instead of asking to be excused, Flynn scowled. "Did you get a kick out of opening all of Jenna Wood's gates last night? You're lucky none of the ostriches was hurt."

"What are you talking about?" Halting his companion's forward motion, Winkleman hitched up his pants and gaped at Flynn.

"Come on. I'd heard you said she'd be sorry she fired you."

The other man shrugged. "Sure, I was steamed. I ran that place for Oscar Martin. But she paid me. I've no reason to drive out there since. You say her birds got out? Good to hear none were hurt."

Flynn simmered. Obviously, Winkleman lied like a rug. He unhooked his sunglasses from where he'd tucked them into the neck of his T-shirt. "Just so you know, I'm keeping an eye on her place."

Putting the glasses on, he brushed past the couple and strode down the street to his pickup. He should have stayed out of it. He had enough of his own stuff to contend with; why insinuate himself in Jenna's trouble? Except that she had a big heart. And no one else had her back.

Wheeling out of the parking lot, he drove straight to the airpark.

He stopped next to Travis Hines's sports car. As Flynn climbed out of his pickup, the kid left the hangar, talking on his cell phone. He met Flynn outside the office and stopped talking.

"Hey, my dad just said you jumped on his idea to add an air show to Pancho Villa Days. Maybe he can finally bring in investors who'll put this jerkwater town on the map."

"I'm more interested in ticket sales going to house our homeless veterans," Flynn said coolly.

"Oh, yeah. Get those old bums out of our park."

"Those *men* fought to keep this town, this country, safe," he snapped.

"Yeah, whatever." Travis rolled his eyes as he sidled past.

"Wait, Travis! The other day I suggested you pull up more sharply when you take off on the east runway. Today I saw you fly too low over the ostrich ranch. Maybe you noticed birds running loose and dropped down for a closer look, but airplanes scare the birds. So keep that in mind for future take-offs, okay?"

"You saw me? How? I went out before you got here." Travis half turned back.

"I was at the ostrich farm and I tried to wave you off. Didn't you see me signal?"

The kid didn't respond. He delivered a stony look, stalked to his car, jumped in and roared off, leaving a rooster tail of dust in the wake of his shiny red Corvette.

Shaking his head, Flynn unlocked his office. Even though Travis's attitude irked him, he put that aside and settled down to do the paperwork he'd put off.

It was as well he spent the day toiling over his books, because in the afternoon he rented two additional hangars to a co-op grain company. They had housed two crop dusters they leased to farmers at an airfield several hours' drive away.

Flynn had showed the men his facilities and given them maps of his runways. He'd waited at the field while they'd arranged to have the planes delivered. The men had assured him they didn't store crop-dusting chemicals in their planes or in the hangars they leased. Since he'd known those materials were highly combustible, for his own peace of mind, he'd stayed to be sure they had told him the truth.

It was dark by the time they'd shaken hands on the deal.

He was hungry. It'd been hours since he'd eaten Jenna's pancakes and eggs. Some stale potato chips had passed for lunch. He could swing into town and eat at the café, but he was tired and his leg ached. He hadn't let on to Jenna that the spots where the doc had removed shrapnel hurt when he'd herded her flock. She'd seen, though.

The way she'd engineered that and had also set out he-man bandages for his use led to why he'd judged her to have a big heart. Plus, she was a good mom. A good mom to a cute, precocious kid.

Thinking about them made Flynn elect to skip the restaurant and go home instead. He had stuff in the fridge for a cheese sandwich or he could eat cereal. Jenna had replaced his Froot Loops. Remembering, he smiled. Then he frowned. He'd thought of Jenna's house as "home." Was he letting her get under his skin?

He thought maybe yes when he drove down her lane, saw lights on in the kitchen and felt a ripple of warmth in his midsection. He parked, got out, locked his pickup and sorted out the house keys Jenna had given him.

Trudging up the steps, he paused with the key poised over the lock on the kitchen door. It was late, well after Andee's bedtime. Not so late that Jenna would have retired. Should he knock? He didn't want to scare her. A knock could wake Andee or cause Beezer to raise the roof barking. And hadn't Jenna provided him keys because she expected him to use them?

He unlocked the door and went in.

He registered Jenna at her kitchen table, a cup of some steaming beverage in front of her along with a stack of papers. She held a pen in her right hand. Her left forefinger twisted a strand of brown hair around and around.

"You startled me," she said, releasing her hair as she half rose.

"You gave me keys." He tossed the key chain from hand to hand and then pocketed it. "Well, it's late. I'll go on upstairs," he said, deciding to forego food.

Jenna looked far too enticing in cutoffs and a T-shirt.

"Don't rush off. I'm sick of crunching numbers. Would you like something to drink? I have tea. Or I can pour you juice or ice water. No doubt you've eaten by now, but I saved a plate of spaghetti and meatballs from our supper."

Flynn pulled out a chair opposite her and sat. "I didn't eat. In fact I missed lunch. The thought of spaghetti and meatballs makes my mouth water."

"It'll take a jiffy to reheat in the microwave. There's garlic bread, too."

"Sounds fantastic."

Beezer stuck his head around the kitchen door. He gave a big yawn followed by an excited little bark and padded up to nudge Flynn's arm.

"Hey, guy. Were you a good dog today? I missed you. We got two new planes in," he said at large.

The dog leaned into Flynn's brisk side rub, then padded off down the hall as abruptly as he'd showed up.

Jenna turned from punching buttons on the microwave. "New clients are good. How did your air-show meeting go?"

Flynn laced his fingers and bent them back until they popped. "We set a date. The last weekend this month... They, ah, will have wing walkers and other stunt pilots."

At the concern in her expression, he quickly added, "The show's owner said they fly over open land."

She pursed her lips and he continued, "The mayor tied the air show to Pancho Villa

Days, where they have food vendors, a carnival and now tours of old planes."

She didn't say anything, but studied the food heating.

"When did you last take Andee to a carnival?"

"Never," Jenna said. The microwave dinged. She removed the plate and set it in front of Flynn, turning to get him a napkin and silverware.

He rubbed the side of his neck and studied her slender, curvy back. Her feet were bare. He found that very appealing. "I pictured Andee loving carnival rides and wanting to collect stuffed animals at the coin and baseball-toss booths. Surely you've been to carnivals."

"I grew up on Army bases. Mostly abroad. My mom took us to museums, ruins and the beach. We've never gone to a carnival, but I'm sure Andee would love the rides."

"You didn't do amusement parks? I thought you lived in Florida."

"Andrew didn't like crowds. On his rotations home he wanted to stay home. He was preparing for a seventh tour in Afghanistan when…he…his accident occurred." Jenna twisted her hands on the table.

"Uh, this spaghetti is great," Flynn said, digging in to this meal.

"Andrew didn't always hibernate. I believe going on so many tours changed him. You haven't asked, but his accident is being investigated as pilot error. His. There were rumors he got into a shouting match with a Navy pilot. Even if it turns out to be true, it's not how I want Andee to remember her dad."

"I get that. My best friend's wife doesn't understand why her husband died in our crash and I didn't."

"That's terrible."

"She was pregnant, about to have a baby, and I've only visited her once." He shook his head. "I guess I felt guilty for making it out when Chip didn't."

"Did your leg injury cause your discharge?"

"No. I got out to avoid being stuck at a desk job. Unexplained high blood pressure would have eventually grounded me. It still may," he muttered, polishing off the last of his food. "The doctor wants me to take pills. I can't. My flying license runs out at the end of the month. If I don't pass the flight physical, I can't teach flying. I have to pass, that's all."

Rising, he took his plate to the sink and rinsed it off.

Jenna stood and moved to stand beside him at the sink. "Maybe worrying is aggravating the problem."

"Could be," he said slowly, inhaling her sweet scent. Flynn didn't know if it was perfume or shampoo.

Their arms brushed as she put the dish in the dishwasher.

His breath stalled. "I, uh, should go up. Thanks for feeding me."

Jenna straightened and smiled.

Flynn did something totally unplanned. He grasped her damp hands and kissed her.

He'd meant to drop a light kiss on her brow. But her eyes had widened and she'd lifted her head. His kiss landed squarely on her lips. She tasted like the mint tea she'd been drinking.

When she didn't pull away, he slid his hands to her waist as their bodies came together. All the pieces fit fine.

He could have kissed her longer, but Jenna set her hands on his chest. From a distance

Flynn heard her make a sound. Perhaps an attempt to take a breath. It was enough for his brain to kick in.

Putting her at arm's length, he stared down on her flushed face and breathed out.

"Sorry. Sorry. Serving me a good meal doesn't give me license to manhandle the cook. I got carried away with my thanks. It won't happen again. I promise."

With that, he left the kitchen.

## CHAPTER SEVEN

SIGHT AND SOUND came back to Jenna slowly. She touched her lips—yes, she had been kissed. Well kissed. So well the kitchen had receded and along with it anything previously on her mind.

Flynn's kiss had taken her by surprise. More surprising—she wished he hadn't said he was sorry.

With her senses returning, she heard his measured tread as he climbed the stairs. She flipped the light switch and plunged the kitchen into darkness.

A night-light she kept on in the bathroom for Andee allowed her to cross the living room without stumbling even though her knees weren't entirely steady.

Out of habit she peeked into Andee's room. In the trickle of light from the bathroom, she could see her curled around Cubby

Bear. Beezer lay angled across the foot of the bed, softly snoring.

Going into her room, Jenna began to prepare for bed. Over and over she wondered when she'd last been so knocked off kilter by a kiss. Her kisses with Andrew had grown more perfunctory and less frequent in the past few years. Why was that? Had it been her fault?

The many long separations had taken a toll on their marriage. Their love life, too, had suffered, about the time she began to notice significant changes in Andrew. He'd become sullen and guarded. And he retreated if she brought it up.

Jenna partially closed her door that led into the bathroom and turned on the soft, rosy glow of her bedside lamp. She crawled under the covers, but stayed sitting upright.

Even though they'd been having problems, it seemed unbearably cruel for a man who'd served his country in remote, dangerous locales to die in a training mission mere miles from home.

Should she have stayed to fight for his reputation? What could she have done? Andrew's crash had been an accident...hadn't it?

She refused to follow that train of thought.

Jenna turned off the light and lay down. What if she'd been remiss in not insisting he see the base psychologist? If he'd been suicidal, would that have come to light? Could it have been prevented, even?

Why had all these questions come up after she admitted to herself she'd liked Flynn's kiss?

Perhaps because he'd acted guilty.

She was the one who should feel guilt, but heaven help her, she didn't.

JENNA WOKE SECONDS before her alarm went off. Rather than hit Snooze, she turned it off and tiptoed in to close the door between the bathroom and Andee's room. She smiled, because now her daughter slept with one arm around her bear and the other around Flynn's big, clunky dog.

A quick shower jump-started her enthusiasm for the day. She secured her hair in twin braids, put on her jeans, sneakers and an old T-shirt in anticipation of her final day of egg gathering before taking them to market. Rick Cline, the wholesaler middleman, said he was anxious to receive her first shipment.

So much had happened during her first two weeks as a bona fide ostrich rancher that it seemed she'd been here forever. But today represented the first income she'd earn. A milestone.

In the kitchen she hummed as she set coffee to brew. She toasted an English muffin and ate it while waiting for the coffee to emit its last gurgle. Pouring a thermal mug full, she went out into the fresh morning air.

She loved this time of day when the first rays of sun streaked the eastern sky the colors of sherbet.

Clipping her iPod to her belt, she affixed her earbuds and went into the pen with the most birds to search for eggs in the holes in the ground the male ostriches dug for the females.

By the time the sun rose full in a Wedgwood-blue sky, she had all the eggs collected. Hoping the sound of the Cherokee's engine firing wouldn't wake anybody, she backed her SUV up to the egg shed as quietly as she could and opened the back to start loading eggs.

The contrast between the morning warmth and the refrigerated shed made her shiver.

She propped the door open and began transferring crates to the Cherokee. They weren't light. Each only held a dozen eggs, but one ostrich egg was the equivalent weight of two dozen chicken eggs. And each egg was cradled in a thick corrugated cardboard pocket. The wholesaler she'd called had said pastry bakers loved ostrich eggs because they whipped up fluffier than chicken eggs.

She still worried that egg and feather sales alone wouldn't provide the income she and Andee needed. While researching ostrich farms, she'd run across two that didn't sell birds for meat or leather. One also raised alpacas. Apparently they were easy-to-raise, gentle animals and their fleece sold well. It was something she wanted to look into, because the second farmer sold stained-glass art on the side to supplement the ostrich earnings. Jenna couldn't do that.

During her fifth trip from the shed, she saw Flynn and Beezer come out of the house. She waited a minute, expecting Andee to emerge. When she didn't and Flynn went back inside, she figured Andee was still eating breakfast. Flynn must have forgotten something, because he didn't remain in the house long.

Jenna carried out two more crates, then saw he'd climbed into his pickup. Beezer occupied the second row of seats in the king cab. At first the dog dashed from side to side and then obviously Flynn said something because Beezer sat.

Flynn drove off without looking in her direction or tossing her a wave.

That hurt, but was in keeping with his apology for kissing her. Jenna hoped his vow to not let it happen again didn't mean they couldn't be friends. However, the possibility of that not being the case hastened her decision to sell her wedding rings if a pawnbroker would take them.

She had two more trips to make. By then Barney should be rolling in. He could feed the birds and reseed the pen he'd cleared yesterday. She only needed to grab her rings, get Andee and head for the market. What a beautiful morning.

Once the last crate was loaded, she carefully closed the back of the SUV. Dusting off her gloves, she locked the shed. While still in the vicinity of the incubators, she stopped to make her customary morning check. Much to Jenna's delight, for the first time, four of the many incubated eggs had hatched out and one was in the process. The gangly little ostriches were so cute.

This was the most exciting thing to have happened on the farm yet. Jenna wanted Andee to see a baby chick break out of its shell. She set her gloves on the workbench and hurried to the house, stuck her head in the kitchen door and called. Getting no response, she went in.

The table had been cleared and cereal bowls set in the sink. Andee was probably playing in her room as she often did in the morning. She'd probably skipped coming out, especially if she was pouting because Beezer couldn't stay.

Jenna went straight to her daughter's room.

It was empty. So was the bathroom. The house was so silent, Jenna's stomach began to cramp and her heart started to pound. She shouted up the stairs, then ran up, even knowing Andee wouldn't venture up to Flynn's area when she'd been told it was off-limits.

His bed was made and the upstairs was empty.

Taking the steps two at a time, she ran back downstairs. Detouring past Andee's room again, she saw that while the bed was unmade, clothes she'd set out on the toy box for Andee to wear today were gone. Her nightgown lay rumpled on the floor. Not unusual. And Cubby wasn't on the bed with her other stuffed animals. Also not unusual.

Jenna's palms began to sweat.

Possibly, Andee had gone looking for her. Jenna might have missed her, what with trekking in and out of the egg shed. Andee knew Barney had moved birds to the next larger pen, where grass was lush. It was the pen farthest from the house.

Outside again, Jenna cupped her hands and shouted for Andee. She ran full tilt along the path flanking the pens. Not seeing the girl anywhere, her panic soared. Anxiously she peered inside the unlocked sheds, all the while shouting Andee's name.

Racing back along the path, she glanced toward the empty highway a short distance away. Andee had promised she'd never, ever go up to the road. Why would she?

So what was left? The empty field between the ranch and the foothills separating them from Flynn's airpark. Jenna recalled hearing the drone of a plane earlier, but it hadn't flown over the ranch.

Almost back to the house, she saw Barney turn down the lane on his motorcycle. She ran to meet him, blubbering, "I'm beside myself, Barney. Andee's missing."

"Have you called the sheriff?" he asked, climbing off his bike.

"No, no. Oh, she has to be here somewhere. Andee really is responsible for her age. She was still asleep when I went out to work. She knew we were going to take the eggs to market and was looking forward to that."

"Where's the dog? They're like a matched set."

"I know. But yesterday Flynn told her he planned to take Beezer. They left a little while ago."

"You checked the ostrich pens and the incubator area? I think a couple of eggs were about to crack. Kids are drawn to stuff like that."

"I saw them and ran to the house to get Andee. That's when I realized she wasn't here! Oh, wait. She mentioned the wildflowers in the field yesterday. I remember she said I should pick some for the table. I'll bet that's it. Barney, if you'll deliver the eggs to Cline's Wholesale, and give me the key to your bike, I'll check the field."

"Sounds like a plan," he replied. "Meanwhile, I'm also going to call the sheriff. Can't be too careful."

"If she's not in the field, I'll call Flynn to see if she said anything to him at breakfast. Both of their cereal bowls are in the sink, so she must've eaten with him." Jenna felt herself babbling from fear.

"Can you ride a motorcycle?" Barney asked, accepting the SUV key.

"Yes. We lived in Italy and that's how you got around." Jenna didn't say it'd been a good fifteen years earlier.

Nodding, the older man started his bike and gave her the spare helmet clipped to one of his saddlebags.

She quickly put it on and straddled the machine, then took a few seconds to familiarize herself with it. Anxious to leave, she roared off, only fishtailing slightly, and she didn't look back to see if Barney was having fits.

In truth she'd only ridden a Harley once

before. The bikes they had in Europe weren't this big. And she hadn't gone off-roading like this.

She spotted clumps of yellow wildflowers blooming in profusion in several places. Shouting over the racket of the motorcycle, Jenna reached the first cluster of blooms. Nothing moved. Her pulse throbbed in her ears even as her heart sank.

Loosening the helmet, she punched up Flynn's cell. His phone rang, then went to voice mail. Ever more frantic, she left a message and pocketed her phone. Was this pointless? Perhaps, but she tightened the helmet strap and rode on to the next patch of yellow, ignoring sweat trickling down her back.

If Andee had walked this far, she would've gotten hot. Jenna prayed her daughter would've sought the shade of the thicket. By this time her morning coffee had turned to acid in her stomach as she bounced over the rocky terrain.

Hoarse from calling, Jenna revved the bike and swerved toward the foothills to check the last patch of flowers.

Nothing.

The silence left her shaking.

She had no choice but to return to the

ranch. Hopefully, the sheriff or a deputy would be there to assist her. She couldn't make herself think that Andee may have been abducted. Oscar Martin had said that sometimes people on the highway stopped to see the ostriches. No one had since she'd taken over. And she'd been in and out of the egg shed and hadn't heard a vehicle except for moving her own, and when Flynn drove out.

She set a beeline course across the empty field. As she got nearer to the house and didn't see any sign of a patrol vehicle, her hopes plummeted.

But Flynn's pickup turned off the highway. As he came closer, she saw Beezer's bobbing head. And right next to him, Andee.

Jenna's heart threatened to explode out of her chest. Yes, her missing daughter's sweet face was pressed against Beezer's ear. As she fought to keep from fainting, Jenna shut down the bike, leaped off it and ripped off the hot helmet. Her legs were so weak she let the bike fall sideways instead of deploying the kickstand. It was all she could do to breathe.

Plunging toward the pickup, her sweat-drenched braids slapped her neck. In a fog, she watched Flynn slam on his brakes to avoid hitting her and the prone Harley.

He vaulted from the cab. "What in all that's holy are you doing? Are you nuts? What if I hadn't been able to stop in time to avoid hitting you?"

"How dare you take Andee off the ranch without telling me? How dare you take her anywhere without my permission? Have you any idea how frantic I've been?"

Clasping her stomach, she bent over as she hauled in great, shuddering breaths. And for a minute she was afraid she'd lose the meager contents in her stomach.

"I didn't *take* her anywhere." Circling around the front of his pickup, he yanked open the back door and leaned in to unbuckle the now-crying child.

Beezer bounded out first. With his tail wagging like a flag, he ran up to Jenna, barking.

Her knees did give out then. She sank to the ground, choked by tears of relief, and suffered Beezer's rough tongue on her face. Through a sheen of sweat and tears, she watched Flynn carry Andee and Cubby Bear to within a footprint away.

He dropped to one knee. "You've got to believe me, I don't understand any of this. I swear until I got to the airpark and got out by the hangar and Beezer started jumping at the bed, barking his head off, I had no idea she'd stowed away."

Jenna leveled a teary stare at her child. "Then how? What? How? Why?" Words failed her.

The girl twisted a strand of her flyaway hair. "Beezer took me."

Jenna scrambled to her feet. "Don't make things worse by lying. Beezer did no such thing."

Andee's face puckered and giant tears tracked down her cheeks. "I wanted to go up high above the clouds where planes fly. I thought I could see Daddy in heaven." She sobbed louder and buried her face in Flynn's neck.

The air escaped Jenna's lungs. Again fighting her own tears, she covered her trembling lips with shaky fingers.

Flynn sat on the rocky ground, flattened his hand across Andee's back, patting gently. "Airplanes can't fly as high as heaven. Only angels do that."

"But...my Sunday school teacher said heaven was above the clouds, and you fly way high, Flynn."

"We humans can only imagine heaven," he said softly. "My best friend's gone to heaven, too. Chip. I talk to him sometimes. I can't see him, but I believe he hears me."

"I don't think Daddy hears me, 'cause he doesn't say anything back."

Flynn shot Jenna a helpless look.

She cleared her throat. "Sweetie, he hears you. Heaven's not a place any of us can see. I understand now why you ran off. You miss him. But I was so scared when I couldn't find you. Promise me you won't ever go off again without telling me."

"But I wanted to fly in Flynn's plane."

Flynn stirred. "When people fly, they need to buckle in. Like you do in the car. So you don't bounce around and get hurt. If you'd managed to get on the plane without me seeing you, you could have been injured. Then your mom and I would feel horrible. Worse than horrible, Andee."

"But you said you were gonna take Beezer flying, so I hid in the back of your truck. Beezer saw me crawl under the black thing."

"His canopy?" Jenna rubbed at her forehead.

Flynn looked distressed. "Andee, you might have fallen out—the road to my airpark is so rough and the tailgate was down."

Jenna blotted away the last of her tears. "That's something else we need to discuss. Right now, though, the sheriff's coming. We can talk more after I explain things to him."

Flynn got up and set Andee on her feet. The girl and Beezer were subdued—as if aware they weren't totally out of the doghouse.

Jenna started to lift the heavy Harley, but Flynn nudged her aside and took over. She flashed him a trembling smile.

He shut both pickup doors and stood by Jenna to await the sheriff.

Andee sidled up. "Am I gonna be arrested?" Her voice quavered.

Flynn answered for Jenna. "No, Sheriff Denton has grandchildren about your age. He'll be delighted to see you're safe and sound."

"Of course you won't be arrested," Jenna added. "Where would you get that idea?"

"From TV," Andee said. "Bad people get arrested."

Jenna paused to frown at that statement. "Another thing we'll have to discuss apparently is what shows you're watching. I do need to apologize to the sheriff for not notifying him the minute you showed up. I was just so rattled. I still am."

Striding off, she met the man exiting the patrol vehicle and launched into an immediate apology.

Sheriff Denton was a big man who wore the trappings of law enforcement well. His expression didn't change one iota as Jenna hastened to explain what had happened.

Andee didn't leave the safety of Flynn's side. She peered out from around his leg and wrapped one arm around her bear and the other around Beezer.

When Denton approached, the girl tipped back her head and gazed up at the tall lawman. "I'm sorry," she blurted out, her voice squeaky. "Don't take Mommy away, either. I did the bad thing, so I don't want her to get arrested, either." Giant tears rolled down her pale cheeks.

Jenna automatically bent and hoisted the

girl to her hip. "Shh. Honey, no one's getting arrested. The sheriff knows I was sick with worry. He's happy it was all cleared up as easily as it was."

Flynn placed a bracing arm around Jenna and Andee.

Sheriff Denton removed his sunglasses and stretched out a hand to Flynn. "Lieutenant Sutton, nice to see you again. Is this your family?"

Flynn's fingers flexed around Jenna's shoulders, and it seemed he couldn't quite decide how to answer.

Flynn finally laughed. "No, I'm Jenna's boarder. But my dog and I were unwitting partners in this morning's debacle. I think we've all come to an understanding, so it won't happen again." He gave an added clasp to Jenna's arm and caught Andee's eye.

Both nodded vigorously and Flynn let his arm drop.

The sheriff tucked a small notebook he'd been holding into his shirt pocket. "Well, I always say all's well that ends well. These are the types of calls I like. Say, Lieutenant, the mayor tells me you've booked an air show to coincide with Pancho Villa Days.

Just so you know, I'll beef up our part-time deputies that weekend. Not that I expect trouble."

His sharp gaze flicked from Flynn to Jenna.

"Ms. Wood, I heard you had a bunch of ostriches loose. How'd they get out?"

She slid Andee off her hip. "The gate latches weren't very secure. I had Barney Fisk, my helper, install new ones."

"Ah. Okay. How's he working out?" the sheriff asked casually.

"Fine. Is there something I should know?" Jenna let Andee skulk away with Beezer.

"No, no. We seem to get more than our share of drifters. I'd say Barney's a cut above. Haven't had any complaints about the odd jobs he's done for ranchers and such."

Jenna stayed behind, listening to the two men begin to chat about the mayor's housing project as they walked toward the sheriff's car. They stopped when Barney pulled in.

Jenna went to meet him.

"Hey!" Barney vaulted from Jenna's Cherokee, a huge grin slashing his gray whiskers. "You found the little miss. Where was she?" he asked, handing Jenna the check he'd brought from the wholesaler.

"It's a long story." She glanced down at the check. Shocked by how small it was, her breath stuttered. Not only wasn't it enough to go with what she hoped to get for her wedding rings to buy Flynn's new air conditioner, this paltry sum would barely cover next month's expenses.

Andee, who stood to one side with Beezer, released her hold on the dog. "I was a bad girl, Mr. Fisk. I wanted to fly with Flynn, but he found me and brought me home. I scared Mommy, and I won't do it again." She shook her head until her fine curls flew.

"Whoa, that's some adventure." Barney scraped a thumb across his chin. "I know your mama was scared, all right. So, I guess you missed seeing the new baby ostriches come out of their eggs."

Andee perked up. "Baby ostriches?"

"I'll take you to see them when I finish talking to Barney," Jenna said. "Barney, did Mr. Cline give you a price list for eggs and feathers? Eggs are supposed to bring in more than this, according to Oscar Martin."

"No price list, but Rick Cline said he'd buy

twice the amount of eggs as you sent today. I gather his market for feathers goes up and down. He said the demand for ostrich meat is high because it's so lean."

Jenna hauled in a deep breath. "I'm squeamish about the thought of slaughter. I need to pursue other avenues. I'm considering a couple."

Still a distance away with Flynn, the sheriff climbed into his SUV and drove off. Flynn moseyed back to where Jenna and Barney stood. "You look worried," he told Jenna. "Has something else gone wrong?"

"I just didn't make as much money from selling eggs as I expected."

"Flynn, Mr. Fisk said we've got new baby ostriches," Andee piped up. "Will you take me to see them?"

"You have chicks?" Flynn smiled. "Are they in the main pen? Sure, I'll take you, if it's okay with your mom. Remember, we don't do anything without Mom's okay."

"It's fine with me if you don't need to rush back to work. They're in the large shed with the incubators. I wonder if there's a market for people to buy chicks. I could advertise in the poultry magazine or the local newspaper."

Barney shrugged.

Flynn shook his head. "What I know about this business you could inscribe on the head of a pin," he said, turning away.

Andee peered back over a shoulder. "Don't sell our babies, Mommy. You said I could take care of them."

"And you can help take care of them until I see if there's a market. Don't get attached," she warned. "Don't name them."

"What else can I do today?" Barney asked. "We didn't collect loose feathers from probably half your flock."

"Sure, but first could you fill the feed bins with cracked corn? I have a couple of errands to run, but I need to clean up. By the way, thanks for the loan of your bike. I'll pay you for the gas I used."

"Your kid is some plucky. But the way you gunned my old Harley and took off, I'd say the girl takes after her mom." He laughed from his belly, reset his baseball cap and went off, leaving Jenna startled by what he'd said.

"Uh, would you swing by the shed and tell Andee I want to see her in the house when Flynn's ready to leave...and tell her no detouring."

He circled a hand over his head to show he'd heard, so she hurried inside to shower.

In less than twenty minutes she emerged from her room combing out her wet hair. She heard Andee's voice coming from the kitchen, along with Flynn's deeper tone. It surprised Jenna that he hadn't left for the airpark.

The pair sat at the kitchen table snacking on crackers and cheese. They looked up when Jenna entered the room.

"Me 'n Flynn are talking about heaven," Andee said.

"Oh?" Jenna shot Flynn a guarded look.

"Yep," Andee said. "Flynn says heaven is way, way far past the sun and moon and stars. Even past the tiny, tiny ones we can barely see. When somebody we love goes there, it makes us sad. But everybody in heaven is safe. Even cats and dogs. So we shouldn't be sad. And now I don't need to worry about trying to find heaven, 'cause Daddy and Flynn's friend Chip are up there together. They're not lonely."

"Uh, that's nice, Andee." Jenna's voice was strained. But when Flynn looked embarrassed, she set a hand on his arm. "I really appreciate how you stuck around, Flynn.

May I fix you something more substantial for lunch? Tuna sandwich?"

"Not for me. I'll head back to work. Barney said you were going to run errands. Anything I can swing through town and pick up for you?"

"No, but thanks. I decided I won't bank with Franklin Hart. I found a savings and loan in the next town—Las Cruces. So, I hope I'll be closer to having money to replace your air conditioner. But I'm not there yet."

Flynn snapped his fingers and Beezer got up from where he was catching a snooze under the table. "Listen, don't short yourself to get that done. Add on fencing if you need to expand your flock to make more money. I'm, uh, well... Beezer and me, we're okay bunking upstairs."

Flynn ducked his head and headed for the door.

"Yay!" Andee fed her last piece of cheese to Beezer. Sliding off her chair, she first hugged the big dog, then ran and threw her arms around Flynn's waist.

That startled him and Jenna. She recovered first. Their eyes met. She ventured a smile. "I must admit, you have a nice way of making ordinary things special."

The red on his cheeks got ruddier. "Uh, ordinary things like having supper together in town? It's Pot Roast Monday at the diner. Their cook makes the best pot roast in the West. We've all had a trying day, so it's my treat. Say, seven?"

His offer surprised Jenna, who hesitated for a second. "I'm not sure how long my errands will take. How about if Andee and I meet you there?"

"It's a da—" He stopped short of saying *date*. Jenna could tell Flynn knew it, and so did she.

Unwinding Andee's arms, he chucked her under the chin and made good his escape with his dog loping through the open screen door on his heels.

Jenna gave a start when Andee piped up to say, "We love Flynn, don't we, Mommy?"

Jenna's mouth dropped open and she shut it. She knew she blushed because her neck and face got hot. She was glad Flynn had charged off the porch and was probably too far away to hear. "We *like* him, honey," Jenna emphasized.

Andee tilted her head and pursed her lips. "Okay. But I don't want him and Beezer to go away. Not ever."

# CHAPTER EIGHT

JENNA WAS HELPING Andee climb into her car seat just as her cell phone rang. She saw her sister's number in the readout and stepped away to answer, leaving Andee to buckle herself in.

"Melody, hi. Are you home from work? I can never remember our time difference."

"Is that why you've only called once since you moved to no-man's-land?"

Thinking back over all the ups and downs of her first weeks on the ranch, including her terror when she couldn't find Andee this morning, Jenna tempered what she might have said. "Ranching isn't a nine-to-five job, Mel."

"Neither is teaching boneheaded college kids US history."

"Listen, I'm just heading out to the bank. Can I call you this evening? Or tomorrow?"

Belatedly, Jenna remembered Flynn's dinner invitation. She wasn't ready to share anything about him with her sister. She could do without the third degree, or worse, Rob running a background check on Flynn. That would be embarrassing.

"I really called to tell you that yesterday Rob heard through a source that the investigative committee finished studying Andrew's accident. They'll be issuing a report."

Jenna clutched her throat, which suddenly felt tight and dry. "Wh-what did they find?"

"Don't know, sis. Rob says those committees never leak. But once they reach their conclusion, the report goes out fairly fast. He asked me to give you a heads-up. You'll probably receive an official update in two or three weeks. Will you be okay being all alone out there? Are you prepared for a worst-case scenario?"

Rubbing her free thumb across a temple beginning to pulse with pain, Jenna strangled out her answer. "Y-yes. All I want is to have it settled."

"Call me after you receive the report, okay? Hey, I have a staff meeting in ten minutes.

I miss you, Jenna. Pinky promise you're all right?"

"Pinky promise. I like it here. I swear."

"Okay. But you sound off kilter."

"I'm standing out in the hot sun. And your news came as a shock. The committee has spun its heels for ten months. I wasn't sure they'd ever reach a conclusion. I know we've both got to run but, Mel, thanks for the alert."

"Don't forget us. And tell Andee I found the cutest cowgirl boots in her size. They're pink. I've shipped them. She should get them today or tomorrow."

"She'll love them. That's so thoughtful of you. But rather than tell her, I'll let them be a surprise. 'Bye. Love you. Don't work too hard."

Her sister laughed. "I only get a week's break between summer classes ending and fall ones beginning. I'd hoped Rob and I would have some time to fly out and see that ranch of yours. Doesn't look like it can happen before my Christmas break."

"Sounds more doable then for me, too. I'll put up a tree and everything."

Jenna loved and missed her sister, but the thought of her coming out made her neck pinch with tension. By Christmas, however, she ought to have a better handle on the business.

And surely by then Flynn's AC would be in and he'd be back in his own place. If he still lived upstairs, she foresaw how her relatives would grill the poor man.

"Okay, I'll log it into our day-planners. 'Bye, kiddo."

"Later, then." Jenna dropped her phone into her handbag and slid behind the steering wheel.

"Mommy," Andee fretted. "What took you so long? Me 'n Cubby are hot."

"Sorry. That was Auntie Melody." Jenna started the SUV and cranked up the AC.

"You didn't let me talk to her. She doesn't know Beezer's come to live with us."

*Thank goodness.* Jenna adjusted the rearview mirror. "She only had a few minutes to talk because she was late for a meeting. She and Uncle Rob may come visit us over Christmas. Won't that be fun?"

"Yay! Then they can see the baby ostriches, and Flynn and Beezer."

Time didn't always compute with a child. And according to Oscar Martin, baby ostriches grew about a foot a month for five or six months. For sure the ones in the incubators now would be full grown by Christmas.

And why upset the applecart by mentioning that Flynn and Beezer would be gone before the holidays? It was likely that the increased pressure to have him back in his own place weighed heavier on her.

She'd soon receive the commission's verdict on Andrew's accident. Regardless of their personal issues, her heart ached when she thought about his death...

What kind of fool risked disrupting her life by falling for another pilot?

"Where are we going? You passed the town."

"Clever of you to notice that we're going someplace new."

"Why?"

"A bigger town has more stores. A larger bank."

"Oh."

It seemed farther than Jenna had estimated. But traffic was light, so it didn't take long to cover the miles.

Her GPS made the pawnshop simple to

find. It sat in a nice strip mall, not seedy, which had been her main fear.

"Andee, I have some jewelry to sell here. You can't wander around once we go inside. Okay? And don't talk while I transact my business."

"What's trans…act?"

"It means I'll discuss stuff with the person in charge." Jenna climbed out, then opened Andee's door and helped her out.

"Mommy, look in the window. A pink bicycle 'xactly like one Brittney got for her birthday, remember?" She frowned. "Daddy said I couldn't have one, 'cause we lived in an apartment."

Andee scampered off for a closer look.

After locking the SUV, Jenna turned, too.

Sure enough, on prominent display in the pawnshop window sat a small girl's bicycle with training wheels. Andee, with Cubby tucked into the crook of one arm, had her nose pressed to the glass. "We live in a house now. Can we buy me the bicycle? Please. I'll be really, really good, I promise."

Her little face reflected hope mixed with worry that she'd be told no again.

The bike looked nearly new to Jenna. Its paint and chrome sparkled in the afternoon sun.

"Let me take care of my business, then I'll ask the price. No promises. You know our money is tight right now. I'm trying my best to save enough to buy an air conditioner for the rental house. For Flynn."

"But he said he likes living at our house."

"He said he was okay with bunking upstairs. That's different from liking it, honey. Maybe we can come back another time to see about buying the bike."

The girl's shoulders slumped as she turned away from the window. "It'll be gone by then."

Jenna sighed. That was probably true. "Come on inside. Put on your best manners, please."

Andee nodded and slipped her hot palm into Jenna's hand.

A bell over the door jingled as they stepped inside the shop, which felt cool thanks to the lazy churn of an overhead fan. Andee peeled off to inspect the bicycle from a new angle.

Jenna approached a bespectacled man seated behind a glass-fronted counter filled with watches, rings, cameras, cell phones and other small items.

"Welcome. I guess you've come about the bike." The man smiled. "She's a beauty, isn't she? Only took her in yesterday. A grandparent bought it new, but the dad lost his job and needed the money."

"Uh, I'm here to sell my wedding rings," Jenna mumbled, suddenly depressed for sounding needy, too.

"Ah, sorry." The man abruptly became very business-like, his expression detached. "Let's see what you've got. Bear in mind I'm overstocked and have to be realistic since times are tough all over."

Swallowing the lump in her throat, Jenna set the rings on the counter with an unsteady hand. The pawnbroker had already fitted a loupe to one eye.

"Three-carat main stone. Four one-carat stones in the band. Set in platinum I'd say. I'll be honest, ma'am. These are worth a lot more than I'm able to advance you."

He put them down and named a figure below what Jenna had hoped for. Calculating quickly, she thought that if she maxed out her new credit card, the two amounts might cover the lowest-priced air conditioner. Which would leave her without funds to invest in the farm.

She ran a hand nervously up and down the strap of her shoulder bag.

"If you need the money to house and feed you and the girl," the man said, lowering his voice, "I can probably raise that by a couple hundred bucks."

Jenna followed his gaze to Andee, who stared reverently at the bike. She saw her daughter finger the pink and purple streamers attached to the bicycle's handle grips. The bike even had a star-studded doll carrier attached to the rear fender, the perfect spot for Cubby to ride.

Clearing her throat, Jenna turned back. "Out of curiosity, how much are you asking for the bike?"

"You could get something cheaper at a discount store. But I'll let you have the bike for sixty. That's half what it cost new."

With a bike to occupy her, maybe Andee wouldn't dream up another adventure like the one that had scared Jenna half to death today.

"Would you be able to deduct the amount from what you're giving me for the rings?"

"I'll even help you load the bike."

While he counted out cash from a drawer stowed out of sight beneath the counter, Jenna saw a blood-pressure cuff in a case on the round table. "Does this work?"

"Yes. It's nearly new. My wife bought it shortly before my mother had to go into assisted living. It may have been used once a day for a couple of weeks. How does ten dollars sound?"

"Subtract that, too, will you? I'd better get out of here before I end up owing you money."

He laughed and exchanged a twenty he'd set out for a ten.

When Andee learned the bike would be hers, she gushed, "Mommy, I love you this much." She spread her arms wide. "I'll take good care of it, like I do Cubby. I can't wait to show Flynn. Can we go by his airplane place?"

Jenna frowned over Andee's dogged attachment to Flynn. On the other hand, she'd just forked over precious dollars to buy him a blood-pressure cuff. Moreover, she'd gone weak-kneed over his kiss. To say nothing of how her heart had jacked up at his dinner invitation.

Plainly he'd wormed his way under defenses she'd erected against pilots. Especially military ones.

Were ex-military flyers less apt to collide in the sky and die?

She doubted it.

True to his word, the pawnbroker loaded the bike, and Andee danced at the back of the SUV.

Jenna tallied the many sleepless nights she'd spent worrying about Andrew's flights. Only an idiot would go soft on another man involved in the same dangerous occupation.

Especially someone like her, who didn't even like to fly.

"There you go." The man shut the back of the Cherokee. "Good luck getting your renter that AC. They're about the only item I've never taken in."

"Thanks for your help. I hope a madly-in-love needy couple buys the rings."

"Then you won't be back to claim them?"

Jenna shook her head. "I'm…widowed." She hated that word. *Widow.*

"Oh, uh, sorry, ma'am…" He backed up a step, clearly uncomfortable.

She hated that, too. The reaction other people had when they found out she was a widow.

"Uh, you two take care, hear?"

A moment later Jenna checked that Andee was buckled in and set her GPS for the bank. It wasn't difficult to find. But she had a tussle with Andee, who didn't want to leave her new bike.

"Honey, the bike's not going anywhere. But the bank's due to close in half an hour. I need to hurry." Jenna cajoled until she coaxed the girl from the car. Even then Andee took her sweet time scooping up her beloved Cubby.

In the bank at last, a woman behind the desk directed her to the office of the loan officer, who took them in immediately. This woman was efficient and couldn't have been nicer. So different from Jenna's last experience at a bank.

"I can't promise our loan board will approve this since you're new to the area. But I do know they'll take into consideration that you own property. And that—" she hesitated a moment before saying "—you're a widow."

Jenna tried not to react; the loans officer was being so helpful.

At the woman's suggestion, she opened a checking account and deposited the money from the rings. She left with the paperwork she needed to apply for a loan for the full price of the air conditioner.

"Yay, now we can go home and show Mr. Fisk my new bike," Andee said, skipping out the door ahead of Jenna. "Mommy, what's a widow?"

Jenna stopped walking even as she clicked the Cherokee doors open with the remote. "It means...I'm raising you by myself, honey."

"Oh."

"Now let me ask you a question." Jenna watched while Andee buckled herself in. "Why don't you call Mr. Fisk, Barney? Like you do Flynn."

Andee shrugged. "Can we go by the plane place so I can show Flynn my bike before we go home and put on dresses?"

"I hadn't planned on changing into a dress. And I have another stop to make. I think you'll find it fun." Jenna tapped on her smartphone, getting an address for the alpaca farm she'd seen signs for on the highway.

She backed out, ignoring Andee, who bobbed around excitedly asking where they were going.

"It's a surprise."

Fifteen minutes later she saw the farm sign. Leaving the freeway, she followed a fence along a dusty dirt road for about a mile. Soon big-eyed alpacas peered over the fence at them.

"What are those? Are they sheep?"

"They're alpacas. They are sheared like sheep. Their fleece is soft and silky, lighter but warmer than sheep's wool. And it sells for more than our ostrich eggs."

Slowing near the farmhouse and a row of low buildings in the center of a large patch of grass dotted with shade trees, Jenna saw a lot of pens like the ones that housed her ostriches. As she stopped beside a pickup and shut off the motor, two lanky dogs loped up to her door.

Jenna heard Andee unbuckle her seat belt.

"Honey, let me get out first to make sure the dogs are friendly."

"One is looking in the window at me. He's not cute like Beezer. What kind is he?"

"I don't know." Jenna stepped out of the

car. The dogs rushed to sniff the hand she extended. As quickly, they ran to meet a woman who had emerged from one of the buildings. They trotted back with her.

"May I help you? I'm Peggy Johnson. My husband and I own Desert Hills Alpaca Farm." She pointed to one of the buildings. "If it's yarn you're after, I have people who card and spin our fleece and dye skeins in glorious colors."

"Actually, I was hoping to get information on raising alpacas. I bought an ostrich ranch the next town over." Jenna spared a glance at the car to check on Andee, who hadn't yet come out. "A wholesaler who buys my eggs suggested he could sell alpaca fleece if I branch out. Frankly, I wonder if it's feasible."

The woman nodded. "I'd love to explore that possibility with you."

The alpacas across the fence were making low honking noises.

"They don't recognize you," Peggy Johnson explained. "Alpacas hum or honk like geese if they sense something new or possibly threatening."

Andee cracked open her door. "Mommy, can I get out and see the alpacas up close?"

Peggy smiled. "I'll show her our three new crias—baby alpacas."

Jenna beckoned to Andee, but said to Peggy, "You have a lot of animals. How many would I need to start with if I built slowly?" Jenna took Andee's hand and closed the car door against the nosy dogs.

Andee patted them gingerly.

"We have thirty acres and currently keep two hundred adults. Let's see…I started with a dozen. Two sires and ten females."

Peggy led them along a fenced enclosure where fuzzy-headed, slender-necked alpacas peered over.

Jenna took it all in. "Your feeders look a lot like those I have for my ostriches."

Reaching into her jeans pocket, Peggy pulled out a handful of pellets. "By nature alpacas are shy. It's better to feed them in groups. But I carry treats." She opened a gate and went into the pen. Soon the mothers crowded around and the babies followed. Peggy picked up one of the babies and carried it over to them. Behind her the mother hummed nervously.

"See how soft his fleece is." Peggy knelt so Andee could stroke the long, silky hair.

"He's softer than Cubby or Beezer." The child stroked the animal with care. "Are all the babies gold-colored?"

"There are two classes of alpacas—suri and huacaya." She pronounced it *wa-kai-ah*. "The suri are blond and silky. The huacaya are darker and woollier."

Rising, she set the baby down near its anxious mother and they all left the pen.

"I'll be in a position to sell you at least six of each, if you're ready to start a herd by fall. A male of both types and the rest females. All of my stock is registered."

Andee clung to the fence while Jenna and Peggy discussed approximate costs to raise a herd.

"I see you have two dogs," Jenna said. "I'm considering getting one from a shelter, but I want one that won't scare the animals."

"Then I'd suggest a herder breed. Ours are Australian blue heelers. A dog or two is crucial to protect alpacas from predators like coyotes."

"There's a lot I need to consider." Jenna turned in a small circle, studying the farm's layout. Her phone rang, which surprised her. She got so few calls and she'd already spoken to her sister. Her heart jumped at the thought it might be Rob.

Maybe he'd found a leak in the investigative committee, after all.

She managed to get the phone out of her purse and say a breathy hello before the answering service kicked in.

"Jenna? It's Flynn."

*Flynn.* She hadn't expected that.

"I stopped back at the ranch over an hour ago, hoping to catch you. I figured it's silly for us to take two vehicles to dinner. Barney said you went to run a few errands. Is everything all right? I mean, it's after six…and… well…I was getting worried."

"After six? Yikes." Jenna cast a quick glance at her watch. "I guess I've let time get away. I should reach the ranch in twenty minutes or so. Could we make dinner seven-thirty or will that totally screw up your plans?"

"Is that Flynn?" Andee left the fence and dashed up to Jenna. "Is he home? Can we go so I can show him my new bicycle?"

Jenna hushed her with a wave of her hand.

"Sorry, I missed what you said. Oh, okay, you didn't make reservations? We'll leave now, then. 'Bye."

She shut off her phone and dropped it back into her purse.

"Peggy, I so appreciate your time. I own more than enough land, but I need to see if I can afford to expand. I don't have the grass and trees you do, and only ramadas for shade."

"Ramadas work, too. Ones made from sailcloth aren't beastly expensive. Anytime you want to come back if you have more questions, I'll be glad to talk. Are you interested in spinning or weaving? I start beginners' classes in August after school opens."

They strolled to Jenna's vehicle. "I'm so new to ranching I should concentrate on learning those ropes first. I'd guess there are tons of things to learn about raising alpacas. You probably have a vet you call, and someone for shearing?"

"A vet immunizes our animals. My husband and I shear them and clip their toenails. My hubby handles most birthings. So, yes, if you're on your own, unless you have experienced help—" She broke off to wave at a man driving past in a flatbed truck. "Speaking of my husband, he's been trading help to a friend who's haying. Enough trade to feed our herd through the winter."

"Can't Flynn and Mr. Fisk help?" Andee asked before she climbed into her car seat. "I like alpacas better than ostriches. Today a baby ostrich pecked me. But the baby alpaca cuddled me."

Peggy laughed. "I can't guarantee you'd be able to handle everything that comes up. You could manage both if you had a full-time employee."

Driving out, Jenna thought about how ill prepared she was for ranching. She liked the outdoor life and being her own boss, for sure. She also liked that it enabled her to be a work-from-home mom.

She'd done a lot of volunteering on base as a military wife. She had a liberal-arts degree... which had prepared her for nothing specific.

Really, growing up in a military family had prepared her to be a military wife. One capable of moving around a lot.

She listened to Andee hum along with a Katy Perry song on the radio. A song about a romantic life. Things she'd learned and a decision to move forward feeling "wide-awake."

It reminded her of Flynn's recent phone call. Jenna wasn't used to having anyone check on her because they were concerned for her. Flynn's concern felt...nice.

Reflecting over her day, Jenna revisited parts she'd been too upset to fully register at the time. Such as the relaxed way Flynn had handled her hysteria and Andee's tearful questions about heaven. It hadn't dawned on Jenna that Andee only needed reassurance that her daddy was somewhere safe.

Even Flynn's voice had exuded calm. As had his firm hand on her shoulder when she'd talked to the sheriff. Flynn continued to claim her thoughts as the Cherokee ate up miles. And suddenly she found herself at the ranch.

It was late enough that Barney's motorcycle was gone.

Jenna wasn't prepared for the warmth that slid up her body when Flynn emerged from the house.

She didn't object when Andee shouted at Flynn to help her out so she could show him her new bike. The brief respite gave Jenna time to slow her pulse and stanch a rush of emotion that welled up when he drew near.

Tonight, backlit as his rangy body was by the orange rays of a sinking sun, a curl of desire built in her. He had on gray pants with a razor crease and a formfitting gold T-shirt that defined his sculpted torso and deepened his tan. His blond hair had grown longer, and its attempts to curl made her fingers itch to ruffle it. To see if his hair felt as soft as alpaca fleece.

Hearing him at the back of the SUV exclaiming over Andee's bike jolted Jenna out of her daydream. Finally curbing emotions she needed to quash, Jenna managed to climb out and join them as Andee said, "I didn't think Mommy would buy me the bike 'cause it cost too much. But she did, and she got you a gray thing with blood before we stopped to see the alpacas."

She let out a surprised laugh.

Flynn questioned her with his eyes.

"I intended to bring that up later because I don't want you to think I'm meddling in your life. We stopped at a pawnshop to… uh… *Anyway.* Turns out they had this bike.

It's exactly like one Andee's best friend has."
Jenna paused to haul in a breath.

"I trust you're getting to the blood part?"
The corners of Flynn's mouth twitched.

"Right. So, the guy also had a digital
blood-pressure cuff that's almost new."

Jenna leaned into the back of the SUV and
brought out the case.

"I saw it and had a fleeting thought that if
you took your pressure each day for a while
and logged it, if it's not high, your doctor
should know. Maybe you get anxious because of being at the clinic, you know?"

Flynn accepted the case. "I suppose it's
possible. Thanks."

"So you don't think I stuck my nose in
where it doesn't belong?"

"Not at all. I didn't fill the prescription.
Before I do, I'll take my pressure for a few
days."

Andee climbed onto her bike. She'd put
Cubby in the doll seat and peddled off toward the ostrich pens, Beezer loping alongside her.

"Don't go beyond the first pen," Jenna
called. "We need to clean up for dinner."

Stretching, she shut the Cherokee's hatch and clicked the remote.

"You look fine as is." Flynn ran an eye down her frame.

"Says you, who looks all spiffed up. Andee and I tramped around a dusty alpaca farm. Anyway, the sun's about gone. I'd as soon she didn't ride at dusk with so many potholes on the paths. I'll have Barney fill them tomorrow."

Flynn nodded. "It's almost dusk. If you'd like to go in and get started, I'll escort her back. Should we leave her bike on the porch?"

"I predict until the novelty wears off, she'll want to store it in her bedroom." Jenna laughed. "I'm okay with that."

"You're a good mother." His voice vibrated with feeling.

Jenna glanced back over a shoulder. "Thanks. But you're the one who settled her worries about her dad. I'll be forever obliged to you for that."

"I was worried you'd thought I'd overstepped my bounds." He gave her a lopsided smile.

Jenna felt light-headed. "Uh, the blood-pressure cuff makes us even, then." She jogged up the porch steps and opened the screen door.

"Hey," Flynn yelled after her. "I forgot… the mailman delivered a package addressed to Andee. I set it on the kitchen table along with your other mail."

Jenna leaned back out. "That'll be the gift from my sister. Andee will be over the moon. I don't mind if you help her open it while I take a quick shower."

"Can do." The screen door banged shut on Flynn's response, followed by a scream from down near the pens and a dog barking.

Immediately, Jenna flew out the door again and down the steps, running flat out toward the noise.

Flynn had a head start and even with his bad leg Jenna couldn't overtake him. They reached a screeching, bawling Andee at the same time.

She lay trapped beneath her bicycle.

Jenna dropped the handbag that had been draped over her shoulder. "Honey bunch, shh."

Beezer quit barking and picked Cubby

Bear out of the dirt. He set the bear down by Andee, then licked the side of her face.

Flynn pulled a penlight from his pocket and flashed it over the scene, shrouded in shadow. A skewed front bike wheel stuck half in, half out of a deep rut.

Andee, still lying twisted under the handlebars, asked through her sobs, "Is my new bike hurt?"

# CHAPTER NINE

"YOUR BIKE LOOKS OKAY, but how are you?"
Jenna leaned down and started to lift the
bike off her daughter.

Flynn's fingers curled around her wrist.
"Wait, Jenna. Her left arm is broken," he
murmured. "Will you go to the house and
bring me a magazine and string or sturdy
tape? I'll splint her forearm so it won't hurt
so much while we drive her to the emergency room."

"Bro…ken?" Jenna clapped a hand over
her mouth. She took a moment to regain her
composure and ruffle Andee's bangs. "Lie
still for Flynn, honey, I will be right back."

Leaving her purse on the ground, she
sprinted away.

Flynn tucked Cubby under Andee's good
arm. "Sugar, I don't want you to move while
I untangle you from your bike, okay?"

"'Kay." The girl's sobs abated some. "I cra...crashed."

"You did," Flynn said, carefully removing the bicycle. "And you've hurt your arm."

"Is Mommy mad?"

"Of course not," he said, taking time to carefully check her for other injuries.

Jenna arrived with magazines and a roll of duct tape.

Kneeling, she said, "Andee, I love you so much. I hate that you fell."

"Is my bike broke?"

Flynn fit a magazine under the part of Andee's arm indented in a deep V.

"Ow, ow, ow," she yelped, then whimpered, "that hurt, Flynn."

"I know. I'm sorry. Your bike looks fine, but I'm afraid your arm needs a doctor."

"Is that why my fingers feel funny? Owie funny?"

"Yes, it is."

Jenna hovered anxiously, touching Andee's cheek until she saw Flynn had finished wrapping a magazine around her tiny arm. Then she tore off three strips of silver tape and passed them to him.

"I hate to hurt you again, Andee, but you'll

feel it when I tape across the magazine. I have to do it to keep your arm steady."

The child gazed trustingly up at Flynn. She only hollered out when he gathered her up in his arms and stood, cradling her injured arm against his chest.

Jenna rescued her purse and the bike. For the second time in one day, her legs threatened to buckle. As if he knew how unsteady she was, Beezer stuck to her side.

"If you're putting the bike in the house, Jenna, grab a couple of pillows."

She nodded and hurried up the porch steps. Beezer followed.

She and the dog emerged from the house in short order.

"Jenna, will you shut Beezer inside?" Flynn called.

Without questioning, Jenna complied.

Sounding shaky, Andee said, "But I want Beezer to go to the doctor with me."

"He can't go into the hospital, Andee. It's better that he stay here."

"But...he went to the doctor with you."

"I go to the veteran's clinic. They let dogs in. The community hospital is different."

Andee whined, "Why can't I go to vet... vet...place you said?"

Flynn smiled. "Because you're not a veteran, sugar."

Jenna returned, clutching two bed pillows. "My SUV has more room inside than your pickup. But would you drive so I can sit in back with Andee?"

"Sure. Let's put her in the middle seat belt and not in her booster, where it'll be more difficult to support her arm."

Jenna opened the back door and propped the pillows against the child seat.

Flynn slid partway in and gently settled Andee, who cried out sharply. He backed out fast to let Jenna climb in.

Starting the SUV moments later, he glanced back to make sure they were okay before he got under way. Andee cried from the jarring until Flynn reached the highway, where the road smoothed out.

The adults refrained from talking. Jenna filled the silence by quietly singing one of Andee's favorite songs. It helped pass the time until Flynn pulled up outside the hospital emergency room. "I'll go grab a wheelchair. Why don't you take her in and get the ball rolling while I park?"

Jenna nodded anxiously.

The girl still held Cubby in a death grip with her good arm. Over the last mile or so she'd stopped crying. But her wailing commenced the minute Flynn moved her to the wheelchair.

"Please don't cry, sweetie," Jenna murmured. "I have to fill out some paperwork so they'll let a doctor see us."

"They'll need your insurance," Flynn said, pausing to hand Jenna the purse she'd left on the floor mat. "Are you guys still covered by the military?"

"No, our benefits are in limbo. I had to take out a private policy." She didn't mention having opted for a high deductible. In fact, his reminder about insurance knotted her stomach. The cost to repair a badly broken arm would probably wipe out everything she'd gotten for her rings. Funds she'd earmarked for Flynn's AC. But it was what it was. Andee's health came first.

Resolute, Jenna navigated the wheelchair through the automatic door. She was relieved to see an almost empty waiting room.

"I want Flynn." Andee fussed.

Jenna filtered her fingers through the girl's sweat-damp curls. "He's parking the SUV." She gave their names to the nurse behind the counter, who then asked the nature of their visit.

The woman murmured sympathetically when Andee spoke up, saying tearfully, "I crashed my new bicycle and broke my arm."

"I see. Well, let's get you into an examining room. Your mom can fill out the papers in there." The nurse turned again as Flynn entered, looked around and joined them. "Ah, here's Daddy," the nurse announced around a smile. "He can lift you up onto the exam table so I can cut off the splint and have a look at your arm."

"He's a friend," Jenna put in quickly.

"But I can certainly lift Andee up onto the table," Flynn responded.

And he did just that, shifting a pillow from the head of the table to tuck it under Andee's arm.

Andee's cries again tapered to loud sniffles.

Before now Jenna had only viewed the injury in a dim light provided at the scene by

Flynn's penlight. Now as the nurse cut away
the duct tape, exposing the misshapen bend,
she shuddered and clamped down on a sob
of her own.

Flynn slid an arm around her shoulders
and massaged the tight muscles on either side
of her neck. "Why don't you sit? You haven't
filled out the registration forms."

Nodding, Jenna sank gratefully into a
straight-backed chair. She popped up again
when a young man wearing a white coat bus-
tled into the room.

"Hi, I'm Dr. Reynolds. Ouch. Did you fall
out of a swing or a tree?"

Shaking her head side to side, Andee ob-
served him with big eyes. "I crashed my new
bicycle."

"Ah. Nurse, we need pictures of that arm
stat."

"Why? My arm hurts." Andee tried to
shrink away from his touch. The movement
obviously caused her pain because she began
to shriek anew.

"X-rays don't hurt," the doctor promised.
"They'll show me what I need to do to fix
your broken bones. Right now your fingers
are swollen up like little sausages. We don't

want them to stay that way. And you'd rather the hurting stop, right?"

Andee nodded tearfully. "I don't want sausage fingers."

"Mom, Dad," the doctor said, "we'll bring in a portable X-ray. It'll take a few minutes to get some shots and set up to reduce that fracture. Mom, you look peaked. If you feel faint, it's okay to step out of the room when I start."

Neither of them corrected his misconception, but at the doctor's statement, Flynn transferred his gaze to Jenna. "You'll hold up. Andee will want you with her."

Tightening her hold on the clipboard, Jenna took strength from how tall, solid and dependable he was. If his blood pressure had increased during this, it sure wasn't obvious. "I'm good," she declared.

The doctor inclined his head. "A tech will be in shortly. I'll leave you to complete registration while Nurse Foster gathers what we need." To Andee he said, "You take good care of that bear until I get back." He left, and a man in light blue scrubs rolled in an X-ray machine. Things moved quickly after that. And it wasn't long before Dr. Reynolds swept back in.

"Good news." He drew Jenna's and Flynn's attention to a computer screen. "Both bone pieces are aligned and there are no muscle or ligament tears."

He then went to the sink and began to wash his hands. Pulling on latex gloves, he discreetly selected a hypodermic from a surgical pack Nurse Foster had prepared. She'd already cleaned Andee's arm with a liquid the girl complained was cold.

"Little bee sting," the doctor said.

It wasn't until after Andee uttered an ear-piercing scream, which caused Jenna's stomach to plummet, that she realized how deftly the nurse and Flynn had held Andee still.

And still Flynn anchored his free hand around her waist, tucking her against his side. She took comfort from the heat radiating through his shirt as Dr. Reynolds eased Andee's bones back into place.

"You're a brave girl," he said. "For that I'll give you a cast with pink-and-white flowers. Would you like that? Or you can have a yellow one with bright green frogs."

Tears still billowed from Andee's eyes.

"Mommy?" A question hung on the one shaky word, sounding so pitiful Flynn relaxed his grip as Jenna moved closer to the table.

"Your choice, honey." Bending, she kissed Andee's wet cheek before the tech moved everyone away to shoot more X-rays.

The nurse kept Andee occupied, leaving the doctor free to explain what was going on. "Her fingers should look more normal by morning," he said. "These porous casts let air circulate around the arm. At her age, bones generally knit fast. Take her to your family doctor to have it rechecked in four weeks."

"I don't have a family doctor yet," Jenna said. "We only moved here a month ago."

"Ah, sorry, I noticed you're favoring one leg," he said to Flynn, "so I assumed you'd seen a doctor recently."

"I go to the VA," Flynn put in, still not correcting his family status.

The tech entered and showed Dr. Reynolds the new X-rays.

"Perfect," the doctor announced. "So will it be flowers or frogs, young lady?"

Jenna fiddled with Andee's hair. "I happen to know Auntie Melody sent you a present that will look nice with pink-and-white flowers. It's waiting for you at home."

"But I want frogs."

That made everyone in the room laugh. "Frogs it is." The nurse opened a cabinet and brought out casting material. In a few nimble moves the doctor had Andee's forearm encased in fabric covered in smiling green frogs on lily pads.

When the ordeal was over, the nurse directed Jenna to an area marked Accounting.

Flynn carried Andee and Cubby into the waiting room, where she just had to show her new cast to the few people that'd come in after them.

"There went my alpacas and your air conditioner," Jenna said to Flynn, who waited at the door for her. "By the way, I'm sorry they all kept assuming you were Andee's dad."

He started to reply, but his cell phone rang. Flynn worked it out of his pocket and managed a "Hello?" on the fourth ring. "Mom, hi. Listen, I'm just leaving the emergency room. Can I call you later? What? No, not me. Jenna's daughter fell off her bike and broke her arm."

Walking beside him, Jenna could hear his

mother's exclamations of sympathy, followed by rapid-fire questions.

He rolled his eyes at Jenna, but asked Andee, "Do you want to tell my mother you're okay?" He waggled the phone toward her.

The girl lifted her head from his shoulder. "Do I know her?"

"No, but I've mentioned you enough that she feels she knows you." He held the phone to Andee's ear, then halted by the SUV Jenna was unlocking.

"Yep, it hurt awful," Andee said. "It's better now 'cause I got my arm wrapped in funny green frogs."

Flynn raised his voice. "They're on her cast. Mom, say goodbye. We're at the car and everyone's tuckered. Especially Jenna," he added, since the powerful parking-lot light he'd left the SUV beneath illuminated dark circles under her tired eyes. "I'll call you tomorrow."

"She said goodbye and remember to call her," Andee relayed.

Nodding, Flynn pocketed his phone.

"Flynn, do you mind if I sit in back with Andee again on the way home?"

"Why would I mind?"

"No reason. I... It's nice to have help. I would have handled it alone if I'd had to."

"I know that," he said. He closed their door and went around to open his.

They hadn't gone far when Andee fell asleep with her head on Cubby Bear. Jenna felt compelled to say "From the time she was born Andrew was away more than he was home. I dealt with her choking on a penny when she was three. And she swelled up with hives the first time she ate a strawberry. It was a holiday and all of my neighbors were gone. Still, I can't tell you how grateful I am that you were there tonight to splint her arm."

"It wasn't a big deal."

"Please. Let me thank you. I'm trying to say it was a big deal to me."

"Okay." He glanced at her over his shoulder just as her stomach growled.

So loudly it embarrassed her.

Flynn eyed her again. "We missed dinner. I don't believe there's anyplace open in town since they roll in the sidewalks at eight. Anyway, you look exhausted. By no means am I a good cook. But I can probably throw together eggs, bacon and toast."

A sigh escaped her. "I've already leaned on you more than I have any right to do."

"Let me be the judge of that."

"Look, I know you didn't want to relocate to my place. You laid out a strict timetable I thought I could meet. Now I doubt I can and I'm sorry."

Flynn gave a self-deprecating laugh. "I should confess... I... Well, I was smarting from having been dumped by my fiancée. I didn't trust you because it seemed as if yet another commitment I'd signed up for was... well...was falling apart."

He shook his head.

"Spending time with you has showed me that relationship was a mistake from the start."

The silence lengthened.

"I don't know what to say," Jenna finally responded. "Relationships can be complicated."

"I should be thankful that her lack of commitment came to light before we got married."

"And had children."

"See, that was part of the problem. She wanted to concentrate on her career. My injury and subsequent decision to leave the military didn't fit her plan, either. Which is why it took me a while to accept any part in our breakup."

"What was your part? Or do you have any idea?"

"Over the many weeks I spent in the hospital and then in rehab, I worked out the future to suit me without consulting her."

He paused, a distant look in his eyes.

"She didn't know I owned the airpark or that I opted for discharge. There are always two sides that you can't separate until the shouting's over."

Jenna thought about her last few years with Andrew. He'd been away so much she had felt neglected. She'd acted like a single mom, giving Andee her undivided attention. When he got home he'd seemed demanding. Perhaps on those rotations, never for long, he might have felt she'd ignored him.

Andee had trailed him like a puppy, but perhaps he'd closed himself off, not because he hadn't wished to be a dad, but because he'd needed time to decompress.

It had been easy to see he'd been under stress. She should have worked harder to get him to see a doctor no matter how much he'd objected.

"We're at your lane," Flynn said, breaking into her reverie. "You'll want to make sure Andee's arm doesn't move on this rough section."

Jenna gathered the sleeping girl close. "Funny how the ruts and dips in the lane and along the paths by the pens feel worse now."

"I can give Barney a hand filling them in tomorrow."

"Thanks, but I'm sure you have your own work to see to."

"Speaking of work… Dayton Hines, a local commercial Realtor, brought the owners of the historic-plane show to the airpark this afternoon." He shot her a glance.

"Dayton is Travis Hines's dad. He's the kid who buzzed your pens."

She nodded for him to continue.

"Anyway, Dayton suggested to the mayor and city council that they sponsor an air show. He's up-front about his motive. He wants to keep the homeless vets out of the park to make the town more conducive to investors."

"What kind of person doesn't want to house the homeless for their sake?"

"Apparently a commercial Realtor." Reaching the house, Flynn parked behind his pickup. "I hear Beezer barking. That'll wake Andee." He hooked an arm over the seat back as he turned. "Shall I go in and try to quiet him?"

"No need. She's zonked." Jenna unfastened their seat belts.

"Shall I carry her?" Flynn got out and came around to open Jenna's door.

"Thanks so much."

Flynn helped her out before he leaned in and carefully collected the girl. "I dropped Cubby. Will you get him?"

She complied then locked the SUV. With no lights on in the house, they were engulfed in darkness. Not realizing Flynn had waited, Jenna bumped into him.

He reached back with one hand and tucked her into his side.

She shivered in the curve of his arm. But not from cold.

Flynn held her steady. "Our eyes will adjust in a minute."

Jenna looked for the moon, which on previous nights had shone brightly. Tonight a crescent of gold stood out in the distant starlight. "Oh, look. There's Orion overhead. Don't you love how clear the skies are here?"

"You should see the constellations from thirty-five-thousand feet. When I fly at night I envy the astronauts."

"I'm afraid to fly."

Flynn had been guiding Jenna up the porch steps, but at her comment stopped dead. "Since your husband's accident?"

"No, since I was a kid. My dad's plane crash-landed in Italy. It was in a remote spot and we didn't know if he was alive for almost a week. I shouldn't have married a pilot. Andrew thought my fears were foolish, but look what happened."

She took out the house key and unlocked the door.

Before Flynn responded, Beezer bounded out, leaping and barking. He woke Andee up even before Jenna switched on the outside lights.

Sleepy-eyed, Andee raised her cast above

Flynn's head. "No, Beezer. You'll hurt my broken arm."

Flynn settled the dog with a couple of words. "He's happy to see us. And he's probably hungry. We took off so fast I didn't think to feed him."

"Sorry, Beezer." Andee yawned and rubbed her eyes. "I didn't eat, either."

"None of us did. I'll fix something and give your mom a break."

Andee eyed him solemnly. "Mommy, can daddies cook?"

"Do you mean can men cook? Some of the world's most famous cooks are men. I'm sure some of them are dads," Jenna said, reaching for her, balancing the girl on her hip. "I'm taking you in to change into your nightgown. That way you can eat and head straight to bed."

"My arm hurts. Can I sleep with you tonight?"

The doctor had said Andee wouldn't be in pain with the lidocaine and to use an over-the-counter children's analgesic if she felt uncomfortable the next day. Jenna guessed she was being played.

"Okay, for tonight."

Beezer seemed torn about whether to follow them out of the kitchen or to stay with Flynn.

Leaning down, Flynn rubbed the dog's sides. "Let's check your food and water bowls, boy." He strode into the laundry room. The dog wiggled all over as Flynn poured out kibble and fresh water.

Returning to the kitchen, Flynn washed up and listened to the murmur of feminine voices drifting from the back of the house. The indistinct sounds mingled with Beezer crunching kibble.

A sense of peace settled over Flynn of the type he hadn't felt in a long time. He considered that as he moved clutter off the table and set out plates and silverware.

Jenna and Andee reminded him there could be good things in his life. Things he'd rejected after his engagement had disintegrated.

If he was honest, his relationship with Saundra had been fun, like a Tilt-A-Whirl. Not peaceful at all.

He moved Jenna's mail to the counter and made a mental note to jog her memory about the package for Andee. She'd said it was a gift from her sister.

He moved on to assemble what he needed for the meal.

Would her sister like him? He had no doubt his family would love Jenna and Andee without reservation. His mom might overwhelm them. She was a born hugger. Picturing the lot of them at a Sutton family gathering had him whistling while he beat the eggs.

"Are you making French fries?" Andee asked from behind him.

Flynn turned, spatula in hand, to find Jenna holding her daughter and looking over his shoulder. "Nope. Toast, bacon and scrambled eggs. Does that sound good?"

"Uh-huh. With ketchup, please."

"A girl after my own heart." He chuckled.

Jenna seemed to sag under the weight of the six-year-old.

"Why don't you two sit? Ah, there, the toast popped. Jenna, can you butter?"

"Gladly."

He put the toast on a plate and set it on the table.

She pulled a chair out for Andee.

Beezer loped out of the laundry room licking his chops. He nuzzled Andee's bare toes and she giggled.

Sitting, Jenna buttered the toast, then poured Andee's milk. "You may need help drinking from this fat glass."

"Why did the doctor wrap frog stuff around my thumb?"

When Jenna, busy opening the ketchup, didn't answer right away, Flynn brought their eggs and bacon to the table and said, "Until your broken arm heals, it might hurt if you wiggle your fingers too much."

"What if my bones don't get well?" The child dipped her fork into the food he'd dished up, but waited to take a bite after her mom squirted ketchup onto her eggs.

"They will heal." Flynn and Jenna spoke with a single voice. Their eyes met, and he suddenly wanted her. It felt like a hefty kick to his gut.

Andee reached for her milk. Hurriedly dropping Flynn's eye contact, Jenna helped steady the glass. When she slopped milk out, Flynn decided she'd felt the gut punch, too.

"I don't like being a baby again." Andee shoved Jenna's hand away. "I don't like a broken arm. How can I get dressed or tie my shoes?"

"I'll help you. Hey, speaking of shoes…" Jenna set down the glass. "Flynn, where is the shoebox you said came in the mail?"

Getting up, he brought it to the table. "I have a pocketknife if you need help cutting through the tape."

"It's a box of shoes?" Andee asked around a mouthful of egg.

"Maybe. You'll see. Do you remember me telling you Auntie Melody sent you a present? Finish eating and then you can open it."

The girl tucked into her remaining food. The adults polished theirs off, too.

Andee finished first and wiped her mouth on the back of her uninjured hand instead of using a napkin. "Why would Auntie Melody send me shoes? Maybe it's a new doll. I want Flynn to open it." She pushed the package toward him, slid off her chair and held up her arms so he'd lift her onto his lap.

He sought Jenna's approval.

"Go ahead. My sister uses more tape on gifts than anyone I know. My dad used to say if he was smart he'd buy stock in a major tape company."

Flynn laughed as he dug out his pocket-knife. He boosted Andee into his lap.

"Hurry," she urged.

"This strapping tape is tough. You need to sit still as a mouse. The last thing we need is for the knife to slip and cut one of us. That goes for you, too, Beezer," Flynn added when the dog nosed in. At last he sawed through. "You open the rest," he said, closing and pocketing his knife. He steadied the box so Andee could more easily rip off the wrapping.

Jenna stacked their dirty dishes to give them more room. They leaned in to watch the child pry off the lid.

"Oh, boots." Whooping, Andee took one out of the box. "Flynn, Mommy, look! They're pink like my bike. I should've choosed the flowers for my arm."

"I don't know. The frogs are cool," Flynn told her. "They go fine with pink."

"If you say they do, okay," Andee said around a giant yawn. "Can I wear my boots to bed?"

"Why not? And let's get you off there right now." Standing, Jenna held out her arms.

Andee burrowed against Flynn's wide chest. "I want Flynn to carry me."

Letting her arms drop, Jenna spent a moment wondering if she'd left underwear lying on her bed. Too late to do anything about it. Flynn had stood and Andee's eyelids were already at half mast.

She scooped up Cubby and led the way.

After snapping on the bedside lamp, she was relieved to see everything in order.

"She's out," Flynn murmured. "If you turn back the covers, I'll lay her down."

Jenna did and tucked the boots and Cubby under Andee's good arm.

"Well," he said, "I'd better get back to the kitchen and put the dishes in the dishwasher. Considering your eventful day, you'll probably want to turn in."

"Actually, I'm thinking about making a cup of chamomile tea." She turned the lamp to low. "You cooked, so I should do the dishes." She slipped past him and out the door. "Didn't you say something about telling me how your day went?"

"It wasn't anything important. I'm excited about the historic planes. We're going to offer tours. And flights in a B-17 Flying

Fortress, as well as the B-24 Liberator. For a hefty fee there will be half-hour flight instruction in a P-51 Mustang fighter. You may not even want to take the tour."

"I don't." Having put a kettle of water on to heat, she helped him rinse and stow their dinner items in the dishwasher. "But Andee will want to see the planes. Are you sure the noise from all of those flights won't stampede my birds?"

He folded the paper that had been around Andee's gift and stuffed it into the boot box, which he put in the trash bin. "I won't lie. World War II planes aren't quiet. They recommend in the brochure that people taking excursions bring earplugs."

Beezer wandered out of the laundry room, where he'd been lapping up water, and through the kitchen.

"Mmm-hmm. Would you like tea?" she asked Flynn distractedly as the kettle whistled. Noisy planes. What about her birds?

"Sure." He took a second cup from a cupboard and passed it to Jenna. Watching her pour boiling water over tea bags, he leaned his hip against the counter and hooked his thumbs in his belt. "I thought you'd throw a fit at the prospect of the noise."

Giving a rueful smile, she handed him a cup. "I'd be more apt to if the money wasn't going to a good cause. I hate the notion of anyone sleeping out in the park. Everybody deserves a bed and a roof over their head." She sat at the table and blew on her hot tea. "I know some might choose the streets, but many would rather have normalcy."

Flynn pulled out the chair across from her and sat. "I'm glad to hear you say that. Dayton Hines asked if I knew of any structures the city could buy now to get the four veterans currently living in the park out before Pancho Villa Days."

She didn't say anything, so he continued slowly, "I started thinking…your rental has three bedrooms, plus a den that could be a fourth bedroom. As worried as you are about finding the money to upgrade the AC, it crossed my mind it may be a relief to sell it to the city on the condition they replace the unit. Unless your heart's set on being a slumlord. Just kidding," he tossed out quickly with a laugh.

Sitting up straighter, Jenna gripped her cup. "Then where would you go?"

He cleared his throat. It took him a minute to speak.

"I thought I could stay here."

# CHAPTER TEN

"Is THAT A no or a yes?" Flynn asked after rushing around the table to pat Jenna on the back as she choked on her hot tea.

She needed to breathe. "I...swallowed the tea too fast."

Flynn was a pilot. He could collide with another flyer in the sky—and...die. "I need time to think this over."

"Yes." Flynn took his seat again and picked up his cup. "Knowing the day you've had, I should've laid it on you with a little more finesse. I assumed you'd want to help the vets."

"The idea is worth considering. I counted the rental income as gravy. That didn't pan out."

"Your income wouldn't change with me paying the same to rent here."

Jenna studied him pensively. "Let me sleep on it," she said, standing and putting her cup in the dishwasher.

He pushed to his feet and did the same.

Their arms bumped. It felt like an electric shot. She hurriedly started the dishwasher and eased away.

"What's wrong, Jenna?" He caught her arm, turning her to face him. "Just say no and we'll forget I brought it up. The last thing I want is to cause you more headaches."

She took a long, careful breath. "You're right. I've had an eventful day."

"Don't lose sleep worrying about it, okay? You go on to bed. I'll set up coffee for morning and make sure everything is locked up before I shut out the lights and turn in."

"Thanks, I'm going." And she fled.

Reaching for the coffee filters, Flynn stared after her and wondered if she had other problems bottled up.

He truly regretted his part in their thorny start. It was just that sticking to a commitment was such a huge deal in his life. He'd committed to the service…and look where that had gotten him: grounded and barely scraping by. He'd committed to Saundra… and enough said about that.

So many things about Jenna were opening his eyes.

Yes, she'd committed to taking over his

lease and making good on his living conditions. No, she hadn't been able to follow
through on that promise. Was Jenna really
any different from Saundra?

Damn. When had he become so rigid and
uncompromising? Was it the military training?

He didn't know.

But maybe sometimes the road paved with
good intentions didn't have to lead to hell.

He set about doing all of the other chores
he'd promised Jenna he'd take care of. Then
he retired for the night.

WHEN FLYNN GOT up the next morning, he
used Jenna's gift and took his blood pressure. It registered normal, making his spirits soar. Feeling like kicking up his heels, he
dressed and hurried downstairs, surprised to
discover he was the first one up.

But if anything spoke about Jenna's previously rough day, her sleeping late was it. He
started the coffee, hoping the smell would
entice her out of bed. His pouring cereal attracted Beezer. The dog beelined straight to
the laundry room, but promptly came out to
gaze accusingly at Flynn.

"Ha, you traitor. Leave me all night then expect me to feed you? Okay, come on." He filled the dog's bowl with kibble and went back to eat his Froot Loops. Since there was still no sign of Jenna or Andee by the time he finished, Flynn took his coffee outside to savor the fresh air and sunshine.

Beezer tagged along and went sniffing in the bushes.

Flynn set out toward the pens to get an idea how many holes needed to be filled. Luckily she didn't need to buy gravel. She owned several acres of sandy soil.

He parked his mug on a shed window ledge so he could see if there was a wheelbarrow inside. Before he got the door open, an airplane crested the foothills flying so low he could count the rivets outlining the aircraft's wheel well.

Hearing a commotion coming from normally quiet ostriches, Flynn crossed to the pens and saw birds in chaos. It was exactly how Jenna had described it when she'd levied her first complaint at the airpark.

He hadn't wanted to believe Travis Hines would deliberately and repeatedly buzz this ranch. Flynn knew his plane. This time the kid had meant to strafe the pens. He'd banked and roared over them, flying lower. Dangerously so.

For all the good it did, Flynn shook his fist at the now-departing Piper Cub. The dog pawed at his good leg and whined. "Sorry, boy, but he's a knucklehead."

Glad Jenna hadn't been up to see the plane today, Flynn idly rubbed the dog's silky ears and tried to think of the best way to deal with Travis. Obviously talking to him hadn't worked. Maybe he'd speak to Dayton about his son.

Steeped in thought, Flynn went back to retrieve his coffee and saw Barney rolling in early. The older man parked his Harley and strode out to greet Flynn.

"Hey, who slashed your pickup tires and cut up your canopy?"

"What?"

Flynn led the way to where he'd parked the previous afternoon—before Andee's accident and their subsequent trip to the hospital in Jenna's SUV. His head spun when he got a look at the damage. If it had happened before they'd arrived home, it'd been too dark to see. And this morning he hadn't paid attention. Now he circled his pickup again.

"Bummer," Barney said, hooking his thumbs in his back pockets at the end of Flynn's tour.

"It could've been worse. Whoever did it skipped the front tires and didn't mess up the paint job. My canopy took the brunt." Flynn lifted several strips of shredded vinyl.

"Probably teens out joy-riding and making mischief. Funny your dog didn't howl."

Flynn went to inspect Jenna's vehicle. It was okay. "It probably happened while we were at the hospital." He straightened and told Barney about Andee's accident.

"That's awful. Poor little tyke."

"Yes. On a normal night I would've noticed since I parked Jenna's Cherokee behind my pickup. I was focused on getting Andee into a dark house. There was barely a moon out last night."

Jenna and Andee emerged from the house. "Here you men beat me out and about. I feel guilty for sleeping late." Jenna took her daughter's hand coming down the steps.

Beezer bounded up to the girl and licked her face. She giggled and shook loose from her mom. "Mr. Fisk, did Flynn tell you I broke my arm?"

"He just did. That's some fine-looking cast you have there, kiddo."

"And see my new boots. Auntie Melody sent them. Oh, Mommy, can we show him my bicycle? It's pink like my boots."

In the middle of sipping her morning coffee, Jenna was slower to make her way to where the men stood. "Andee, honey, he can see it later. I want Barney to fill in the potholes along the path before you ride your—" She got her first look at Flynn's pickup. "What in the world happened?"

"Vandals," he said. "I intended to help Barney fill potholes, but I either need to call a tow truck or borrow your SUV to run into town and pick up a couple of new tires. I have one spare, but that won't get me on the road."

"What'll you do about the slashed cover? It's a mess," Jenna said.

"Let my auto insurance replace it. They should pay some on the tires, too."

"We need to take photos," Jenna advised. "And call the sheriff. He said to call if we had more trouble. Did Oscar Martin have to put up with this? Is that why he sold the ranch?"

Shrugging, Flynn took out his cell phone and began snapping pictures. "Ask Sheriff Denton."

Andee, who'd tossed Beezer's ball, ran back. "You got holes in your tire," she announced. "How will your truck go, Flynn?"

He tweaked her nose. "It won't go. Not until I buy new tires."

The sound of a vehicle approaching garnered everyone's attention. A silver pickup kicked up plumes of dust that rolled toward them in waves.

Jenna scooped back tendrils of hair blowing in her eyes. "Is that the sheriff? Did you already call him?"

He shook his head, stepping forward so the driver would see him and stop.

The driver braked. The dust began to settle. Jenna gasped when Don Winkleman climbed out of the cab.

Flynn stabbed a finger at the man. "Well, well. Have you come to gloat over your most recent sabotage?"

Stopping short, Winkleman resettled his ball cap. "What are you talking about? This is the second time you've accused me of something. I don't know what your problem is. I've come to do business with Ms. Wood."

"I suppose you have no idea how my pickup got slashed?"

This time the man removed his cap and scratched a spot on his head. "Is that Barney Fisk?" Winkleman sidestepped Flynn. "Barney, you've been in town longer than these folks. Have you ever heard of me doing anyone dirt?"

"Can't say that I have."

Flynn bristled. "You tell Jenna she'll be sorry for firing you and, funny thing, things inexplicably start to go wrong around here."

Jenna moved closer to Flynn. "Maybe we should let Mr. Winkleman say why he's showed up on this unfortunate day."

"Yes, ma'am," the newcomer said. "Two weeks ago I learned I'd inherited some land in Arizona. It belonged to an uncle who raised a few sheep and goats."

"I'm sorry for your loss," she replied.

"Thank you… Well, I went to see if I should keep the farm or sell it. The place is perfect for starting my own ostrich flock."

She and Flynn shared a look.

"The cattle pens are empty, and I hoped you'd sell me a hundred chicks now and another hundred in two or three months."

You could have knocked her over with a feather. He wanted to buy from her?

"I can't afford to install incubators. And I know Oscar's birds are top of the line."

He twisted his cap between gnarled hands.

"I probably should've started by apologizing for mouthing off to you like I did. I'm real sorry. This was the first job I ever had where I fit. I—I got to know the birds."

Jenna was surprised to discover she had to blink back tears. She'd fired a man who had taken the time and effort to get to know the birds.

And here she was fumbling away at caring for the ostriches without really having a clue.

"I was mad at Oscar for selling out to an Easterner who wasn't a rancher," he continued, "and I honestly thought my work deserved more money."

"So you really didn't open my gates and set the ostriches free?"

"I'd never do that. I love those birds. They could've been hurt."

She had to look away at that. He *loved* them.

He turned to Flynn. "Is that what you were talking about that morning you met me in town? I told you I hadn't been out here."

"I didn't believe you."

Jenna glanced from man to man. "I believe him, Flynn."

He nodded. "Which leaves me no suspect for today's dirty work."

"Kids, I tell you," Barney chimed in. "Teens on alcohol with too much time on their hands. Our camp got ransacked twice."

Jenna studied him thoughtfully. "Barney, would you move to a room in a house if the city provided a safe place you could stay?"

He bent and patted Beezer. The dog and Andee stood between him and Jenna. "I'd consider it if the rent wasn't outlandish."

"Can we get back to my offer to buy the chicks?" Winkleman put in. "I brought travel crates. I'd like to load them and head back to Arizona pronto," he said and named a price he'd pay per chick. "That's two bucks more for each than Oscar charged. I figure I owe you extra for the way I acted, Ms. Wood."

Andee tugged on Jenna's shirt. "I don't want the bad man to take our baby chicks."

"Shh, honey. He's not bad. He apologized. And we'll get more babies. This way, we can use the money to build pens and buy alpacas."

The girl kept eyeing Winkleman from under her long, dark eyelashes.

"I'll sell you chicks," Jenna said with finality. "Barney, will you help him load up? My rough estimate of hatchlings is a hundred and twenty. Give him one hundred and put twenty chicks out for our birds to care for. We'll start replenishing the incubators right away. Andee, please go inside and get my car keys off the kitchen counter so Flynn can take his tires to town in the Cherokee. I'll go feed the birds and fill water troughs."

Barney headed to a shed and Don Winkleman returned to his pickup. He backed it behind the pens to where they could load the birds into his crates.

"Can we go with Flynn?"

Flynn jumped in to say, "I was planning to ask if you'd keep Beezer here, Andee. The tire store isn't really the best place for kids or dogs."

The girl pouted. "I thought we could get ice-cream cones."

Jenna turned her daughter toward the house. "This afternoon is your first story hour at the library. I'll take you for ice cream after it's over."

"And Beezer? He likes hearing stories. I bet he loves ice cream. But not chocolate."

Flynn grinned at Jenna, who was plainly fighting a losing battle. "You can almost see the wheels turning in her head. She's always thinking one step ahead."

He hooked a playful arm around Jenna's neck and buried a laugh in her windblown hair.

"The car keys, Andee," Jenna said, pointing to the house. As she darted away, Jenna reared back to look at Flynn. "How can you be so cheerful when your pickup has been decimated?"

He pressed his lips against her mouth, saying, "You make me happy. You and Andee. And I didn't have a chance to tell you, but I took my blood pressure this morning. It was normal."

Jenna's voice deserted her.

Rallying, she managed to say, "Ah, that

explains why you kissed me after saying you'd never do that again."

"Hmm. Dare I say that was a mistake on my part? What I said before was an error," he added, releasing her as Andee and Beezer popped back out of the house.

"Thanks," he said, taking the keys from Andee. "You take good care of Beezer and your mom while I'm gone. How does your arm feel this morning?"

"Better, but Mommy had to help me dress and pull on my new boots." Her lips turned down.

Jenna ruffled the child's bangs. "I don't mind. I'll go help you with breakfast, too. We should let Flynn go to get tires."

She started to turn away, then stopped. Hesitantly she said, "By the way, I slept on your suggestion about my rental. If the city council is interested in buying it as is to house vets, I'll discuss selling. I think I'd be better off to concentrate on raising ostriches and alpacas."

"I'll mention it to Curtis. Someone can contact you if they're interested."

Jenna returned to the house with Andee and Beezer.

Flynn bent to the task of jacking up the pickup and removing the back tires. He saw Barney and Don go to the house, so he loaded the tires and left.

In town, the first thing he did was buy new tires. While they were being mounted on his rims, he phoned his insurance agent. "I'm covered 100 percent for vandalism? That's good. No, it didn't happen at the airpark, but in the yard where I'm renting." The men talked a while longer. Flynn asked his agent to fax the authorization to purchase a new pickup canopy to his office.

Since he was in town, he decided to make another stop.

Giving his name to the mayor's secretary, Flynn was ushered into Mayor Parker's private office. He was surprised to see commercial Realtor Dayton Hines and residential Realtor Bud Rhodes in the room. They shook hands all around.

"Sorry for butting in on your meeting, Mayor. Your secretary didn't say you were occupied."

"No problem," Curtis Parker said. "In fact Dayton said he told you that our hope is to move the homeless guys out of the park before Pancho Villa Days, and he said you may know of a house."

"That's why I'm here." Flynn silenced his phone so they wouldn't be disturbed. "Bud knows I rented a home from Oscar Martin, who later sold to Jenna Wood. The air conditioner fell apart at my rental. She doesn't have funds to replace it, so I'm renting the upstairs at her ranch."

The other men shared pointed looks.

Flynn hesitated before continuing, "Her rental has three bedrooms, two baths and a den that could be a fourth bedroom. She'd sell, but as is. Bud, you handled Oscar's sale. You'll know what the house is worth."

Dayton turned to Rhodes. "Bud, this sounds ideal. I can get an AC wholesale." He glanced at the mayor. "The city can write off the price and may even recoup some of the cost from one of the area's veteran groups."

The other three talked over and around Flynn. He got to his feet. "I'm just the messenger. You'll need to contact Jenna."

He opened the door.

Rhodes glanced at his watch. "What do you say we all go to the café for an early lunch? I can write up our offer. Since you're staying at the ranch, Sutton, you can take it to her and then the ball will be in her court. Curtis, does it take a council vote?"

"They voted to buy a suitable property and put a dollar figure not to exceed. If this home falls within the guidelines, we're good." He stood and rang his secretary. "We're going to lunch, Rachel. Take messages, please."

Outside, Rhodes fell in beside the mayor. They chatted about the house, leaving Flynn behind with Dayton Hines. Flynn debated whether or not to mention Travis, then thought, *Why not?*

"Dayton, I hesitate to bring this up, but I've spoken to Travis more than once about flying low over Jenna's ostrich pens. He came really low today. It sends the birds into a frenzy. So far none of them has been injured, but if they are Jenna will file a complaint with the county."

"With the county, holy cow!"

"Maybe he'll listen to you. If he keeps ignoring me, I'll have to ask him to move his plane to another facility."

Hines pinched his lower lip. "My wife and I hoped flying would teach Travis discipline and respect. He's a moody kid, but he loves flying. I'm sorry to hear he's not listening to you. I'll speak to him."

"That's a load off my mind," Flynn said.

"Could you give me until after the air show? We have guests at home and I'm snowed under with business."

"I can, but Jenna Wood is her own woman. She may report him if he strafes her flock again. If I see him I'll tell him that."

Hines clapped Flynn on the back. "Meanwhile I'll try to keep him busy helping with the historic planes. Travis wants us to pay for him to train in the P-51. I'll set some conditions."

The men walked into the café, where talk turned to ordering. After that Bud Rhodes wrote up an offer on the house for Flynn to give Jenna, and he gave Bud a key so the Realtor could evaluate it.

Once lunch ended, they parted and Flynn drove back to the ranch.

Jenna paced in front of the house and Andee sat on a step. The minute Flynn parked, Jenna ran up. "Where have you been? I tried phoning you. I have to take Andee to her first library story hour. You need to unload those tires ASAP."

"Sorry. I stopped to see the mayor and... Never mind, it can wait." Flynn got out and quickly removed the tires while Jenna settled Andee in her child seat. He'd no more than closed the back door than Jenna took off.

Barney hiked over from the direction of the sheds. "Hey, Flynn. I'm done filling pot-holes. I'll give you a hand replacing your new tires."

"Thanks. Squatting is hard on my bum knee. I appreciate the help. Where's Beezer?"

"Jenna left him in the house. That was a bone of contention between her and Andee. She insisted your dog likes hearing stories, too."

"What a kid. I'll take the mutt with me to the airpark and leave Jenna a note. You did a great job filling holes. Andee should be able to ride her bike without falling now."

"Yeah. I wet the new sand and smoothed it out. It's a shame she got hurt. But she's not letting a broken arm slow her down. The ball she threw around for Beezer lodged on the roof of one of the sheds. Jenna caught Andee stacking egg crates to climb up there. Man, I wish I had half her energy."

Flynn laughed. "Do I need to go get it?"

"Nah, I brought out a ladder and retrieved the ball."

"Jenna needs to get her a pony. When I was a kid we all had horses. That would burn a lot of energy."

Once they finished with the tires, Barney helped remove the shredded vinyl canopy. It was a hot job. "I appreciate your help. Can I offer you a cold drink before we take off, Barney? Jenna keeps a pitcher of water in the fridge and usually has lemonade."

Flynn washed his hands under the hose by the pens. Beezer must have been napping earlier; now he was barking up a storm.

"Thanks, but at three o'clock I'm filling in at the Legion bar. I'll go in early and buy a cold brew before regulars drop by. Haven't seen you there in a while."

Flynn realized he preferred coming straight here once he left work.

"I'm pretty busy at the airpark," he said. "I'll be even busier if I can keep my blood pressure down and pass my flight physical so I can offer lessons."

The older man dried his hands on his shirttail. "I've got buddies who suffer white-coat syndrome. Is that your problem?"

Flynn cocked his head to one side. "Anxiety leading to raised BP at the sight of a doctor, huh? Well, it's been suggested."

"A buddy started taking some fruit powder. He swears his BP dropped. Now he flies equipment out to the oil rigs off the coast of Texas. I bet you could look on the computer and find out what it is."

"Worth checking. You sure he wasn't pulling your leg?"

"Nope. He's dead serious about flying."

"If this pans out, I'll owe you big time, Barney."

"Gotta stick together. Still, you young guys get a lot more help than we Nam vets ever did. Listen, I need to take off."

"Sure. Thanks again."

Barney walked his motorcycle down the lane before firing it up. Like Winkleman, he cared about the ostriches. Flynn would tell Jenna, knowing she'd be pleased.

He went inside and fended off sloppy dog kisses. "You are such a people animal," Flynn told Beezer as he took a few minutes to pet him. "Okay, okay, we'll go in a minute. Quit licking me so I can leave Jenna a note."

He set the house offer on the table and laid

his note on top of it. He hadn't read the offer, because it felt wrong, like an invasion of Jenna's privacy. He assumed it'd be fair. But if she wanted his opinion, he'd look it over.

Flynn locked the house, but stood a few minutes gazing around at the place that felt like home after such a short time. He hadn't been attached to the rental, even though, as Jenna pointed out, it had flowers and a yard. Maybe this place reminded him of the farm of his youth.

Or maybe he'd gotten attached to the people who lived here.

He loaded Beezer and drove out, still contemplating why that was, when he'd sworn to himself and everyone he knew that he was going to remain a bachelor forever.

Forcing his mind to other things, he mulled over what Barney had said. Instead of going to the airpark straightaway, he detoured to the VA clinic.

Parking, he clipped on Beezer's leash and got out. The closer he got to the door the more hyper he felt. Entering the familiar space he watched the hustle and bustle of lab-coated doctors and uniformed nurses going in and out of examining rooms. His throat closed and he dropped Beezer's leash. Consumed by jitters, he backed out the door as another patient walked in.

Catching his breath, he rescued Beezer.

"Okay," he said as he returned the dog to his seat. "I need to read up on white-coat syndrome."

Driving to the airpark, he'd calmed down by the time he got there and unlocked his office.

The fax from his insurance agent had arrived. Kicking back, he returned the calls on his answering machine—inquiries asking about lessons.

"I still have work to do on my runways," he told both callers, but he invited them to the air show.

Antsy again, he left the office and wandered through the hangars. It wasn't until he stared up at one of his planes that he admitted he'd put off firing up his computer.

He was afraid if it turned out he didn't have white-coat syndrome that whatever did ail him would ground him for good.

But he'd never been a coward, so he went back to the office. After Beezer flopped down at his feet, he started a search and got deep into reading about white-coat hypertension.

The recommendation to live with it wasn't an option. His flight physical had to be signed by an FAA-approved MD.

So he typed in alternatives to blood-pressure medicine. Voilà! There were holistic remedies. He wrote down one, hoping it was available without driving to Albuquerque.

"If this works I owe Barney a high five and a six-pack."

Flynn left his office when he heard the deep drone of a B-17 overhead. It was the first of the historic fleet to arrive. A thrill shot through him.

Even as he watched the big plane circle twice before setting down on his longest runway, a van pulled in. Its side panels bore the logo of the foundation that owned the planes. A tall, lanky man stepped out.

"Hi. I'm looking for Flynn Sutton."

"You found him."

"Ah, good. I'm Russell Tolliver."

The men shook hands.

"You have a sweet facility. No mountains. No close power lines. Lots of parking. Perfect site for our show. My brother, Hank, is bringing in the flying fortress. Would you like a close-up before we head back to Albuquerque to ferry in the Liberator?"

Flynn grinned. "Like a kid wants into a candy store." He put Beezer back into the office to the dog's displeasure, then fell in beside the other man.

The sun had begun to set before three strangers who needed nothing in common but the love of planes quit talking about a flagship of the WWII Strategic Bombing Fleet. By then Flynn had sat as a bombardier would have and stood in the spot of a waist gunner.

"Watching you land, I couldn't help thinking those pilots were sitting ducks compared to the F-15s I flew," Flynn remarked on the walk back.

"Maybe so," Hank Tolliver said, waiting for his brother to unlock the van. "I think of the people below seeing thirty or so of those babies ready to drop their payload."

"For sure. I can't wait to see the other planes. Are you the only pilot ferrying them?"

"No. Tomorrow I'll drop off a list of our crew." Russell glanced back at the plane, a dark silhouette in the fading light. "What's your security?"

Flynn gave a start. "The sheriff said he'd handle it. I'll give him a call and make sure he has someone canvassing the area." His thoughts went to his tires.

When the others left, he phoned Sheriff Denton immediately. It was only after he hung up that he realized he hadn't mentioned the latest vandalism at the ranch. Should he have? He chewed that over as he and Beezer headed home.

He dismissed the thought as he turned down Jenna's lane. Light shone from her kitchen windows. Unlike his hesitancy to go right in the other time he'd showed up late, he used his key. As before, Jenna sat alone at the kitchen table.

She raised her head and smiled.

Flynn returned her smile.

This homey contentment was something he hadn't let himself want. Hadn't realized he needed.

"The coffee's fresh," Jenna said. "If you didn't eat I can warm up some leftover tuna noodle casserole."

"Don't get up. I'll fix a plate. Where's

Andee?" he asked, noticing Beezer padding aimlessly, whining.

"I wore her out today. She met some kids her age at the library and we all ended up at the elementary school's swings. Andee practically fell asleep in her plate."

The dog figured out on his own where to find Andee. They heard him pad through the living room, woof and then the creak of the bed under his weight.

They traded smiles while Flynn spooned out some of the casserole.

"What do you think of the city's offer for your hou—uh, my house?" Jenna asked.

"I didn't look at it."

"It seems all right. I checked comparisons on a housing website. Considering it needs a five- to eight-thousand-dollar AC, I guess the offer is in line."

"Dayton Hines said he can get them an AC wholesale. You could counter upward." Flynn removed his steaming plate from the microwave, poured coffee and sat next to her. He thought it was telling that she didn't shy away. "Did they break out a price for your furnishings?"

She nodded. "For as fast as they put this together, everything seems in order."

"But…?"

"Because they did it so quickly, am I being hustled?"

Flynn swallowed a bite, then said, "You said the price looks fair. Bud Rhodes wrote the contract. He knows our real-estate market. The mayor and others just want the homeless to quit camping in the city park."

"So do the mothers I met today. They're uneasy. They say families no longer picnic at the park. Of course, no one lets their kids go there to play. But they sure were excited about the carnival coming to town."

"And the first historic plane landed at my airfield today. It's a beauty."

"So soon? Aren't there two weeks to Pancho Villa Days?"

"A week and a half." Flynn touched her arm. "I learned about alternative therapies for white-coat syndrome from Barney today. I'm going to buy fruit powder tomorrow and start taking it."

"Fruit powder, huh?"

"I mean, what do I have to lose?"

"Do you have to fly to teach?"

He chuckled and gestured with his fork. "Would you take flying lessons from someone who couldn't demonstrate how?"

"I wouldn't take flying lessons period. I moved here to get away from air bases and naval air stations."

"Ouch! Where does that leave me?"

She studied him with a troubled expression and he felt a chill.

"You're an enigma, Flynn. Don't get me wrong...I like that you're here. I feel safe. I like how you admitted to changing your mind about Don Winkleman. It was big of you. Andee's crazy about you and I'm... torn," she said carefully. "I feel things I shouldn't."

"Shh." Flynn held a finger to her lips. "You're making it too hard. I'm not asking you to suddenly love airplanes."

"Okay, that's good. Listen, I'm signing it as is," she declared, pulling away from his touch.

Flynn watched her gather the papers and leave the kitchen.

## CHAPTER ELEVEN

JENNA WOKE EARLY and once again felt buoyed by hope and promise. She had money from the sale of the chicks to bank, and if the city bought the house, she could quit worrying about the AC. If and when the sale came to fruition, she'd owe Flynn for suggesting she cut her losses on the second property.

Flynn had played a large part in that. Who was she kidding? He'd played a large part in her life recently.

She fairly danced into the kitchen to flip on the coffeemaker and begin her chores for the day.

Admitting out loud to having feelings for him she didn't think she should feel had actually opened her mind to thinking she might be ready for a relationship. This morning in the warm light of day, it didn't seem wrong to risk her heart again.

Neither one of them had been looking to

meet a significant someone. Oh, but perhaps she'd read too much into what she saw as progress between them. As Flynn suggested last night, maybe she was thinking too much, making them...this...difficult. Melody always told her she overthought things.

There was no denying how glad she'd been that Andee's call to thank her aunt yesterday had gone to voice mail. Andee wouldn't have held back about not only her broken arm but also Beezer and Flynn.

Hopefully, by the time Mel slowed down enough for them to talk in person, Jenna would be more comfortable explaining Flynn and his dog's arrival in their lives.

For the time being, though, she had other thoughts to occupy her. Jenna poured a mug of coffee and went out to gather eggs.

She'd put half in refrigeration and half in the incubators, she decided. Egg production had been up the past few gatherings in spite of earlier disruptions to the birds.

This morning as she watched some of the hens fluff out their feathers to shade the chicks Barney had turned into the pens, Jenna was glad she hadn't sold Don Winkleman all of the babies.

Who would've thought from their inauspicious beginning that they'd end up having good business dealings?

Since he swore he hadn't opened the gates and freed her birds—and she believed him—then who had?

Being targeted for sabotage left her feeling uneasy and vulnerable. And jumpy, being out here alone with the birds.

With the last eggs stored, Jenna locked the sheds and retrieved her now-cold coffee. Before she returned to the house for a warm-up, she walked to the end of the pens and theorized how best to extend them to house alpacas.

She had the land to build out in a straight line. But it would be cozier and easier to care for the birds and animals if she added on at a right angle.

At Peggy's alpaca farm she'd had some beautiful old shade trees. All Jenna currently had on her property were creosote bushes, a few honey mesquite and sundry cacti like yucca. On the drive in from the East, she'd seen fields of chili peppers and some orchards of pecans. Come to think of it, big old pecan trees may have been what Peggy

Johnson had. But buying trees of any size would cost more than new pens. Since she planned to live here a long time, she could plant smaller trees. Until they grew she'd still need to install canvas ramadas.

She turned back to the house with a clearer idea of an end result.

Steps away from the house, she saw Flynn come out onto the porch. His sun-kissed blond hair still looked damp. But he always looked so put-together even when he wore an olive-green flight suit, as he did today.

Flynn did his own laundry; she'd seen his flight suits and shirts hanging in the laundry room. Andrew had always sent everything he owned to the dry cleaner's. Her friends on base used to think she was lucky. Many of them hated to iron the requisite creases in their husband's uniforms.

Somehow, seeing Flynn's things hanging in her laundry room evoked a sense of domestic bliss.

"Hey, there, I was just coming to find you," he called, stopping at the edge of the porch. "Andee's up. I helped her finish dressing. But she wants ribbons in her hair. That is above my pay grade," he said, laughing.

"I thought I'd get through chores before she woke up. You should have yelled for me." Jenna drew even with him.

"Why? Since her arm is in a cast, it seemed a logical request."

"But she's *my* responsibility." Jenna saw Flynn's gaze lower to her mouth, which caused her to get weak in the knees.

They stood for a few seconds locked in awareness, until Jenna sucked in a sharp breath and Flynn hurriedly opened the door to let her pass.

Beezer charged out of the laundry room yipping.

"Hi, Mommy," Andee called, dripping milk off the spoon she waved through the air. Jenna thought it was almost funny how quickly the momentary flame of passion was extinguished by the ordinary world.

"I want ribbons in my hair like Keisha had yesterday."

Jenna stopped in the process of adding hot coffee to her mug. "Honey, we don't have that many ribbons. And I don't have Mrs. Taylor's talent to give you so many tiny braids."

"But her hair looked like a rainbow of ribbons."

Jenna smiled. "Next time we see them, you'll have to tell her mom that."

"Can we all play at the school again today?"

"Not today. I have several errands to run. Maybe next week after your story hour."

"Can I still have ribbons today?"

Jenna met Flynn's eyes over top of Andee's head. She couldn't resist rolling her eyes.

"I have to go. You ladies enjoy your day." Flynn refilled his travel mug with coffee and tapped Jenna's nose on his way to the door.

"What?" she teased. "You don't want to stick around and learn how to braid hair and tie ribbons? Mouse," she accused as Flynn collected Beezer.

Tossing back his head, Flynn gave a hearty laugh.

It had been years since she and Andrew had bantered like this. Certainly not the last three years, she thought with sadness.

By then Flynn and his dog were outside and he'd closed the screen door. Then he stuck his head back into the kitchen. "If you ladies are going to get all gussied up, that calls for dinner out. I owe you one. Shall we try again? Meet at the café. Six o'clock?"

"What's *gussied*?" Andee asked.

"Prettied up," Flynn supplied.

"Yeah, Mommy. Let's. I have a dress that is pink like my boots."

"How can I say no to that?" Jenna said softly.

Stepping all the way inside, Flynn dropped a kiss on top of Andee's head and then did the same to Jenna, making her feel diminutive next to his superior height, and cherished, too. So much so that she dusted a finger across the dimple in his chin.

Teasingly he nibbled her finger. Or it may have been a kiss, Jenna thought after he disappeared again. She heard him whistling as he trod lightly down the steps. Happiness pulsed through her.

The feeling stuck with her while she ate toast and yogurt. And while she divided Andee's hair and wove two neat braids, which she tied off with pink satin ribbons.

Barney arrived and Jenna left Andee playing with her dollhouse. "After you're done seeding the empty pen, would you be able to go price the materials we'd need for three new pens? Could you and I build a setup like the one that's already here? Or do I need to pay a fence company for labor, too?"

"I'd like to help you save money, and they do rent posthole diggers. But a lot of this ground is like cement. I'm not a young dude any longer," he said as if it pained him to admit it.

"So would you be able to find a couple of quotes for labor? If their fees are by the hour or a flat charge?"

"Sure. I'll see if they'll give you a discount if they bid the whole job from delivery to setting posts, stretching wire, on through hanging gates. I can muscle them a little."

Jenna tried to scrutinize him from a salesman's perspective. He was a big man with a lived-in face. Sometimes, like today, he was clean-shaven except for a droopy mustache. Other times he didn't shave at all. His longish graying hair, the part not covered by a skull-tied bandanna, looked brassy in the sunlight. The total package put Jenna to mind of Hulk Hogan. She could well imagine a stranger thinking he was the type to use muscle.

"Don't act too tough. I doubt there are a lot

of fence companies in the vicinity. We don't want them turning us down. In fact, if you think it's a good deal, have them call me. I want to get this done as soon as possible."

"Hard hit as the local economy's been, there's no danger of anyone refusing a job."

A big hawk careened overhead. Ostrich hens scuttled around until all of the baby chicks were shielded. The males strutted back and forth until the predator left.

Jenna slowly let out her breath. Her chicks were safe. But the hawk was beautiful. She hoped he found a field mouse. She parted from Barney and went in to do a load of laundry before rounding up Andee to head off on errands.

She sat in the car when it dawned on her that she should have asked Flynn if he'd like her to pick up the fruit powder he wanted to try to lower his blood pressure. Their small town might not have it, and her first stop was at her bank in the larger city of Las Cruces.

Digging out her cell, she punched in Flynn's number. He answered on the first ring. "Hi, it's Jenna. I'm off to my new bank and wondered if you'd like me to see if I can find a health-food store that carries the fruit powder you told me about last evening."

"That'd be great if it doesn't put you out. I may not be able to get away. The air-show folks brought in two more planes. The crew wants to meet, so we'll all know the schedule for refueling, how many passengers fit in each plane, and so everyone has the rules for safety. They brought their own rope fencing to cordon off the planes, but I'll help them set up observation areas."

"You sound excited."

"I am. I've visited a couple of air museums. I've never seen takeoffs or landings of historic planes. And to actually get to fly in one or take the throttle of one is a rare treat."

"You're going to fly one?" Jenna couldn't help it—fear streaked through her.

"You bet. It's the chance of a lifetime." Flynn's excitement traveled over the airwaves.

"Listen, I'll let you go. I'm in the car, ready to leave."

"Sure. Have a good day. I'll be tied up here for most of it. So, I'll meet you at the café as we discussed."

Swamped by uneasy concerns that gave

her goose bumps, Jenna said, "If you're too busy we can skip dinner. Last time we tried to go didn't work out so well."

"Nonsense. Andee's arm was a once-in-a-blue-moon accident. Hey, someone from the air show is hollering for me. If you find the supplement, buy enough to last me till the end of the month. And hang on to the sales slip so I can pay you. 'Bye."

"Uh, 'bye," Jenna murmured. Shutting off her phone, she covered her face with her hands and rubbed hard, attempting to abolish fears Flynn would say were uncalled-for.

"Mommy, what's wrong?" Andee asked from her seat behind Jenna. "Was that bad news, like when Daddy's plane fell? I thought you were talking to Flynn. Is he all right? And Beezer. Beezer didn't get hurt, did he?"

Jenna dropped her hands and sat straighter. She hadn't thought Andee, who wasn't quite six at the time of Andrew's crash, had in any way been aware of that initial devastating phone call. Obviously she absorbed more than anyone realized.

"Sweetie, it was Flynn, and everything is fine. I just needed a minute to decide where to start on our errands."

Adjusting the mirror, she gazed at her daughter. Andee had Cubby hugged tight. Her little forehead remained puckered and her mouth looked pinched. "Truly, Flynn is fine," she reiterated. "And I heard Beezer bark in the background. Flynn's busy right now with those old planes he told us about. I thought he might not have time to meet us for dinner tonight. He said nonsense." Re-adjusting the mirror, she started the SUV.

"I heard him say that. Was he mad? He never gets mad like Daddy used to. When people get mad my stomach doesn't feel good."

*That was an eye-opening revelation.*

Jenna reached the end of the lane and turned onto the highway. "Flynn wasn't mad," she said firmly. She probably ought to explain that Andrew's bouts of temper were a form of post-traumatic stress. But that wasn't easily explained to children. She hadn't been able to understand Andrew's mercurial moods. And any time someone mentioned to him about seeing the base doctors, he'd closed himself off.

By the time she reached the bank, she'd managed to shake off her melancholia. After her banking, her second stop was the health-food store. She found Flynn's supplement and started for the checkout counter, but Andee stopped her.

"Look, they have fat raisins that aren't in boxes."

Indeed, they were in the bulk bin. "Okay, we'll buy a small bag for you to eat in the car." Crossing to the next aisle, Jenna sniffed the air. "Wow, they have coffee and a machine to grind beans." Since she and Flynn both loved their coffee, she ground a Kona blend and a rich, dark high-mountain roast. "This is all," she said, only to pause again next to tables of fresh produce.

Andee's eyes were level with mounds of tomatoes. "Those are as big and red as Beezer's ball. And are those watermelons? Mommy, I love watermelon."

"No more," Jenna announced after filling a basket. "Yikes, I still need to drop papers off with Mr. Rhodes. If he wants to chat, this will cook in the car."

Another shopper overheard Jenna's comment. "They have that covered," she said. "On the back shelf they have foam coolers and, of course, ice."

"Thanks, that's what I'll have to do. Andee, choose a medium-size melon so we only have to buy one cooler."

THEY'D PULLED ONTO the highway when Andee asked, "Do you think Flynn likes watermelon? Before we moved in with Auntie Melody, we got a giant watermelon. Daddy cut it up and we ate a lot. You said we were gonna get sick, but we didn't."

"Mmm. Two things you and your father could eat way too much of, ice cream and watermelon."

"But not together. Daddy said that would curl in my stomach."

"Curdle. That means they'd sour if you ate them together."

"I better tell Flynn. He really likes ice cream. I hope he likes watermelon."

Jenna debated shutting down Andee's line of thought. But how could she when she'd caught herself comparing Flynn to Andrew?

And wasn't it healthier for Andee to talk about her dad? After his death, she had withdrawn. That had been one of the reasons for their move. However, Jenna saw danger in letting Andee get too invested in Flynn Sutton. Especially now that he was going to be living with them.

Maybe she and her daughter were already too invested.

She'd dickered with herself about that all the way to their town. Entering the restricted-speed zone, she slowed and said, "I have one more stop to make at the realty office. Why don't you bring your raisins and Cubby inside? But be careful to not drop any on the floor. They're sticky and I'd hate for anybody to squish one underfoot."

"Are we getting another ranch?"

Jenna smiled. "No, we may be selling back the house that needs the air conditioner.

"That's enough with the questions for now, Andee." She parked, gathered up her purse and the folder with the contract. "There's a lot of traffic on the street today. Will you scoot across the seat and get out on the sidewalk side?"

"Did you see those big trucks that passed us? One had a big, big octopus-looking thing with red and blue and yellow boxes on the end of its legs. Except they were round."

Circling behind the Cherokee, Jenna tried to sort through Andee's narrative to make sense of it. "I must have missed the truck you saw. Maybe it passed when I was parking."

"No, it wasn't on this street."

"Hmm. Okay, well, we're here." Jenna opened the door to the office and held it so Andee could enter first.

Bud Rhodes got up from his desk. "Mrs. Wood. I just returned from touring your house in town. I tried to call you, but my call went to voice mail."

Jenna dug out her phone. "Oh, sorry. I silenced my phone when I went into the bank and forgot to turn it on again. Is there a problem? I have the signed contract."

"Mayor Parker had a bit of cold feet. He's spending the city's money, you see." Rhodes laughed. "Once he saw the home, he was fine—I hope you don't mind that Flynn Sutton gave me a key. I have the cashier's check for the property and another for furnishings. All I need is for you to sign the closing papers."

He went to his desk, brought another folder to the counter and handed Jenna a pen.

"I must say this is the quickest I've ever turned a property around."

She began scribbling her name on the pages

as Bud Rhodes explained each one. After the last one she put down the pen. "I hope this works well for men like Barney."

"Most of the homeless are vets—some are on board with the project. One has decided to move on. He's been footloose a long time."

"I don't have any say in how the city handles the house, but Barney works for me at the ranch. He said he'd be open to community housing if the rent was reasonable. How will that work?"

"Curtis, that's the mayor, set out a plan with the city council. They'll charge rent by the week or month. There'll be no smoking inside and a no-drug policy that will be enforced by our sheriff. Most homeless veterans have a pension or social security. Some like Barney find work, too. The city will take referrals from the Legion Post." He stacked the papers. "I've no idea how word travels among the wanderers, but they seem to have an effective underground. I think that's why our legion and our park became a haven."

"I've lived in a military community almost my entire life. I just find the homeless situation, especially among veterans, so sad."

"It definitely is. It's not only Nam vets.

Lieutenant Luke, who is in charge of our Legion Post, says he's fed a lot of young guys over the past several years, too. Anyway, here's your check, Mrs. Wood. I understand from Lieutenant Sutton that you plan to add to the ostrich ranch."

*Lieutenant Sutton.*

She didn't think of him that way. It gave her pause.

"Yes." Jenna folded the check. Since it was like cash, she needed to go back to her bank. "I'm sorry you had to bother Flynn. He's extremely busy preparing for the air show."

"He didn't seem to mind." Bud Rhodes peered over the counter at Andee, who sat eating her raisins. "And, Miss Wood, the lieutenant told us about your unfortunate bike accident. I see your cast. I hope that doesn't keep you from enjoying the carnival. This morning the café was buzzing over the carnival starting to set up today."

Andee slid off the chair and skipped to the counter. "How did a lieutenant know about my arm? And what is a carn…carnival? I don't think we're doing that, are we, Mommy?"

"Honey, Flynn used to be a lieutenant."

"Like Daddy?" Andee's face lit up.

"Yes, like Daddy. And, uh, a carnival is hard to explain."

"Carnivals have fun rides and games and things," Bud said. "Never met a kid who didn't think it was a highlight of their summer."

Andee blinked owlishly as Jenna took her hand. "I need to make another trip to the bank. I hope this all works out for the city and the veterans," she said. "Selling the house came at a good time for me. Come on, Andee. Tell Mr. Rhodes goodbye."

"Goodbye," the girl parroted. They were nearly at the car when she said, "I thought we were meeting Flynn for dinner next. You said I could wear my pink dress that goes with my new boots. I want you to wear a pretty dress, too. So let's go home now."

"We have plenty of time to return to the bank then home so you can change out of your jeans. I've got no reason to put on a dress. Flynn's probably going straight from work. Besides, we're only going to the café."

Andee stuck out her lower lip. "This morning I told you I wanted us to wear dresses. I want Flynn to think we're...what did he say? Gus-something."

"Gussied up?"

"Please, Mommy."

"Okay, already. I'll wear a sundress. But if Flynn feels bad because we're overdressed for the occasion, I'll tell him to blame you." She made a face at Andee in the rearview mirror and then checked to see the street was clear so she could pull out.

Andee sank into her booster seat wearing a satisfied smile.

Reaching the bank and depositing the check didn't take long. But traffic had picked up in the interim. After slowing to a crawl for several miles, Jenna noticed a uniformed cop stood up ahead, directing drivers to move their vehicles over a lane. She crept along for several more car lengths before spotting the problem. A big rig had apparently broken down and hadn't been able to pull off onto the shoulder.

Inching past, Jenna saw it was a long, flatbed truck carrying the pieces of a Ferris wheel. Then it dawned on her the thing on the truck Andee had tried to describe earlier must've also been a carnival ride. She'd likened it to an octopus. Which wasn't too surprising since one of Andee's favorite things in Florida had been going to an aquarium. But—wasn't there an amusement ride called an octopus? Wow, for six, Andee was astute.

"Mommy, you said it wouldn't take long to go back to the bank. It did. And I have to go potty."

"I'm sorry, sweetie. We're almost home, I promise. Can you hold it a little longer? There's no place to stop for a bathroom without going way out of our way."

"Okay, but the road is bouncy."

Jenna smiled. It was. If she had any extra funds once she'd built the fence and bought the starter group of alpaca from Peggy Johnson, she'd try to gravel the lane.

They did luckily make it home for Andee. Jenna leaped from the car and dashed up to unlock the door. "I'll get Cubby," she called back to the girl. "You hurry on inside."

Her whole gamut of errands had taken more time than Jenna had allotted.

"Instead of giving you a bath, let's just get a washcloth and clean your face and hands."

"Are we going to be late? I don't want Flynn to think we aren't coming. Then he might leave and we'll miss dinner with him again."

"Not to worry. We won't be too late. Besides, I have his cell number and can call him."

"But it's not nice to be late. Daddy said so," Andee said into the damp washcloth Jenna was using on her face.

She paused in the act of scrubbing. "We won't be that late," she said staunchly. Punctuality had been another of Andrew's bugaboos. The military honed that. And Andrew thrived on being regimented.

Flynn had also served in the military for quite a while. Maybe he would be angry if they showed up late. If so, better to find out now.

"Please hold still, Andee, so I can rework your braids. There. You look snazzy, Ms. Wood."

Andee giggled. "Now you hurry and get ready."

Jenna slid hangers around in her closet. Mostly she'd worn skirts and blouses with jackets to gatherings on base. The commander's wife, the unofficial head of wives' events, had stressed looking professional whether or not you worked or volunteered.

So she owned more office attire than clothes suitable for the desert heat.

Andee squeezed in front of her mother. "Wear this." She pulled at the skirt of the green Hawaiian-print spaghetti-strapped dress Jenna had worn to a dinner out when Andrew'd had a layover in Honolulu between short hops.

Her mom had babysat Andee so Jenna could fly to Hawaii for three days. Andrew had been so exhausted she doubted he had noticed what she'd had on. As it turned out his unit shipped out a day early. She'd spent her last day in the hotel alone, not knowing a soul. She hadn't taken beachwear because Andrew had said they wouldn't have time to visit Waikiki.

She might have worn this dress in Florida if they'd ever gone out. By then Andrew had grown averse to noise and they'd stopped eating out or attending neighborhood events.

It was so easy now to see she should have pressed Andrew harder to seek professional help.

"I don't know if Hawaiian print is suitable for a New Mexico café."

"It's pretty and it goes with my green frogs."

That generated a laugh from Jenna. And with time of the essence now, she thought, *What the heck?* and slid the full-skirted dress from its hanger.

"WHAT DO YOU s'pose Flynn is going to do with Beezer?" Andee asked as they drove toward the café.

"I've no idea." It was still too hot for him to stay in the truck while they ate. Undoubtedly the restaurant didn't allow pets inside.

She had to park across the street and halfway down the block, which made them even later. "Andee, take my hand while we cross the street. This must be a popular night for people to eat out. Oh, look. Beezer's tied to the bench outside the café."

The dog had spotted them and barked excitedly as Andee broke loose from Jenna and ran to hug him and be licked in return.

"We're going inside to eat with Flynn. You be a good dog and I'll bring you a treat," Andee said seriously. "I can bring him hamburger, right, Mommy?"

"Possibly. Look, Flynn left him water

under the bench. Now you have to wash before we take our seats."

The hostess directed them to the ladies' room, which was at the front of the building and took the pair more time they didn't have. In total, they were about twenty minutes late by the time they emerged.

She was kicking herself that she hadn't called his cell to at least give him the heads-up.

It surprised Jenna to see a back room had been opened up for a robust dinner crowd. The candlelit oak tables were filled. It was quite a festive atmosphere. Some women were fairly dressed up, she noticed.

As she spotted Flynn, who saw them and rose from his seat, she was glad Andee had chosen this dress for her. She was even happier when they drew near and Flynn ran his eyes from her head to her toes and back, and his face lit with appreciation.

"Hi," he said, taking her hand and bending to kiss her cheek. "I was beginning to worry that maybe you'd gotten tied up in that breakdown on the highway. I heard about it on the radio."

"Were you waiting long?" she asked. He

didn't sound as if he had an issue with punctuality.

"Not really. I went by the rental to box the rest of my belongings. The mayor asked if I could do it today."

"Flynn, did you just kiss my mom?" Andee bellied up to the table and gazed up at him with open curiosity.

"I did at that. She just looked so pretty. And so do you." With that he lifted Andee and gave her a noisy kiss on her button nose.

She smooched him back, then asked, "Mommy, do I hafta go wash again?"

Pretending to give it serious thought, Jenna finally said, "It's not necessary," and grinned.

Flynn parked Andee in a chair across the table. Then he pulled out the one next to him and seated Jenna. "I took the liberty of ordering you ladies iced tea and milk. If you'd like something stronger, Jenna, they serve alcohol."

"Tea is good," she said, taking the opportunity to admire how handsome he looked in the low, flickering light cast by the candle.

He'd changed into khaki pants and a hunter-green dress shirt. It accentuated the gold streaks in his hair and complemented the background color in her dress.

"I've never seen this part of the café. It's really nice." She set down her purse and willed herself to relax.

Before the dinner of parmesan-crusted chicken, red potatoes and baby carrots was over, Jenna acknowledged to herself that she was falling for Flynn Sutton.

And falling didn't feel so bad.

# CHAPTER TWELVE

AFTER DINNER FLYNN unhooked Beezer from the bench.

Andee knelt and said, "I brought you a piece of chicken. Sorry, I didn't get a hamburger."

The dog scarfed down the meat and licked his chops. He nudged Andee's hand for more and lapped at her fingers.

"Hey, mooch." Flynn pulled him aside. "You'll get plenty of food at the house."

"Can he ride with us?" Andee pirouetted under the streetlamp on one foot until the skirt on her pink dress swirled like a ballerina's tutu.

"Sure, if it's okay with your mom. Where did you park?" Flynn stepped to the curb and looked both ways on the street.

"I'm on the other side, down the block. It's fine with me. Are you heading someplace else?" She reached for Andee's hand and the dog's leash.

"No. I'm coming home. Come on, I'll walk you to your car." He settled his hand on the back of Jenna's waist.

She liked the warmth and weight of it, and gave him points for his thoughtfulness in seeing them to their car. Most of all, hearing him call her place *home* opened little fissures of desire she'd failed to keep in check. It made her think she was ready to move on—ready to venture into another romantic commitment even though she knew only too well it could be risky.

"You've grown quiet all of a sudden. I hope you didn't eat something that disagreed with you."

"Heavens no. Dinner was lovely. I enjoyed the whole evening. Possibly more than I should have," she lamented.

They reached the Cherokee and she unlocked it. Flynn opened the back door, boosted Andee inside and let her settle in her car seat before he removed Beezer's leash and had him climb in.

He shut the door and turned to Jenna, "Explain what you meant. How can you enjoy yourself more than you should? Based on what scale?" He slid his hands under the wrap she'd draped over her shoulders.

She stared at his mouth, but finally said, "I guess I feel guilty for going out and having a good time with you when Andrew hasn't been gone a year and his...accident is still... in limbo."

Flynn stopped rubbing her arms. "That makes sense. But, Jenna, he's not coming back no matter the outcome." He said it gently.

She imagined her mouth under Flynn's as she said, "I know, but it seems...unfinished. Is it too soon for me?"

Flynn didn't answer. Instead he said, "You're shivering. Are you okay to drive home? I had such a great evening, the last thing I want is for yours to end on a downer." He escorted her to the driver's door.

Jenna felt his soothing hand slide to her hip even as he reached up with the other to open her door. Her momentary somber mood vanished. "The wind's picked up, that's all. I'm good."

"Are you up for coffee when we get home? I have something I want to discuss. It's best left until after you put Andee to bed," he murmured.

She nodded, feeling a weight descend on her. What could he want to talk about? Had he rethought staying on?

"I'll follow you home." Flynn waited while she buckled in and started the engine. He closed the door and gave it a tap for good measure. Then he dug out his keys and swiftly made his way to his pickup.

PULLING IN AT the ranch some twenty minutes later, the place looked in good order. Jenna stepped out of the Cherokee and beckoned Flynn. When he joined her, she said, "Andee fell asleep two minutes into the drive. Would you mind carrying her in? I'll get the door."

"I'll feed Beezer and put on coffee. Unless you'd rather have tea."

"Coffee. You have me curious and kind of worried about what you want to discuss."

"Nothing bad. At least I don't think so," he said, lifting out a limp Andee.

Her head lolled on his shoulder as Flynn followed Jenna into the house. He deposited the girl carefully on her bed, then coaxed Beezer into the laundry room for his kibble.

Flynn washed up and started the coffee. Beezer gobbled down his food and came out for a few pats before he padded back toward Andee's room.

Again Flynn scrubbed dog off his hands. He was drying them when Jenna walked into the kitchen rubbing the back of her neck. "Headache?" he asked.

"Just tired. That coffee smells good." She pulled out a chair and sat.

Crossing behind her, Flynn set his hands on her shoulders and worked her tense muscles with his thumbs.

Her head fell back. "That feels marvelous. You have untapped talents."

Chuckling, Flynn walked his thumbs up her spine, under her hair, to the base of her skull. "Why are you tense? I thought you were relieved since the house sold so fast. You even approved an order for fencing to be delivered tomorrow."

"I'm having second thoughts whether I should have sold the house. Income from the rental helped Oscar Martin make a go of this ranch."

"But you're going to get alpacas. And I'll be contributing."

"Until you want to spread your wings and find greener pastures. I'm not about to rent my upstairs to just anyone."

Flynn stopped massaging her neck. "My blood pressure was normal again today, so I'll spread my wings teaching flying. And this pasture is green enough. I like being here with you and Andee. You've...uh...become important to me."

He stumbled over the last part and went over to retrieve the coffee. Once he'd filled their mugs, he put the pot back and sat across from Jenna.

"Let's go back to a remark you made earlier. You enjoyed our evening out more than you should. I think we both know something is growing between us. And neither of us was looking for anything."

"That's an understatement. I—I'm a fairly new widow."

"Aren't we both moving past our issues? I know I am," he said earnestly, looking her directly in the eye. "I'm beginning to see that I can trust someone even if I can't predict exactly what will happen next. Even if I can't count on life to fall into the neat slots

I've carefully scheduled. Even if I have to give up some control."

She nodded slowly. "But as I tried to tell you, I feel guilty. Or I sh-should," she stammered. "You're easy to lean on. And Andee is opening up. She's fallen for you."

He reached over and took her hands. "I hope you've fallen a little, too. But we've no reason to rush. I don't want you to feel guilty. Can't we just let happen what will?"

Jenna warmed to his comment. "I suppose. Is this what you wanted to talk about out of Andee's hearing?"

"Uh, yes and no. I had something else to discuss."

"Don't tell me she ate your Froot Loops again?" she teased.

"Nothing like that. Friday, the carnival opens. Saturday and Sunday I'll be tied up with the air show from 6:00 a.m. to pretty late. Last time I brought up the carnival you weren't excited. Now, me…I love all of the rides and silly games on the midway. I've been thinking a lot about taking you and Andee, but I didn't want to ask in front of her. Will you go with me Friday afternoon?"

Her coffee had cooled enough to drink.

Jenna took a swig and turned over in her mind what it would be like to spend an entire afternoon on fun. *With Flynn.*

"Okay. Yes." She touched her cup to his. "Andee and I saw sections of the rides being trucked in today. Can we just go without advance warning and surprise her?"

"Why not? I'll come home for lunch, leave Beezer, and we can ride together. We'll toss jackets in the car and later dinner can be corn dogs and cotton candy."

"Sounds ghastly, but when in Rome... right?"

He laughed, half rose and leaned across the table to kiss her. He didn't make it quick. Instead he took his time and ended with a nibble of her bottom lip. By the time he settled back in his chair, Jenna's cheeks were bright pink. "I'm not going to apologize," he said. "I like kissing you."

Rattled, but with her heart tripping like mad, she maintained a death grip on her coffee mug. "If you noticed, I didn't exactly push you away. I hope you won't take it wrong, though, if I end the day now. I—I do feel better."

She had to look away and regroup.

He didn't say anything.

"I told Barney I'd move the ostriches to the inner pens early tomorrow morning before the fence people deliver at daybreak. They want to get the postholes dug before it gets hot." Jenna knew she was babbling and suddenly stopped.

"Don't let me keep you up. I'll pour another cup of coffee to take upstairs. Think I'll catch the news on TV. The owners of the old planes asked if there was danger this weekend of summer thunderstorms."

"Thunderstorms?" Jenna paused at the sink, where she went to dump her coffee and rinse her cup. "Are they bad? Is that another worry?"

"They'd stop the carnival and air show if we got a real bang-clanker. And that might upset your birds. But no need to borrow trouble." Rising, he brushed his lips across her pleated forehead. "I'll keep a check on the weather for the air show."

She stifled a yawn with a hand. "Sorry."

"No problem. Go on to bed. I'll take a walk around outside and make sure everything is locked up tight. Shall we leave this coffee to microwave?"

"That's a good idea." She yawned wide again, patted Flynn's chest, then ducked around him and hurried off toward her room.

IN THE MORNING when her alarm went off, Jenna was surprised at how well she'd slept. She assumed she'd gotten up ahead of Flynn again. Until she'd filled her travel mug with coffee and went out to start working. He was sitting on the top porch step drinking from his own mug.

"We need some Adirondack chairs for the porch," he said, smiling up at her.

"Oh, *we* do? Feel free. I'm sinking all of my spare money into making the ranch profitable."

"Hmm. Like a certain pink bicycle and a blood-pressure cuff?"

She paused as she passed. "Smart aleck! Speaking of blood pressure… Should you be drinking so much coffee? Doesn't caffeine drive blood pressure up?"

"Mine has registered normal every time I've used that cuff. And I started the supplement, too. Or it could be it's leveled out because I'm happy again."

Jenna studied him. He did look totally at

ease sitting on the steps in blue jeans and a white T-shirt. He was barefoot and hadn't shaved, which shouldn't add to his appeal but did.

"So, the very prospect of continuing to fly makes you that happy?"

"Yes. But it's mostly because of you, Jenna. I like how you get out at first light and attack the day. I especially like the way you look in jeans, boots and with your hair tied in pigtails."

She gave a snort. "I don't like what I see in my morning mirror. Maybe next time you go for a BP check, you should have them monitor your eyesight."

"Twenty-twenty," he said smugly. "If you'll wait until I have a few more slugs of java, I'll help you herd the ostriches into one pen, since I don't see that Beezer's gotten up to help you."

"I won't turn down assistance. However, I think you need shoes." Smirking a bit herself, she set off along the path.

"Hey," he called. "Did I tell you that I find a woman with attitude sexy?"

Jenna didn't trust herself to respond. Their banter had her imagining spending a lazy morning with Flynn instead of attacking the day. The idea was so tantalizing that she merely offered a backhanded wave over her head.

As it turned out, she had the birds corralled before Flynn showed up.

"Sorry to stand you up," he said right off. "By the time I'd shaved, changed into work clothes and boots and come downstairs, Beezer and Andee were up. He was more interested in her breakfast than his. I saw you'd bought her chocolate Rice Krispies. I stayed to eat so I could be sure Beezer didn't con her into sharing her cereal again."

"She wouldn't."

"I know that now. Because when he put his paws up on her chair and tried to horn in, she told him no and moved her bowl out of his reach. By the way, I helped her on with her boots. She'd pulled on shorts and a T-shirt. I assume she'll be out in a minute. If you no longer need my assistance, Beezer and I will go on to the airpark."

"I'm good. Thanks for giving Andee a hand. Oh, hey, I see Barney wheeling in. That truck behind him probably has my fencing."

Barney had set the kickstand on his Harley and strode up to them before Flynn left. "Notice I'm early. That's what sleeping in a real bed in a real house with a working alarm clock does for a man."

Jenna was shocked. "You slept at the house? Wasn't it beastly hot?"

"I think the minute you handed the mayor the deed, Dayton Hines had a crew up on the roof removing the old AC and hooking up a new one. The mayor and two council members came out to the park with pickups and helped us move. They supplied new bedding and the house was cool as a cucumber."

"Speed comes if you deal with power brokers," Flynn said. "Listen, I've got to dash. If I stay, your fence team might twist my arm to pitch in. Jenna, if you need anything, call. Otherwise I'll try to make it home by eight."

"Shall I fix you a plate and leave it to warm?"

"Sure. Thanks." He bobbed his head in the affirmative even as he grasped Beezer's collar and moved out of the way of the approaching truck.

"None of my business," Barney said, staring after Flynn. "Are you and Flynn...? Uh...?"

Jenna shot him a dark look. "Never mind. I tried marriage three times. No kids. That might've made me stick."

He slanted his eyes toward Andee, who ran to Flynn and hugged him and the dog before they climbed into the pickup.

"Flynn's real good with your kiddo. You don't want her to be an only child—"

"Enough!" Jenna sliced a hand across her neck. "And don't make comments like that within her earshot. I'd think someone who tried marriage three times would know there's a lot to consider before walking down the aisle."

He grinned cheekily. "Obviously, I hit a nerve."

The fence men unfolded out of the truck, reaching Jenna at the same time as Andee. After she signed for the materials and paid the bill, she left Barney in charge of showing the crew where to dig postholes.

Adroitly she steered her daughter to the feed shed. Together they filled bins in the pens, then Jenna dragged the hose to the troughs. Her mind wandered from the task to recount her late-night chat with Flynn. Struck by longing, she overran the water trough. All thoughts evaporated as she helped Andee hop over the stream of muddy water.

"Why did Flynn take Beezer? I don't have anybody to play with."

"Beezer is Flynn's dog."

"Why can't he be all our dog?"

Jenna cast a sideways glance at her. "Because."

Andee kicked dirt at the puddle. "My teacher said *because* is not an answer."

Shutting off the water, Jenna coiled the hose.

A light plane suddenly loomed overhead, so low Jenna ducked, held her breath and gathered Andee close. She tensed all over as she waited for the plane to crash into her pens. It pulled up, but she saw that even the fence workers had hit the ground.

It was that same red-and-white plane.

"I'm scared, Mommy. What if he fell on our ostriches? Or on us?"

Hating how Andee shook, Jenna sighed and said to distract her, "I have Keisha's mom's phone number. Shall we see if Keisha can come for a playdate? You'd have to stay inside and keep out of the way of the fence installers."

"Maybe she can bring her dolls and have lunch with me."

"Maybe." Jenna took out her cell phone, but realized it was still very early. "Andee, a lot of people don't get up until later. How about if we run out to the alpaca farm? I want to buy some."

"The soft ones? But how will we bring them home?" the girl asked, skipping ahead to the Cherokee.

"We can't actually get them until the pens are done. Mrs. Johnson said she'd have some available by the end of summer, so I'll order them." She helped Andee climb into her seat.

"Wait, I need to go get Cubby."

IT TOOK FORTY minutes to reach the alpaca ranch. Jenna again hailed Peggy Johnson, who was hand-feeding a cria. Andee ran to watch, enthralled.

"I expected to see you again," Peggy said. "Just not this soon."

"Things fell into place. I thought I'd come order the animals you indicated you'll have to sell by this fall. My new pens are being built as we speak."

"We talked about a dozen, didn't we? Males and females. If you want pregnant females, they, of course, cost more." Peggy cited prices.

The baby sucked the last milk from the bottle as Jenna frantically added in her head. "Maybe I'll get one pregnant female to start."

Nodding, Peggy returned the baby to a listless mother.

"Does that happen a lot? Where you have to bottle-feed?"

"That mother is on antibiotics for an infection. Her baby doesn't need medication."

This was a new wrinkle they hadn't discussed the first time Jenna had stopped by.

Noting her hesitation, Peggy tucked the bottle into a bag she carried over one shoulder. "I'll have a vet certify the animals I sell you. Will you be ready to receive them Labor Day weekend?"

"That's perfect. Andee's school starts the Monday after the holiday. Helping out when she gets home each day will be the first chores where she'll earn an allowance."

The girl straightened away from the fence. "What's that mean?"

Jenna took a minute to explain while Peggy wrote up a bill of sale.

"Do I pay now?" Jenna opened her purse.

"No, just write down your address and phone number. You can pay my husband when he delivers."

Driving off, Jenna felt a real sense of accomplishment.

"Can we stop for drinks at Dairy Queen? If we buy Flynn one, we can go to his work and maybe he'll let Beezer come home with us."

Her kid had a one-track mind.

She was about to remind her that they were supposed to be calling Keisha's mom when she spotted a plane overhead that returned her thoughts to their earlier low flyer.

Flynn had said he'd talked to the pilot. Perhaps it was time she did, too. "We can do that. Flynn may be busy preparing for the air show. If he doesn't have time to chat, or if he'd rather Beezer stay there, promise you won't fuss."

"I won't." Andee kicked her feet against

the back of Jenna's seat. Something she only did when she was excited.

They pulled into the drive-through and Jenna ordered iced tea for herself and Flynn. Andee got lemonade and a cup of water for Beezer.

They were under way again when she said, "Look. What's that?"

Having turned onto the road to the air-park, Jenna saw it was the carnival that had caught Andee's attention. Maybe this hadn't been a good idea. She offered a few sketchy details about it being Pancho Villa Days.

"The kids we went to the school playground with called it a carnival. And said they have better rides than the ones at the playground."

To divert her attention, Jenna stepped on the gas and pointed out changes at the airpark. "Heavens, I can't believe how fast they've put up a chain-link fence to cordon off all those airplanes."

"Will Flynn take us up in one?"

"No." Jenna's shoulders tightened.

*This definitely isn't a good idea.*

She gripped the wheel and drove to the office, where Flynn stood in full sun talking with two men.

As she'd done at their first visit, Andee threw off the shackles of her seat belt and exploded from the backseat. Unlike the first time, Jenna saw when Andee ran to Flynn, her arms up, a smile wreathed his face. Catching her, he swung her high.

The air around Jenna stilled. She fought mixed emotions as she collected their drinks and got out.

The men smiled and said something to Flynn, then walked off. He set Andee down and, déjà vu, Beezer charged out of one of the hangars. The laughing girl tackled him as Flynn strode up to Jenna.

She passed him the cold cup. In spite of condensation cooling the plastic, Jenna felt the warmth of his fingers when they brushed hers. "Why are you looking at me like that?" Her voice held a tremor.

"I'm parched and you're a sight for sore eyes." Leaning in, he kissed her full on the mouth.

She took a deep breath and let it out in a rush. "I bought alpacas. Andee asked to see if you'd let Beezer go home with us." By then, girl and dog had run to the car, so they made their way over. She reached in and got the water.

The adults watched the dog slurp it down to the bottom.

Flynn's smile tilted. "I should start leaving him at home. With all his fur, the next month or so it'll be too hot even in the shade. I'll install a cooler on the office once I get money coming in from flying lessons."

"I hope you give the guy lessons who owns the red-and-white aircraft. I thought he'd crash into my pens today. The fence builders hit the ground."

Frowning, Flynn gestured with his cup as a lanky kid left the hangar. "Speak of the devil, there's Travis now. He flew in a while ago." Flynn raised his voice and called the young man over. "Travis, this is Jenna Wood. She's telling me you buzzed her ostrich pens again this morning. That has to stop. We discussed it before."

The kid glared at Jenna and she scowled back. "Stop or I will report you to the sheriff and the FAA."

Travis swept past, stalking to a spit-polished red Corvette. He jumped in and roared off.

"Wow. Charming fellow." Jenna signaled Andee to get in the SUV. Beezer followed, so Jenna closed the door.

"I told his dad if he doesn't shape up I'll refund their money and ask Travis to park his plane elsewhere. Dayton, that's his dad, promised he'd find time to talk to his son."

"That's good. Hey, I'll leave you to your work. I see the men you were talking to when I drove in are unloading a ticket booth. Looks like you're set for the air show."

"Almost. What do you think of the monster B-17 in the field?"

"I hope it doesn't fly over my pens or the birds will die of fright."

"It won't. And neither will Travis. He'll be back after lunch, and I'll make that abundantly clear."

Jenna nodded. "We drove by the carnival. Andee asked questions. It may be hard to keep taking her as a surprise."

"Even if you tell her, since neither of you has ever been it'll be special." Flynn held her cup while Jenna got into the car. He stretched across her to set her cup in the holder and extricated himself slowly. At one point their breaths mingled, leaving the air in the front seat so supercharged Jenna assumed he intended to kiss her goodbye. He only smiled a killer smile that left her knees trembling as he shut her door.

She reached home before the feeling faded and decided then and there that, yes, she wanted to explore their relationship.

THE REST OF the week sailed by. Different groups of fence workers showed up to set posts, pour concrete and stretch wire to form the new pens into an L shape off the old ones.

Jenna drove to Albuquerque one day to buy canvas for shade canopies. While there, she stopped at a nursery and bought half a dozen small trees to plant strategically outside the pens.

Barney laughed when she returned home and showed him. "Ms. Jenna, those won't shade a mouse."

"At the nursery they said these trees are water thrifty and perfect for xeriscapes. They don't grow fast, but give them time."

Barney helped her plant them.

Friday came before Jenna thought about what one wore to a carnival.

"What are we doing?" Andee asked when

her mom insisted she take a midmorning bath and change clothes.

"You'll see."

Surprisingly, it was Jenna who anxiously paced, awaiting Flynn's lunchtime arrival. "Ah, here he is." She hastily gathered their jackets, told Beezer to stay and hustled her daughter out. "Do you need anything from the house?" she belatedly asked him.

He shook his head as they climbed into his pickup.

"Why can't Beezer come with us?" Andee sounded mystified.

"It's a people outing, Andee."

Jenna loved seeing how big Andee's eyes got when fifteen minutes later Flynn pulled in behind a line of cars being directed to park in a vacant lot adjacent to the carnival.

Jenna had folded cash into her jeans' pocket, but Flynn had pre-bought tickets that allowed them to pass the waiting families and go straight in.

"Look, look!" Andee squealed. "There's Emily and Joey. They were at story hour."

On hearing their names, the other children turned. Spotting Andee, they dragged their parents over. This wasn't the Lipmans' first carnival. Their kids advised starting at the Tilt-A-Whirl. "Then do the Zipper and Drop Tower before you eat, or you'll barf," Joey, wise for seven, said.

Jenna and Sue Lipman declined to go on the first two rides. Darrell Lipman and Flynn had no such compunction. They were as excited as the kids.

Standing below the Zipper, Jenna could see Andee clinging to Flynn once the equipment fired up and made its first spin around. Screams and laughter rose from the riders.

Jenna, who'd only ever seen TV ads for amusement parks, stood transfixed. The whole area was awash in noise and light. The carnival breathed out pungent odors. Some tart. Some sweet. Jenna thought she'd feel lost after they parted from the other family, but Flynn slung an arm around her, holding her close as Andee chose the Scrambler.

Two rides later, the girl was beside herself because they went on the ride she'd tried to tell Jenna days ago looked like an octopus, and it was indeed called that.

"You have to ride the Ferris wheel with us," Flynn insisted.

"Are you kidding me?" Jenna pressed the

tips of her fingers against his chest. "I'm squeamish about heights."

He hid his disappointment in delight after Andee dragged them to the carousel, and convinced Jenna to go along. "Mommy, we can all ride the white horses with the golden saddles and crowns. There are three in one row."

"That I can do," Jenna said and leaned her head against Flynn's shoulder. They rode twice, and then because Andee discovered a sparkly pig she wanted to try, Flynn cajoled Jenna into joining him on a bench seat, bracketed by a pair of swans. He caught hold of her hand and draped his other arm around her, hugging her close.

Jenna reveled in the feel of his muscular torso. She let out a sigh. "I can't believe how all these years I could've missed such fun," she confessed.

"I haven't been to a carnival in ages. I'm getting the most fun out of watching you and Andee soak in the sights and sounds."

"It's really like a magical world," she said, snuggling closer.

Flynn pressed a kiss to her temple, then

dropped one on the tip of her nose. Jenna's sense of well-being blossomed like a rose.

Afternoon gave way to a lazy, warm summer evening. At a duck shoot on the midway, Flynn won Andee a giant stuffed panda. They moved toward the baseball throw, but stopped to see what had caused a small boy, age three or four, to be sobbing his heart out. The harried parents were quietly trying to explain they didn't have any more money for rides or games.

Andee shook loose from Jenna's hand. She went up to the boy and gave him her panda. "Here," she said. "I have my Cubby Bear at home. I want you to have this one."

She had such a good-hearted girl. Tears blurred Jenna's sight for a moment.

She saw Flynn rub his thumb and forefinger quickly across his eyes before he went to the boy's dad and pressed a string of tickets into the man's hand. Then boosting Andee up in his arms, Flynn left the startled couple, who struggled to say thanks.

He smiled, took Jenna's hand and they melted into the crowd. "Your mom and I are proud of you, Andee," he said. "What you did was generous."

"I only gave him a stuffed toy. You gave them all our tickets." Andee looked sad until Flynn tossed her up, then caught her, saying, "I didn't give them all away. I have plenty more for us to ride Bumper Cars, and buy corn dogs and cotton candy."

Which they did. The junk food was surprisingly more satisfying than Jenna imagined. But once they wound down and she stopped to take stock of their time at the carnival, it wasn't the event but sharing it with people she loved that left her floating in pleasure as Flynn drove home and Andee fell asleep in the backseat.

"You're smiling," he noted, his voice a low rumble.

"I am." Burrowing into the leather seat back, Jenna turned her head toward him.

He reached out and cradled her hand in his. Stroking her knuckles, he said, "Are you overanalyzing again? I want this to be the first of many enjoyable family outings."

"Isn't that putting the cart before the horse?"

"Maybe. But we're not kids. I think we make a good team." He promised something in his tone.

"Perhaps I'm dense, but it sounds as if you're asking, uh, suggesting... Sorry if I'm misreading signals. What are you saying?"

"When I examine my life, I want you in it." Flynn's fingers tightened around hers. "You must think I fall in love all the time. I don't. What I feel in my heart for you... It's dug in. You may not be at the same point. All I'm asking you to do is think about us together for the long haul. Keep an open mind."

"Flynn, are you proposing?"

"Not doing a good job of it, obviously."

"I...can't say yes. But I'm not saying no, either." She looked up and out the window. "How long have we been parked in front of the house?"

"Awhile. Let's call it a great night and go in, shall we?"

He carried the sleeping Andee to her bed and kissed Jenna good-night, leaving her wanting more.

# CHAPTER THIRTEEN

JENNA DIDN'T SLEEP WELL. She wrestled with the notion of marrying Flynn. Was it too soon? He hadn't said he loved her. But he had kissed her like a man who loved her. And he'd put his heart out there by asking her. Or had he asked? He'd implied it...

Her bedside clock ticked past 2:00 a.m., then three. Maybe she catnapped, because she dreamed of living with Flynn as husband and wife. At 4:15 a.m. she fluffed her pillow and began compiling a list of positives and negatives.

He was easy on the eyes. His smile caused butterflies in her stomach. He helped around the house and the ranch. She'd seen he kept his room tidy. She moved to the top of the list how good he was with Andee.

Then she got stuck on imagining having a baby with Flynn. She'd always wanted more kids. Flynn would be a wonderful dad. When all was said and done she had a long list of positive attributes—and only one negative. A big one.

Flynn loved flying. How could she ask him to give that up? It was part of his fabric. An integral part of the man she'd come to love. There it was—the crux of what caused her dilemma—his career.

*He might crash and die.*

She picked up the clock. It was 4:45 a.m. Slamming it back down, she got up and took a shower. She shouldn't be surprised to see a light on in the kitchen or to find Flynn in there eating Froot Loops. He'd said he had to be at the airpark at six o'clock.

"I'm sorry if I woke you," he said, looking up. "I tried to be quiet."

Jenna was glad to see the coffee perked. Grabbing a mug, she filled it and went to stand beside him. "Yes."

"Yes, I woke you? I am sorry."

Clutching her mug in both hands, Jenna slugged some down. Looking over the rim at him, she said, "Yes, I'll marry you."

His mouth dropped but he didn't say anything even though he tried to speak.

"You didn't wake me," she continued. "I

didn't sleep all night for thinking about how you half asked me so casually. You'd say I overanalyze, but I'm in love with you, and that's the truth of it."

Joy chased surprise across Flynn's face. He dropped his spoon, shoved back his chair and sprang to his feet, tracing her cheekbones with his thumbs. Steadying her head, he kissed her long and deep.

Jenna closed her eyes. He tasted like cereal, milk, morning coffee and man. Feeling all tension leave her body, she feasted on his kiss and longed to touch him—to run her hands over the hard dips and muscles of his chest. Instead she gripped her mug tighter to keep from spilling hot coffee down both of them.

Flynn finally took a breath. Even then he ran his tongue over her lips and pressed his forehead to hers. "I was prepared to wait months. We aren't finished talking. It's a heck of a note that I have to work from dawn to dark for a while."

Jenna felt his frustration. "It's okay. We don't need to rush to the courthouse or anything."

Straightening, he let his fingers outline

her chin. "True. But time is sometimes too short. We both know it," he said, guiding her to a chair before retaking his.

Now Jenna felt shy. "I... My family will be surprised. Shocked is more like it," she said, thinking of Melody and Rob, who were so sure she'd regret leaving the East Coast. "My sister teaches college. She and her husband plan to visit me over her Christmas break. We...uh... Could we get married then? Maybe my parents can come from Costa Rica."

She stopped talking and looked at him.

"What about your family? I know you talk to your mother often. Won't she want to be here? Unless she disapproves of you marrying someone who's been married before and has a child."

"Are you kidding?" Flynn swirled his spoon in his cereal. "She asks about you and Andee every time we talk. Mom will love you. So will my sister."

"That's nice." Jenna feigned interest in the contents of her cup. "Nice, since you've not said you lo...love me." She finally got it out.

"Oh." Flynn chewed quickly, then swallowed in haste, too. "I thought I did, when

I said I had fallen in love with you. I said that, didn't I? I guess I supposed I'd made my feelings evident when I said, 'You must think I fall in love all the time.'"

"You need to get better with words. I'm not the best at guessing. So...I don't think you fall in love all the time. But...?"

He tipped her chin up. "I love you." Each word hung between them as their eyes met, and his turned an intense midnight blue.

"I love you back." It felt good to really make it clear.

Standing again, Flynn pulled her up and against him. "I can see there may be a big problem with waiting half a year to tie the knot."

This time when he kissed her, Jenna agreed. When he released her and strode to the door, she was the one left without words. He went out and the screen door banged closed.

With knees of jelly, Jenna had to sit again. She registered the sound of his pickup starting and saw the headlights flash past the window and cut through the misty lavender of morning.

*Maybe Melody and Rob could get away to visit at Thanksgiving. Or Halloween.*

The sun rose, but she still dawdled.

Andee burst into the kitchen, bubbling over as she ate and recounted what she liked about every aspect of the carnival. After slurping milk, she said, "I'm glad Flynn left Beezer today, so he can play ball with me."

"I guess he figures he'll be busy with people attending the air show."

"Can we go see the planes?"

Jenna jerked upright from where she'd gone to unload the dishwasher. "Uh, no, honey. I already hear them flying over the foothills. Some may stray our way, but the fence people haven't finished, so you can't be wandering. If you stay on the porch, you may see some of the old planes."

"You said after they finish the fence I can ride my bicycle. Is that today?"

"They may finish today. But you're due for another X-ray to make sure the bones you broke are fusing well. I'd rather you didn't ride until the doctor says it's okay."

"What's fusing?"

"It's that the broken parts are growing back together."

"How can they see my bones?" Andee gazed down at her cast.

"By the X-ray. You must have been too upset to look at the ones they took the night you broke your arm. I'm sure they'll show them to you if you ask."

"I remember the doctor said X-rays don't hurt. The shot hurt. Will he do that again?"

"No, honey. This is only a checkup."

"Isn't Monday story hour at the libary?"

"Lib*r*ary." Jenna emphasized the letter Andee left out. "And yes."

"I don't want looking at my bones to make me miss going to that. Now that I know some kids, you don't have to stay for the story, Mommy."

Jenna smiled, then felt bleak. Not wanting Mom around was the first sign of growing up. She toyed with mentioning her decision to remarry. Something stopped her. Perhaps it still seemed surreal. "Our appointment for your arm is at eleven-thirty and story hour is at one o'clock."

"I love you!"

After she'd installed Andee and Beezer on the porch with toys and she went out to start morning chores, Jenna realized she was also holding back from phoning her parents and

Melody. Really, though, since Flynn agreed to wait until Christmas, there was no rush.

Barney rolled in and stopped beside the porch for a bit. He hailed Jenna next. "The kiddo just bent my ear about how much fun you all had last night at the carnival."

"Broken arm or not, she opted for all the scariest rides and came back grinning from ear to ear."

They began carrying eggs to the cooler. "I'm going to the air show this afternoon," he said. "Will I see you and Andee there?"

"No. I had my fill of planes all the years I lived on base."

"Huh, I saw you stop a minute to watch those flying now."

She didn't want to admit they made her uneasy. "Flynn promised none would fly directly over the ranch. I'm relieved to see he was right."

"I want to go again tomorrow. Part of the entry fee goes to house guys like me. The mayor stopped by yesterday to see how we're doing." Barney laughed. "I think he was relieved to see we hadn't trashed the place. Beats me why folks think Nam vets are hooligans. Although John isn't a vet, just Mike and me."

"Is that really how Mayor Parker feels? It seems a good thing that city officials put money into veteran housing. They could've had the sheriff or his deputies order you all out of the park and out of town."

"Yeah. The mayor said they'd like to fund a second house. I explained that some guys roam looking for work. Jobs aren't plentiful for men my age."

Hesitating a minute, Jenna said, "If you need more hours, I may be able to swing it once I add alpacas. There are chores Mrs. Johnson said her husband handles that I'll probably need to hire out or at least have help doing."

The man shrugged. "I wouldn't mind a six-hour day. No rush. I'm doing okay. I have a few government bennies. On occasion I fill in at the Legion."

Jenna nodded her head and stored the last of the eggs. "What made you stop here in the first place? I mean, what made you choose to camp in this town?"

"It probably doesn't sound too good, but we have an underground network."

"Ah, sort of a hobo code?"

He laughed. "Not quite like that—no marks over any doorways or anything. But with the Legion post here, and a veterans' clinic not far away, and townfolk who tolerate us hanging around…well, it gets high marks."

"I suppose the weather helps. I know some cities close to active military bases are collection points. It hurt to see men huddled in doorways in bad weather. Why wouldn't they move to someplace warmer?"

Barney spared a wry look as if she was naive. "Military family is more generous with handouts."

"Ah. That's good, but sad. Sorry, Barney, but I have to run in and check on Andee and Beezer. Meanwhile, if you'll clean the small pen, I'll come back and gather feathers."

When Jenna returned, they worked steadily until noon. Glancing at her watch, she stopped and took off her gloves. "Time for lunch. Would you like a grilled-cheese sandwich before you go to the air show?"

"Thanks, but don't bother. They'll have food vendors there. I'm meeting my buddy Mike. His pa flew P-51s. He said they used to have pictures of his dad by his plane. Mike's never seen one up close."

"It's amazing they're still able to get parts so those old planes will fly." Jenna scanned the sky as they walked toward the house. "Flynn said the bigger ones have booked passengers, but the P-51 they're actually offering flight instruction."

"Too pricey for Mike and me. Hey, I almost forgot to ask if you mind me coming to work in the afternoon tomorrow. In the morning they have stunt flyers and wing walkers. I'm keen to see those up close."

"Did you forget that tomorrow is Sunday? You've only been putting in six days a week."

The big man tipped back his head and laughed. "Now I got me an alarm clock. Next I need a calendar!"

Beezer charged down the steps, his tail wagging. He brushed his nose against Barney then Jenna. They both rubbed his head and gave him pats.

Andee left whatever she was doing and asked, "Mr. Fisk, are you going home?"

"Nah, I'm off to the ai—" He broke off when Jenna drove an elbow into his ribs.

"I hear you're going to make grilled-cheese sandwiches. Your mom invited me to stay, but I have to watch my figure."

Andee gaped at him and Jenna snorted. "We don't have to worry about getting belly fat yet," she said, steering the dog and girl toward the house. She heard Barney kick-start his bike when he got to the end of the lane.

"Is *belly* and *figure* the same thing?" Andee asked once they were inside.

"Not really." Jenna washed before assembling bread, butter and cheese. "*Figure* has more than one meaning. One is a person's shape." She made curves in the air with the spatula.

"Sometimes I don't understand what adults say. Should I give Beezer water? I think his bowl is empty."

"By all means. Then wash your hands and I'll pour your milk."

They soon sat to eat. "Andee, tomorrow is Sunday. Would you like to go to Sunday school?" All day Jenna had been thinking how they would be married. Although she didn't want a pomp-and-circumstance wedding like her first one with white gown, military crossed swords and all, she did want to be married in a church.

She probably should ask Flynn's preference. If he didn't have one, and she already had a church, she couldn't see him objecting.

"Will it be like the one in Florida or at Auntie Melody's?"

"Probably smaller than the one by Auntie Melody." Jenna had been raised a Methodist. But she'd spotted a charming brick community church at the edge of town.

"Maybe Emily and Joey or Keisha will be there."

"Possibly, but if not there will be other children I'm sure."

After lunch Jenna wrote out a list and they went grocery shopping. It had sounded to her as if one of Flynn's favorite foods was pot roast. She bought one to prepare for dinner, then remembered he'd be late because of the air show.

That night she tried to stay up until he came in so she could ask about a church wedding. Except she'd barely slept the previous night, so once she put Andee to bed and even Beezer had retired, her eyes got too heavy for her. She had made Flynn a plate to go in the microwave and left him a note. Even at that she thought if she heard him come in she'd get up and keep him company while he ate.

It was a failed plan.

In the morning she vaguely recalled thinking she'd heard the door and the clink of Beezer's tags as he'd left Andee's bed. She had opened one eye and seen the clock said midnight. Her eyes had promptly closed again.

Flynn had left her a note on the table praising her pot roast and saying he was sorry to get home so late. Tonight could be later, it being the last night of the air show.

He'd signed his note "Love, Flynn."

Jenna held it to her heart a minute, then went to her bedroom and tucked it away in her dresser.

Humming an old church hymn, Jenna whipped through her morning chores. Hurrying inside again, she called out, "Andee, I'll lay out clothes for you to wear to church. Will you feed Beezer?"

"Can he go with us?"

"No dogs in church."

"Why? God likes dogs."

"He does. But he likes them staying at home to guard the house."

ABOUT AN HOUR LATER, at the church, Jenna asked directions to Andee's classroom. Turning shy, the girl clung to Jenna's hand until she spotted someone who'd been at the library story hour. Her name was Madison, and her mother introduced Andee around before walking next door to the sanctuary with Jenna.

Jenna liked the minister. She loved the cozy interior of the church and thought it perfect for a small, holiday wedding. She'd have to talk to Flynn soon. Probably people booked holiday events early.

She pictured a late-afternoon ceremony followed by a casual family dinner. They hadn't discussed specifics, but probably only their families would attend. That was providing more than Melody and Rob could come. Six months wasn't really long to plan even a small wedding. Maybe they could hold the reception in the back room at the café. It was special because Flynn had taken her and Andee there on their first date.

In fact she and Andee could stop at the café for lunch and make some inquiries.

Jenna suggested her idea to Andee, who was all for it.

Because the place was busy, Jenna felt lucky to snag a table for two. They ordered burgers and fries, and when the waitress delivered the meal, Jenna asked her, "Does the café hold special events? Say, something like a small reception?"

"Yes. On your way out, you'll pay at the register. Ask the cashier for a brochure. We also list individuals who cater barbecues and graduation parties."

"Wonderful. Thank you."

"Are we going to have a barbecue?" Andee asked, dipping a fry in ketchup.

"No. I'm thinking ahead to maybe having a party when Uncle Rob and Auntie Melody come to visit in December." She was still hesitant to tell Andee about the wedding.

"We'll know lots of people then 'cause I'll be in school."

"You will. Did you like the church? I noticed you made some new friends."

"Uh-huh. Peter and Paulina are twins. Most everyone else had little brothers or sisters. Why don't I have some, Mommy?"

Jenna put down her burger. She didn't really want to say that Andrew hadn't wanted more children. But it was true. "Some people don't, honey."

Andee's question started Jenna thinking how she was on the high side of thirty-one. She knew military wives who'd had babies at thirty-eight or nine.

Having a baby with Flynn was on her mind when she paid the bill and asked for a brochure. Suddenly multiple vehicles fitted with screaming sirens roared past the café.

Jenna was nearly bowled over by two men who burst through the door. One shouted at large, "There's been an accident at the air-park."

Jenna froze.

"My brother is a volunteer fireman. He got the call saying a light plane crashed. Some people at the air show were hit by debris. That's all I got. Seth had to get to the fire-house. Anyone here able to help?"

The room began to buzz and several men left.

Jenna hadn't moved. Her ears rang and she couldn't get air into her lungs.

"Mommy, you're hurting my hand," Andee exclaimed, trying to shake loose of her grip.

Jenna braced a hand on the counter for support.

"Who crashed? Was it Flynn?"

Andee's words penetrated a gray fog engulfing Jenna's brain. "Let's go, Andee," Jenna said through tight lips.

"But I love him. I don't want him to be crashed like my daddy."

"Shh, honey, let me think. We need to hurry to the car and go to the airpark." The words tasted metallic and Jenna discovered she'd bitten the inside of her lip so hard it bled.

Practically running to the Cherokee, she boosted Andee in before she vaulted into her own seat. Then she found her hands shook too much to put the key in the ignition. She scrubbed them over her face, knowing she had to calm down or she wouldn't be in any shape to drive.

Ultimately she clamped down on the fear that sat like a fist in the center of her stomach and managed to shave ten minutes off the drive.

She had to park a ways away from the entrance.

Unbuckling Andee, Jenna hoisted the girl

to her hip and stumbled her way toward a crowd milling around inside the fence. The smell of burning rubber hung heavily in the air and smoke rose in plumes a distance away from the hangars and Flynn's office.

Jenna didn't have tickets. But no one seemed to be in the ticket booth, so she dashed through the gate and shouldered her way to the front of the gawkers.

Her searching gaze honed in on Flynn at once. His face was sooty, and his blue flight suit, which had probably been pristine when he'd left the house, was wet and splotched with the red earth from around the charred remains of what had been a small plane.

She wished she felt relief. Instead a crushing dread left her queasy as she was assaulted by déjà vu.

"Flynn. Flynn!" Andee screamed. "Did he crash? He looks okay."

Flynn straightened and turned.

The child pushed out of her arms, hit the ground and ran, launching her whole body at the plainly shocked man.

"Andee, what are you doing here?" Whirling right then left, Flynn limped over to Jenna. He reached out for her.

"Jenna? You're ghost-white. I'm so sorry, but I'm tied up. One of our guest pilots had engine failure. His wing walker, thank goodness, parachuted to safety, as did he. But a burning wing broke off and landed in the crowd. Some bystanders were burned. Look, why don't you two wait in the office until things calm down?"

He lifted Andee and hugged her a moment, then thrust her into Jenna's arms.

Her lips felt numb as did arms now wrapped around her daughter. Actually, her whole body felt wooden. "No. No, I'm not going to wait. I thought it may have been you who crashed. Flynn, I can't do this. What we talked about. I ca…can't. Moreover…you have to leave the ranch. Move out ASAP. I care. I care too much."

With legs of lead, but hardening her heart to stone, Jenna blindly plowed through people she couldn't see for the tears obscuring her sight.

Flynn called her name.

She didn't turn back or stop running until she reached the gate. There a man in uniform grabbed her elbow.

"Ma'am? Are you hurt? Were you or the child burned?"

Jenna jerked loose. "No. No, but it's just so terrible."

Agreeing, the deputy let her go.

At the SUV, which she hadn't even locked, Jenna sat Andee in her booster and mopped at tears while trying to buckle the child's harness.

"Why does Flynn have to move? Did he make the plane fall out of the sky?"

Jenna brought order to her cartwheeling emotions. "Sweetheart, no."

"I don't know why you told him to move," Andee wailed. "He'll take Beezer."

Climbing into the SUV, Jenna fumbled to clasp her seat belt. She gripped the steering wheel with both hands and sucked in a deep breath.

"I'm sorry. I can't explain. It's complicated. And it hurts me to send him away. You have no idea how much it hurts."

She fumbled a tissue from her purse, wiped her eyes and blew her nose.

"Trust me, it's better that Flynn find a new place to live before we come to depend too much on him. Before he gets too deep in our hearts."

Clearing her throat, Jenna put on her sunglasses and, with jaw set, backed out of the parking spot.

"He and Beezer are already in my heart. I told everybody at Sunday school Flynn's going to be my new daddy."

Jenna gasped. "Why on earth would you say that?"

"'Cause the teacher said God answers prayers. When we prayed, that's what I asked for. I want a dad like all the kids at the libary story hour have."

Jenna's throat was too clogged with tears to respond.

# CHAPTER FOURTEEN

IT WAS SUPER late when Flynn drove in after a very long day. He wasn't surprised to see the house mostly dark except for a night-light Jenna had left on in the kitchen.

He'd hoped they could talk, but dreaded it, too. Probably he was too tired to do justice to serious conversation and combat fears he knew she harbored. Considering his day, some of her worries were legitimate.

He shut off the engine and headlights, and sat for a moment surrounded by darkness and a few night noises drifting through his open window. Circling the steering wheel with his arms, he dropped his forehead onto his hands. The sting from the minor burns he'd suffered to his palms when he'd yanked a piece of hot metal off an observer reminded him to go easy.

An EMT had treated him. He and the show owners were lucky the accident hadn't been worse. There'd be inquiries, but the plane whose engine failed and its pilot were insured. So were the show owners and promoters, as was he.

After some time, he rolled up his window and crawled out. If he didn't go in, he was in danger of falling asleep in his truck.

He needed to remember to set his alarm. The show owners were moving to the next site and planned an early start. That meant he wouldn't have a chance to see Jenna in the morning. The longer he gave her to brood, the harder it would be to convince her to give their fledgling love a chance.

Not wanting to wake her or Andee, Flynn removed his shoes and tiptoed into the kitchen. A note lay on the table. He was almost afraid to read it.

Lo and behold, it said she'd fixed him a plate of leftovers and put it in the fridge. A roast-beef sandwich and macaroni salad. Good, no need to microwave it and make noise. He got out a fork and a bottle of water and decided to eat upstairs.

At the stairwell Beezer came to greet him. Shifting everything to one sore hand, he awkwardly petted the dog. "It's okay, boy," he whispered. "Go back to bed."

The dog sniffed Flynn's boots, yawned and padded back to Andee's room.

Flynn glanced longingly at Jenna's closed door, then trudged upstairs where he turned on a lamp, set his alarm and sat on his bed to eat.

The next thing he knew, his alarm was blaring. His plate and fork were on the floor. He'd slept where he'd toppled over, still in his dirty clothes.

He made short work of a shower. That and clean clothes left him refreshed.

Downstairs, all remained dark. He expected it, but was still disappointed. The clock on the microwave showed he didn't really have time to brew coffee. He took a minute, turned over the note Jenna had left him and scribbled her one of his own.

The crew is breaking down the show and ferrying out the historic planes today. If I can carve out time to get away for lunch, I'll run home. Jenna, I'm sorry. Don't toss my clothes and things out of the house. I love you.

After he'd backed his pickup around and driven far enough away, he felt okay about turning on his lights. He wished he'd written that last line in capital letters.

JENNA'S ALARM RANG, shaking her awake. Murky light filtered through slits separating the panels of her bedroom drapes. When she'd gone to bed, she hadn't expected to fall asleep. Now she discovered she'd slept like the dead.

Slightly rattled, she assumed Flynn hadn't come home. That lanced a sharp pain through her midsection. This morning there was no light from the kitchen and no smell of coffee.

After all, she had ordered him to leave. What had she expected?

Plunging her head beneath the cool spray of the shower, she let it wash away her tears. Instead of feeling revived afterward, she felt drained. Flynn had said he liked her enthusiasm for attacking a day. This morning she felt off kilter as she went into the kitchen and switched on the coffeemaker. Her gaze lit on the note she'd left Flynn. She wondered where he'd spent the night.

This morning, staring out the window at

the slowly rising sun, she felt ashamed of how she'd lashed out at him. He had looked pasty and drawn. She'd acted out of a place of petrifying fear welling up from her past loss.

But he'd also lost his best friend in a crash—the same one where he'd been injured. Yet he didn't see all planes as death traps.

Looking back, she saw she'd had a panicked reaction. Flynn probably thought she was a crazy woman. Maybe she was. Was it crazy to now not want him to leave?

How could she take back what she'd said? She'd never been good at pouring out her heart. Even if she tried, would Flynn listen?

The sun had risen enough to dust the foothills in muted pinks and gold. Jenna prodded herself to move. Barney would arrive soon and they'd planned to seed grass in the new pens. She wasn't hungry, but she should eat.

Reaching for her cereal, she saw Flynn's box of Froot Loops. She ran a finger around a grape-colored O and almost cried. Quickly closing the cupboard, she poured her wheat flakes, sat and then remembered she hadn't gotten out milk. It was when she opened the fridge that she noticed the plate she'd made up for Flynn wasn't there. She moved things around, thinking Andee had maybe gotten up in the night for a glass of milk. *Still no plate.*

Jenna spun around to look at the note on the table. The paper wasn't exactly where she'd left it. She turned on the overhead light. With heart thumping, she picked up the paper, read it once, then read it again. A third time the last line got splotchy with tears.

Flynn hadn't left. He didn't think she was crazy. The wonderful, forgiving man still loved her. Drying her eyes on her shirttail, Jenna folded the note and tucked it into the pocket of her capris. At last she was able to sit and eat something.

It wasn't until she'd finished, rinsed the bowl and stored it in the dishwasher that she remembered Andee's doctor appointment today at eleven-thirty. She also had story hour at one o'clock. Flynn had said in the note he'd try to come home for lunch. She'd have to call him. Would he think she was making up excuses?

Grabbing a pair of gloves, she went out. Probably she was overthinking again.

Barney saw her and waved. He'd parked his Harley in the shade of the porch. "Did you hear the big news about the plane crash at yesterday's air show?"

Jenna barely inclined her head. The memory of how the plane looked smoldering on the ground still made her heart cramp.

"This morning the guys at the Legion Post couldn't stop talking about the dumb luck of everyone involved to get out alive."

"People were hurt," she told him. "I saw fire trucks and ambulances galore headed out there."

"I had a ringside view. If you take our weekly newspaper, you'll see my picture and my name mentioned for shoving a couple of families back who'd have otherwise been hit by debris."

"Wow, you must've been close." Shivering, Jenna opened the shed and got out the seed. She wished Barney would stop talking about the accident. But, being ex-military, he wanted to describe each nauseating detail.

Finally she just unrolled her earbuds, turned on her iPod and tuned him out. She had to tell him to stop talking when Andee and Beezer came out from the house to watch them spread topsoil over the seed.

"Mommy, where's Flynn? He always eats breakfast with me. Is he mad at you?"

Jenna saw Barney's ears perk up. "No, honey. He left really, really early. The men who own the old planes are taking them somewhere else today."

"Yep," Barney broke in. "I talked to the flyer giving lessons in the P-51. The next show is in El Paso."

Andee climbed onto the fence. "Did you ride in one of the planes, Mr. Fisk?"

"I did, Miss Boots."

She giggled.

"I went in the B-17," he said. "At one point we could see all the way to Arizona. That was cool. But when they flew those planes in the war, they often flew through fog so thick they couldn't see their targets below."

"What's a target?"

"Barney," Jenna warned. "TMI. Andee, stop bouncing on the fence. The men only finished installing it yesterday. Did you have breakfast? Did you feed Beezer?"

"Uh-huh." She jumped down, sank to her

knees and looped her arms around the dog. "Can I wear my blue dress to the doctor and story hour?"

"It's pretty dressy. I thought you might wear it the first day of school." Really, she'd pictured Andee wearing it in the wedding.

"Can we afford to buy me new school clothes? At the carnival Emily said her mama is taking her school shopping. They go to a city. I can't remember the name."

"We'll buy a few new things. I think you've grown taller."

"Am I too tall to ride my bicycle when my arm gets fixed?"

Barney laughed and Jenna shook her head. "You didn't grow that fast. Maybe you'll be okay to ride after you see the doctor today."

The pair worked steadily thereafter. They weren't quite done when Jenna realized it was a quarter to eleven. "Yikes. I need to clean up and take Andee to her appointment. I want to get there early since it's a new doctor. There will be paperwork."

"You run on. I'll finish, lock up the wheelbarrow and spreader before I head out. I'm tending bar later at the Legion, but I've got plenty of time."

"Thanks. If you work overtime, be sure to write it down."

In the house, Jenna sped through getting ready. They were in the Cherokee driving out when she realized she'd forgotten to call Flynn. It was as well she stopped at the end of the lane to dial him, because the mailman drove in and flagged her down. Flynn's cell went straight to voice mail anyway. Dropping her phone back into her purse, she rolled down her window to see what the mailman wanted.

"Are you Mrs. Jenna Wood?"

"I am."

"I have a registered letter for you. Here's a pen. Sign that card by the X."

The priority document mailer's return address read SID, Washington, DC. Jenna's stomach did a double flip. The acronym stood for Special Investigative Department. This was the report from the Air Force team who'd reviewed Andrew's crash. She dropped the envelope on the adjacent seat where it lay, innocent and terrifying all at once.

"What did you get, Mommy?"

"Uh, just some documents. I'll look them over later."

The envelope preyed on her mind throughout Andee's appointment and while they removed her cast. She could have opened it after she walked her daughter in for story hour. But the kids all had to exclaim over Andee's arm. Jenna finally broke away, saying she'd return in an hour. On many levels she craved the calming comfort of home while she read the report.

Once there, she unlocked the house and let Beezer out. Taking the envelope, she sat on the porch steps and slowly slit it open.

ON THE PORCH steps was where Flynn found Jenna when he drove in. She sat hunched over. He heard her sobbing the minute he shut off the pickup's motor. Leaping out, he ran to her and had to scoot Beezer aside to fold her in his arms.

"What's wrong? Stop crying. Tell me." He held her so tightly she couldn't pull away. "Is it Andee? Did you get bad news about her arm?" Flynn looked around. "Where is she?"

Jenna tried to talk, but her nose ran and tears blocked her throat. She slid her arms around Flynn's torso and buried her face in his neck, crying like a baby.

He saw a sheaf of papers flutter off her lap. It was awkward, but he scooped up a couple of sheets. He saw an official gold seal and below it rows of black type. Flynn guessed this was the report she'd said was coming from Air Force investigators.

"Is it terrible news? Look, Jenna, you need to keep in mind that nothing the commission says about him can hurt him now."

She loosened her arms and wiped her face on his flight suit. "It's not bad news. Especially for Andee. She can be proud of her dad's military record." Sniffling, Jenna raked a hand through her hair. "The Navy pilot's F-18 Hornet malfunctioned and caused the crash." Her garbled words ran together.

"Then why, for Pete's sake, are you crying your eyes out?" Flynn worked a partly clean red rag out of his pocket and patted her puffy eyes and red face.

"The Navy guy and Andrew argued before the flight. Also, Andrew's squadron commander testified that he'd been sent home with orders to see a base psychiatrist and be evaluated for possible PTSD. He didn't follow through. No one checked to see he did." Jenna snuffled on Flynn's shoulder again. "I knew, as did friends and family, that something was wrong. Oh, Flynn, I should have pushed him harder to go see the base doctor."

"No way. That was the job for his CO."

"I feel so guilty. And look how I yelled at you yesterday. Because I can't bear to think you might die like Andrew."

Flynn spoke into her hair. "Accidents can happen anywhere, sweetheart. In a car. In a house. Flying. Playing sports. Life's a risk."

"I'm not a risk taker. I won't make you a good wife."

"Listen to me. You risked marriage to a man headed to war. You risked having a baby. You risked moving here, where you didn't know a soul. Please, won't you risk spending whatever time either of us has left, living with and loving each other?"

She traced the hollow of his cheek with a damp finger. "When you put it like that it doesn't sound so risky. Are you sure you want to hook up with a hysterical, unlikely rancher?"

"There's not a doubt in my mind. And in my spare time I'll help you ranch."

"That's good enough for me." She picked up the scattered papers and shoved them back in the envelope. "Flynn, are you absolutely sure? Before yesterday I'd begun to plan a small church wedding. Remember, I said at Christmas so my sister and her husband can attend. I thought we'd invite my folks, too, and your family."

"Um. I'd hoped for sooner. We can get our blood tests done at the VA when I go for my flight physical. I'm counting on you holding my hand so my BP stays down."

"I'll do that anyway," she said solemnly.

"Then all is good. Perfect, in fact!" He kissed her thoroughly.

Beezer flopped down and Flynn straightened. "You proved you aren't hoping I'll fail the test so I have to quit flying."

"I'd never ask you to change who you are for me."

For a time they held hands and talked about the wedding and their future.

Suddenly, Jenna sprang up. "I only have ten minutes to pick up Andee from the library. Will you lock the house? Beezer can ride with me unless you want to take him back to the airpark."

"Nah. Frankly he's become more Andee's dog than mine. Drive carefully. Hey, don't break the news to her about us. Let's do it together tonight at dinner."

"Okay, but she said at Sunday school she prayed you'd be her new daddy. She could've already told the world. She was upset I yelled at you and ordered you away."

"We'll assure her that's behind us. From now on our lives will be nothing but roses."

Jenna left with a somewhat lighter heart and hoped she didn't look too much of a mess from all her crying.

She hadn't let herself grieve for Andrew. Now, in the solitude of the SUV, she did.

She wiped her eyes before going in at the library. None of the other mothers remarked on her appearance. In fact, they voted to take the kids to the park now that the homeless were housed elsewhere.

Keisha's mother had heard of Jenna's involvement. "You paved the way for a wonderful project, Jenna. Our neighbor owns a duplex. A Realtor talked him into selling to the city, too. Dayton Hines first looked at the place to rent for his son. I guess the kid is twenty, still lives at home and is a pain in the you-know-what."

Jenna didn't mention her encounter with young Hines. She wasn't one to gossip.

Driving home after playtime, she spotted a Chinese restaurant. "Andee, would you like fried rice for dinner?"

"Yum. And lo mein noodles?"

"One or the other and a vegetable-beef dish."

"Will Flynn be there? Does he like Chinese food?"

"Who doesn't?" Jenna had to contain herself to not spill their news.

Flynn was waiting when they arrived. As Jenna pulled in, he left the house and came over to help them. "I was worried. You didn't say you planned to go anywhere after the story hour. Ah, I see you picked up dinner. I thought we could call for pizza. This is better."

Andee hurtled herself at Flynn. "You're not gonna go away, are you?"

"No, sugar. After we wash up and set the table, while our food heats in the microwave, your mom and I have something to tell you."

"Good stuff?"

"We think so."

"Don't keep her in suspense," Jenna said,

stopping at the sink to wash. "Flynn, you can do the honors."

He cleared his throat. "Andee, your mom and I are going to get married."

The girl looked from one to the other. "Huh. I thought maybe we were gonna get the alpacas sooner."

Jenna dissolved in laughter over Flynn's deflated expression. "Honey, us marrying means Flynn will be your new dad. Although not until around the time Santa Claus and Auntie Melody and Uncle Rob visit us."

"I knew it, Mommy. Because I asked God."

And that was it. They all helped ready dinner. Afterward Andee took Cubby and Beezer and went to her room to play.

"That was anticlimactic," Flynn said, helping Jenna load the dishwasher.

"Kids are like that. Say, would you like to walk around the pens? I need to see that the birds all have water. It was very hot today. The moms of Andee's new friends said the next two months will be more humid."

"Right, when the monsoons kick in."

They walked hand in hand and watched the sun settle over the foothills. The breeze

Jenna had grown accustomed to sprang up on their return.

Once inside, each of them went about their usual routines. Jenna helped Andee get ready for bed. Flynn set up coffee for morning.

"Our evening was so banal," he said later.

Jenna chuckled. "You expected maybe fireworks? Married life can be boring."

His eyes lit and he pulled her against him for a hard, satisfying kiss. "Once we make it legal, I can think of any number of ways to spice up our nights."

Ducking away, Jenna set out cups for morning. "Hold that thought for six months. Or maybe there'll be fireworks before then. Tomorrow I'm telling my parents and my sister."

"I'll phone my mom tonight. She'll ask why we're waiting so long."

They stayed up talking for longer than either should have since their mornings came early. But Jenna went off to bed thinking it'd been a productive, getting-to-know-more-about-each-other evening.

Flynn was open about his life. He didn't hold back. Andrew had always been reticent.

She filed away the SID report. It was time to close that part of their lives.

Andrew had died a hero. As she climbed into bed, she hoped Melody and Rob would also accept that, move on and be happy for her and Flynn. She spent some time rehearsing what she'd say to them.

IN THE DEAD of night, Jenna woke to Beezer barking and snarling. Jumping from bed, she put on slippers and shrugged into a robe. Rushing to the kitchen, she was stunned to see Beezer lunging at the door.

It was so out of the ordinary that she ran back to make sure Andee was in bed. Not that she was a sleepwalker, but Jenna couldn't imagine what else might turn the dog into a maniac.

Andee was sleeping peacefully, her arms over her head. How she could sleep through the yapping was beyond Jenna. Backing from the room, she pulled the door closed.

The noise had woken Flynn, too. He charged down the stairs, zipping his jeans and carrying his boots. "Something is going on out by the pens. There's not much moonlight. It could be coyotes or a bobcat strayed down from the foothills. You stay here. Hang on to Beezer. I'm going out." Bending, he yanked on his boots.

Jenna grabbed Flynn's forearm. "Don't go. You have nothing to use to fend off a wild animal. All the tools, including the pitchfork, are locked up."

"I'm not going to let something slaughter your flock, Jenna. Hand me a kitchen pot. I'll bang on it and scare whatever it is away."

She reluctantly did as he asked. Shivers climbed her spine as she latched on to Beezer's collar. It was hard to hold him when Flynn opened the door. The dog was in a frenzy. Because she hated the very idea of Flynn facing some wild beast alone, she dashed to the laundry room, found Beezer's leash and hooked it on, telling herself she'd go no farther than the porch.

Once outside she heard cursing and shouting. Beezer strained at his leash. She would've rushed down the path, but concern for Flynn had her dragging Beezer back inside long enough for her to pocket the cell phone she'd left charging on the kitchen counter.

As she jogged behind the straining dog,

she was glad Barney had filled the potholes. All the while she expected the problem to be in the big pen that held all of the birds. They passed it and Beezer didn't slow down. He continued on to the new fence.

By then her eyes had adjusted to the darkness. Enough for her to make out men on horseback. At least three riders were the ones swearing. She saw Flynn spring up and grab one man by his shirt. Two others still astride demanded Flynn turn loose the intruder he held fast by the scruff of his neck.

Not knowing how to assist him, Jenna shouted, "Stop, all of you. I've phoned the sheriff, and I'm about to sic a killer dog on you."

The men on the horses practically sat the animals on their haunches in their haste to depart. They galloped off, leaving their pal behind.

Jenna was near enough to Flynn to smell beer on the one who'd been caught. He continued to kick and curse and flail at Flynn, but it was too dark to see his features. She let go of Beezer's leash. He leaped, toppled the assailant and stood over him growling until he begged for mercy.

Yanking the guy upright, Flynn marched toward the house. "How long did the sheriff say he'd be?" he asked Jenna, who followed with Beezer.

"I, ah, didn't actually call. But I will. Let me turn on the porch light. Shall I get some tape to bind his hands first?"

"I don't know. He's falling-down drunk. What idiots. They tore out some of your new fence." Flynn shook the man, who kept his head down.

"Oh, no." Jenna reached inside and turned on the porch light.

"Travis Hines? What in blazes?" Flynn ducked as the kid came up swinging again.

Jenna stepped back, dialed 9-1-1 and explained what had happened.

THE SHERIFF ARRIVED in a jiffy. He was followed by Dayton Hines.

"Sutton, I'm sorry as anything. I told you I'd talk to Travis after Pancho Villa Days, and I did today. Travis, what's gotten into you, son? Who were your cohorts? Don't tell me. The Carver twins. They own horses."

At first Travis clammed up and looked sullen—until the sheriff threatened to lock him up and let his pals go free. The young man snarled at Flynn, "Because you belly-ached to him, my dad took away my plane."

"Good, it's high time you assume responsibility for your actions," Flynn snapped. "You've blitzed Ms. Wood's pens since the day she moved in. This is your third mischief out here. You slashed my tires and canopy the other day, didn't you?"

"So what?"

Dalton Hines exploded. "You did what?"

"Your attitude stinks," Flynn said.

"He'll make restitution for everything," Dayton promised. "Lock him up for the night, Sheriff. Send a deputy to pick up the Carvers." The elder man gazed at his son in disgust.

Eventually they all left and Flynn and Jenna took Beezer back into the house.

"How much damage did those jerks do to my new fence?" Jenna muttered.

"A few top rails gone. Some of your trees trampled. They were so drunk they couldn't rope the fence posts. Was your old life this exciting?" Flynn teased, brushing a finger down Jenna's nose.

"It was positively monotonous before I moved here and met you."

Flynn kissed her and aimed her back toward her bedroom. "We can't check anything until daylight. I'm betting Papa Hines will have a crew out to repair the damage at first light."

"It'd do my heart good if he hauled Travis and friends out here to do the work."

"He may. Dayton didn't become a business mogul by being a pushover."

IN THE MORNING that was exactly what happened. Dayton Hines and Lew Carver were at the fence overseeing three young men suffering major hangovers. All mumbled apologies to Jenna.

Lew Carver forked over some cash. "I want you both to know these lunkheads will spend their summer and possibly fall mucking stalls and harvesting hay for minimum wage until they pay me this money back. If they don't learn their lesson, their mothers are dreaming up chores to last until they get their heads screwed on straight."

Leaving the men to deal with their offspring, Flynn took Jenna, Andee and Beezer to town for breakfast. Afterward he drove to the VA clinic.

Jenna did hold his hand. And he passed his flight physical. "What shall we do to celebrate?" he asked, all but kicking up his heels on the way out.

Slipping her arm through his as they walked to the Cherokee, Jenna leaned close to his ear. "Can we stop and book the church, just to be sure we have our ducks in a row?"

"What ducks?" Andee asked, skipping along. "Are we getting ducks and alpacas?"

"It's a saying, sugar. It doesn't mean real ducks. It means your mom and I are setting in motion everything it'll take for the three of us to be a real family."

"And Beezer? He makes four."

Jenna touched Flynn's arm. "Maybe we can have that written on our wedding cake. 'And Beezer makes four.'"

He grinned. "Hmm. I don't suppose you'd put a dot-dot-dot after it, then add 'and counting'? That might be…too, too…"

"Yes, it would be 'too, too,'" Jenna said. "Behave yourself. My sister teaches history.

She owns and lives by a gazillion calendars.
I don't want her crossing off days."

Flynn threw up his hands in capitulation.
"Okay. December it is."

# *CHAPTER FIFTEEN*

CHRISTMASTIME IN NEW MEXICO, Jenna discovered, meant outlining the roof of the wide front porch with electric strings of luminaria. And multiple strands of a glorious red chili ristra tied with a huge raffia bow hung from the screen door to welcome visitors.

Jenna and Flynn had spent the previous six months painting the house inside and out. And now, for the past two weeks, the old house overflowed with their families.

Today, the morning of their wedding, was the first time the two of them had managed to sneak off alone to savor their coffee. They used the pretext of checking the new pens that were now home to woolly alpacas, and watering the newly replaced trees that had even grown a couple of inches.

Flynn set one foot on a lower fence rung and tucked Jenna tight under his arm.

"I'm thankful our paint job turned out so well. It looks like a prosperous ranch."

Jenna glanced back, admiring how the pale yellow siding gleamed in the frosty morning sun. "I wouldn't have picked dark green trim. It's exactly right. You did well, Mr. Sutton."

"Glad to oblige, soon-to-be Mrs. Sutton," he murmured. Kissing her, he commented on how she tasted of the cinnamon coffee her mother brought from Costa Rica.

Jenna sighed happily, basking in his warmth.

"Have I said I like your family?" Flynn gestured toward the house with his mug. "Although I can't believe Rob ran a background check on me."

Wincing, Jenna burrowed deeper. "I knew he would. But your sister didn't do so shabby giving me the third degree."

"You must've passed. Yesterday our moms and sisters sounded as though they were enjoying one another's company in the kitchen after Andee asked them to make Christmas cookies for her school party."

"How much of their jovial camaraderie was due to the jugs full of eggnog your dad whipped up?" Clearly, Jenna had found that amusing.

"I've got to admit, it tasted great."

They turned in one motion as Beezer woofed and struck them from behind. The giant red bow the dog had gotten at the groomer's hung askew.

Jenna handed Flynn her mug and straightened it for the umpteenth time. "We'd better go back. If someone let Beezer out, it means the masses are up and raring to start the day."

"A very happy day," Flynn said, his gaze softening on his bride-to-be.

She threaded her fingers with his. "Do you teach any classes today? I heard you tell Rob you'd added a new student."

"I did. He's number six. But no classes this week. We men are going to play golf today at the request of your dad. I hope it'll work the kinks out of my back. You've no idea how glad I am last night was my last sleeping on Andee's short mattress with her gobs of stuffed animals."

Jenna patted his chest. "At least we accommodated everyone by having her share my bed temporarily. Your sacrifice freed the upstairs for my family."

They walked past the massive motor home Flynn's folks had parked at the side of the house. Looking at it, he shook his head. "I cringe every time I think of my dad driving that monster out on the highway."

"Well, it made me a believer that everything in Texas is truly bigger."

"Don't you know it!" Leaning down, Flynn winked at her.

Jenna blushed and dragged him back to the house, where her dad already had a fire burning in the fireplace she'd been so sure would never be used.

Beezer claimed his spot on the rug. And Andee sat on the couch between her two doting grandmothers.

MUCH LATER, WITH everyone assembled at the church, Melody straightened the pretty blue necklace Flynn's mother had loaned Jenna. "Your something borrowed and blue," she said.

Staring in the mirror, Jenna smoothed a hand down silk of such pale lavender her wedding dress appeared iridescent in the soft light of the church foyer. "I can't thank you enough for buying me this perfect dress, Mel."

"I'm really happy for you, sis."

The gathering was the size Jenna had envisioned. Outside of family, a few of Andee's new friends and their parents had been invited. It touched Jenna to see that Barney had bought a suit for the occasion.

Her attendants were Melody and Flynn's sister. His were their respective brothers-in-law.

Over the course of the previous two weeks, the grandmothers had found time to take Andee shopping. They'd outfitted her in a long dress of sea-foam-green layers. She wore sparkly shoes and looked like a princess carrying a wand, which was really the lighter to use on the tapers that flanked the unity candle down front.

Flynn's youngest nephew wore a navy suit. He'd asked to be the ring bearer. His brother, at ten, insisted he was too old to be in such a girlie event.

On impulse Jenna had invited Don Winkleman when he came to buy a second set of chicks from her. She was surprised to look out over the pews and see him seated next to Barney. And Andee's school-bus driver, a jolly woman who stopped each day at the end of the lane, was there. Jenna spied the mayor, the sheriff and his wife, and Dayton Hines and his wife. Flynn had invited them.

What an eclectic group of friends they'd collected, she thought as the organist started to play and the sanctuary fell silent to watch the wedding party precede the bride down the aisle.

She tightened her hold on her dad's arm and on a small bouquet of white baby roses. Next year she hoped to have blossoms like them on bushes Flynn had bought and planted along the house as his special gift to her.

Thinking of Flynn, of her love, he walked out of a side room and stood near the minister, facing her.

Tall, with wide shoulders and slim hips accentuated by the charcoal suit he wore so well, Jenna didn't need the murmured reminder from her father to start her moving down the white satin runner toward him—to where they'd both speak the vows that would join them through good times and bad for however many years they were meant to have together.

Flynn reached out and Jenna placed her hand in his, fully committed and finally without any lingering fear for his career.

Her dad stepped back, leaving her with Flynn, who gazed into her eyes, raised her left hand and kissed the knuckle on the finger that would soon wear his ring.

Andee sidled over and clutched her mother's dress.

Jenna and Flynn glanced down at her and smiled. Flynn slid an arm around Jenna and ruffled Andee's curls. "Reverend," he said, "the three of us are ready to get married."

But the next instant, their ceremony took a turn into pandemonium of the type they'd come to expect practically since the day they'd met.

Beezer, who'd been parked by the entry, must've nosed open the door. With his red bow untied and flapping and his leash banging against each pew, the big dog slid and scrabbled his way along the satin runner until he reached his family.

Flynn calmly picked up the leash and

shrugged at a near-apoplectic minister. "Um, and Beezer makes four," he announced to the delight of everyone in the church.

* * * * *

# LARGER-PRINT BOOKS!

## GET 2 FREE LARGER-PRINT NOVELS PLUS 2 FREE MYSTERY GIFTS

*Love Inspired*

### Larger-print novels are now available...

LILPDIR13R

# LARGER-PRINT BOOKS!

**GET 2 FREE LARGER-PRINT NOVELS PLUS 2 FREE MYSTERY GIFTS**

*Love Inspired®*

## SUSPENSE
RIVETING INSPIRATIONAL ROMANCE

### Larger-print novels are now available...

**YES!** Please send me 2 FREE LARGER-PRINT Love Inspired® Suspense novels and my 2 FREE mystery gifts (gifts are worth about $10). After receiving them, if I don't wish to receive any more books, I can return the shipping statement marked "cancel." If I don't cancel, I will receive 4 brand-new novels every month and be billed just $5.24 per book in the U.S. or $5.74 per book in Canada. That's a savings of at least 23% off the cover price. It's quite a bargain! Shipping and handling is just 50¢ per book in the U.S. and 75¢ per book in Canada.* I understand that accepting the 2 free books and gifts places me under no obligation to buy anything. I can always return a shipment and cancel at any time. Even if I never buy another book, the two free books and gifts are mine to keep forever.

110/310 IDN F5CC

| Name | (PLEASE PRINT) | |
|------|----------------|--|

| Address | | Apt. # |
|---------|--|--------|

| City | State/Prov. | Zip/Postal Code |
|------|-------------|-----------------|

Signature (if under 18, a parent or guardian must sign)

### Mail to the Harlequin® Reader Service:
**IN U.S.A.:** P.O. Box 1867, Buffalo, NY 14240-1867
**IN CANADA:** P.O. Box 609, Fort Erie, Ontario L2A 5X3

**Are you a current subscriber to Love Inspired Suspense books and want to receive the larger-print edition?
Call 1-800-873-8635 or visit www.ReaderService.com.**

* Terms and prices subject to change without notice. Prices do not include applicable taxes. Sales tax applicable in N.Y. Canadian residents will be charged applicable taxes. Offer not valid in Quebec. This offer is limited to one order per household. Not valid for current subscribers to Love Inspired Suspense larger-print books. All orders subject to credit approval. Credit or debit balances in a customer's account(s) may be offset by any other outstanding balance owed by or to the customer. Please allow 4 to 6 weeks for delivery. Offer available while quantities last.

**Your Privacy**—The Harlequin® Reader Service is committed to protecting your privacy. Our Privacy Policy is available online at www.ReaderService.com or upon request from the Harlequin Reader Service.

We make a portion of our mailing list available to reputable third parties that offer products we believe may interest you. If you prefer that we not exchange your name with third parties, or if you wish to clarify or modify your communication preferences, please visit us at www.ReaderService.com/consumerschoice or write to us at Harlequin Reader Service Preference Service, P.O. Box 9062, Buffalo, NY 14269. Include your complete name and address.

LISLPDIR13R

# *ReaderService*.com

## Manage your account online!

- Review your order history
- Manage your payments
- Update your address

> *We've designed
> the Harlequin® Reader Service
> website just for you.*

## Enjoy all the features!

- Reader excerpts from any series
- Respond to mailings and special monthly offers
- Discover new series available to you
- Browse the Bonus Bucks catalog
- Share your feedback

*Visit us at:*

## ReaderService.com